Taming the Singularity

Daniel J. Soeder

 www.trafford.com

North America & international
toll-free: 1 888 232 4444 (USA & Canada)
fax: 812 355 4082

"It's the end of the world as we know it, and I feel fine..." R.E.M.,
Eponymous

To Susan

Chapter One: The Big Oops

The first time that Professor Barnard Freeman heard about the singularity was when he came into the Physics Department office one day before class to pick up his mail. Jodi said that Dr. Luxley wanted to see him. Jodi was the office manager, an attractive brunette, and a flirt. Her only failing as far as Barney was concerned was bringing in donuts several times a week, which did not help his waistline. Like today. Against his better judgment, Barney helped himself a jelly donut with his coffee before heading to see Dr. Luxley.

The department chair had a rather spacious office with a conference table at one end and a massive walnut desk at the other. The door was open. Dr. Reginald Luxley waved at Barney to come inside and take a seat. He was a thin, colorless man with gray hair, a neatly trimmed beard, and watery, pale eyes. Barney considered Luxley to be a better politician than a physicist. Which was just as well, he mused, because department chairs usually need more expertise in politics than anything else.

"I received a call from the Dean's office this morning," Luxley began. "It seems that the United States government needs your expertise to help out with some kind of problem."

"What problem is that?" Barney asked.

"I haven't got a clue," Luxley replied, clearly vexed. "They wouldn't tell me a thing. The Dean wants you in his office at 1:30 PM sharp to meet with the Feds. I'll cover your afternoon class for today. Find out what they want and how much of your time they will need, and let me know. Anything beyond a nominal effort will require funding to support

4

your salary. We can't afford to be doing charity work for the U.S. government."

"Of course," Barney replied. He had been funded by soft money on government projects often enough to know the rules. Give them a little bit for free, suck them in, and then ask them to fund all your non-classroom time, support a gaggle of grad students, and pay to produce a couple of publications out of it. If he played his cards right, he might even get Uncle Sugar to pony up for some nice, new equipment for the project, whatever it was, which would remain behind in the UM Physics Department labs like shells washed up on a beach. Loading up the labs with cool toys was always a great way to stay in favor with Luxley and the other faculty members. Barney's last project working with ultra-dense materials had netted the department a very nice atomic force microscope, which was capable of visualizing the individual atoms in a sample. Since the government had come looking for him specifically this time, it was likely to be another lucrative project. Still, it was curious that Luxley didn't know any details – he was almost always on top of stuff like this.

"So what do you think this might be about, Reggie?" asked Barney, pressing. "You must have heard something – maybe just scuttlebutt or rumors..."

"I'm sure the Dean and the Feds will fill you in with the details, Barney. The rumor mill says it has something to do with CERN and the LHC, because that is where the original request for assistance supposedly came from. With all the weird science and crazy experiments they have going on over there, who knows? This could be almost anything. Listen to what they have to say, figure out what you need to do to make them happy, and then come back to see me, and we'll figure up the costs."

"Who are the federal representatives? Anyone we know?"

"Again, I don't have a clue. However, the Dean's assistant asked me if you needed a reserved parking space. I told her you would just walk over. Whoever they are, it sounded like they were bringing an entourage."

****

The Large Hadron Collider (LHC) was an enormous atom smasher in Europe, capable of crashing subatomic particles together at energies far higher than anything previously created by humans. As a physicist, Barney Freeman was of course aware of the controversy that had swirled around the LHC ever since the beginning of its construction by the European Organization for Nuclear Research, more commonly known by its somewhat confusing acronym, CERN, derived from the French *Conseil Européen pour la Recherche Nucléaire*, or European Council for Nuclear Research, the provisional body preceding the official Organization. The name CERN had been retained even though the Council had been dissolved upon the formation of the Organization in the 1950's. Barney had always wondered why OERN, or the English version, EONR, wasn't used as an acronym by the Europeans. He suspected that it might resemble an obscene word in the language of a member country.

CERN had generated a great deal of concern in the early years of the 21st century as the LHC was constructed and brought on-line. The giant atom-smasher was built into a tunnel 27 kilometers in circumference, located 75 to 150 meters beneath ancient villages and pastoral farmlands near the Jura Mountains in the French-Swiss frontier region. It had been designed for concentrating very large amounts of energy into small spaces. Particle energies of tens to thousands of tera electronvolts (TeV) could be generated by the machine, using lead ion beams moving in opposite directions at

6

nearly the speed of light. Collisions between the accelerated ions could create energies as high as 1150 TeV in each lead nucleus, equivalent to that of a one-ton automobile traveling at 2,100 kph. Collisions at these energies would drive the atomic nuclei deep into each other, creating incredibly dense agglomerations of microscopic particles. If the density of these specks of crammed-together matter was high enough, they could potentially form singularities with event horizons at subatomic scales, or in other words, tiny black holes.

In the early years of the LHC, doomsayers had come from every quarter of the compass, claiming that a black hole created in the machine might remain intact long enough to gobble up additional mass and become self-sustaining. The rate of accretion would increase exponentially, consuming Planet Earth entirely in less than seven minutes. We would never know what hit us.

The CERN physicists, joined by others, had replied that such a scenario was preposterous. They showed from calculations and models that atomic collisions of even higher energy occurred in the atmosphere of the Earth from cosmic rays, and no black hole had destroyed the planet in 4.5 billion years. They showed that even if a black hole could be created in the LHC, which was by no means certain, the tiny structure would evaporate away via gravity radiation in a fraction of a second. Even if the black hole hung around for a longer period of time, it would possess a strong electrical charge from the ionizing radiation inside the LHC, and would be contained by the powerful magnets. Barney thought that although the explanation was reasonable, it contained far too many "ifs," and sounded a bit like famous last words.

Some of the CERN physicists had responded to the doomsday worriers with an air of superiority that bespoke of big-league egos, with an underlying message of "we understand all this stuff and you don't, so stop questioning our genius." Barney thought these folks with oversize egos had apparently lost sight of the fact that they and their fancy toys were supported by taxpayer money, and the taxpayers were scared. Scaring the people with the funding and then acting arrogant about it was bad business for any venture, but especially for high energy physics, which few people understood to begin with. Scare them enough, and they'll simply pull the plug. Then try running your arcane experiments with no money to pay the electric bill, smart guy! It had happened to the U.S. supercollider in Texas, the Yucca Mountain nuclear waste storage site in Nevada, and dozens of other projects.

Barney was a physics professor at the University of Maryland in College Park, and also one of the world experts on the care and feeding of black holes. He had observed galaxy-sized black holes by their influence on gravity, as starlight was bent in its path by the hyper-dense matter. He had detected star-sized black holes from their x-ray emissions, as matter fell into the event horizon at nearly the speed of light. He had listened to the radio emissions of matter swirling around a stellar-mass black hole in close orbits that produced radio sparks. He had done the math for smaller black holes, including bodies of planetary mass or less, and determined that if the Earth was compressed down to black hole densities, the entire planet would have a diameter equivalent to that of a ping pong ball. If the U.S. government needed his black hole expertise for a problem originating at CERN, this could be a lot more worrisome than he thought.

****

Dr. Barnard Freeman arrived in the Dean's office at precisely 1:30 in the afternoon, and was ushered into the executive conference room. He shook hands with the Dean, and turned to the other four people seated at the conference table. To his astonishment, they appeared to be the President of the United States, the Secretary of Energy, the National Science Advisor, and a Navy officer. A Secret Service agent in sunglasses and earpiece stood quietly in one corner. Barney's jaw dropped.

"Good afternoon, Dr. Freeman," President Jackson said. "Thank you for coming."

"Wow," said Barney, gathering his wits. "It must be one hell of a problem."

"It is," replied the President with a nod. "It is indeed."

An hour later, Barney Freeman had gotten the gist of it. It seemed that the CERN researchers had actually been successful at creating pairs of micro black holes from the high-energy lead nuclei collisions under certain beam alignments and acceleration voltages. These tiny black holes spiraled around in the LHC magnetic containment field and evaporated away within a few milliseconds after being created, just as advertised. Then a British researcher by the name of Sir Geoffrey Finch came up with the bright idea of placing opposite electrical charges on the black hole pairs as they were created and immediately crashing them together to make a larger black hole that could be studied. Finch and his team had managed to combine several million of the lead nuclei black holes into a larger black hole with the mass of a grain of sand, and a calculated lifetime of a decade or so. They were able to put a charge on it, and move it to one of CERN's adjacent experiment labs, where they had it tethered inside a strong magnetic field.

This was strictly against the rules, of course. Barney knew Doctor Professor Sir Geoffrey Holmes Finch and detested the man. Sir Geoffrey was a duke or earl of someplace small and rugged in the British Isles, with a complicated Welsh name that eluded Barney's memory. Finch possessed a number of advanced degrees to go along with an ego the size of the moon, and was the most arrogant, sarcastic and cocky bastard that Barney ever had the misfortune of meeting. The man was a firm believer that as long as the end justified the means, there was no moral dilemma to speak of. His attitude toward rules was that they were put in place to protect the incompetent, and since he was nothing but supremely competent, they obviously didn't apply to someone of his genius. With a sinking feeling in the pit of his stomach, Barney had an inkling of what was probably coming next.

Another of the endless series of strikes among French utility workers meant that only a few managers were trying to cover all the operations of the national power grid. While the brilliant Dr. Finch was busy figuring out the title of his next glorious scientific paper, parts of southern France, which included the CERN complex, suffered another of the region's innumerable power failures. Having been through this umpteen times before, the lab's uninterruptible power supplies and back-up generators kept the lights on and computers running with barely a hiccup. But that hiccup was enough. It untethered the black hole for nearly a tenth of a second, which was long enough for it to be pulled by the Earth's gravity out of the temporarily unpowered magnetic cradle. Unlike other subatomic particles, which have very little mass and are affected much more strongly by electromagnetic and nuclear forces than by gravity, Finch's black hole had the mass of a sand grain packed into a diameter of far less than an

10

attometer. And just like a grain of sand blown by the wind off the top of a desert dune, it fell.

Barney asked why Finch hadn't tethered such a dangerous object inside a superconducting magnet, which would have retained a magnetic field for several minutes at least after a loss of power. The Secretary of Energy, who held a Nobel Prize in physics for his work on subatomic particles, explained that Finch had in fact demanded access to such a containment vessel from CERN management, but given the current high commodity prices for the liquid helium required to make it operate, they were simply not able to supply one. The lab director told Finch they would try to help if he would prepare a justification statement for why he needed a superconducting storage magnet, which of course he could not do without revealing the illegal research. So he had quietly tethered it with a conventional neodymium electromagnet, and when the power tripped, the black hole skipped.

Because the diameter of the black hole was so small, it dropped majestically through the vastness of open space between the nuclei and the electrons making up the atoms of the magnet, vacuum pipes and support structures. It fell out of the bottom of the containment vessel without creating so much as a pinhole, landed on the floor of the lab, and continued without pause to fall *into* the floor, because of its enormous density. The difference in the density of the matter making up the mini black hole and the normal matter making up the floor of the lab beneath it was millions of times greater than the difference in density between a lead brick and a cloud. And in the same way that clouds cannot support lead bricks, the laboratory floor could not support the mini black hole. Down it went. By the time they noticed that it was missing from the cradle, it had fallen many

11

kilometers and was well on its way toward the center of the Earth's mass, near the inner and outer core boundary.

Oops!

Dr. Karl Barski, the presidential science advisor, told Barney that the lost black hole was consuming mass slowly. The events had happened nearly a week ago, and the CERN physicists calculated that the current mass of the black hole was now about that of a rice grain. The singularity itself was still well below subatomic particle size, so it was orbiting about the Earth's center of mass, moving freely through the empty space that makes up most of matter. It would occasionally collide with an electron or a nucleus, which would increase its mass by a small amount. There was a debate raging at CERN about whether or not the singularity could gain mass fast enough to offset the gravity wave evaporation. If it could gain mass quickly enough to remain stable, it would grow larger, consuming ever increasing amounts of mass and last for millennia.

Again, oops! This was getting serious.

The Naval officer was a young woman named Lieutenant Nicole Marie Shelton, a graduate of Annapolis, a carrier-qualified F/A-18 fighter pilot, and an astrophysicist with a PhD from Johns Hopkins. Barski introduced her as an expert on orbital dynamics. She taught astrophysics and celestial navigation at the Naval Academy, and had been the Pentagon liaison officer to the Space Telescope Science Institute located at Hopkins. She had been assigned a few days earlier to assess the problem with Finch's black hole, and determine what the United States could do, if anything, to help solve it. Lieutenant Shelton decided immediately that a lot more people and brainpower needed to be brought in on this. This meeting with Dr. Barnard Freeman was her idea. It was Lieutenant Shelton's considered

12

opinion that based on the plausible rate of mass gain, Finch's black hole would grow large enough to accrete the entire Earth in two to five years.

Yet another oops! This time with an "Oh, Crap!"

It just keeps getting better, Barney thought. They needed his help. No one knew what to do, or how to stop this thing, or even if they *could* stop it. How much time did they have? Should the planet be evacuated, or was this all a big fuss over nothing? Finch was unrepentant, claiming that the black hole was too small to do any damage, and it would evaporate away harmlessly in a few years without gaining any additional mass. Dr. Shelton disagreed. Finch's black hole was sitting near the center of the planet, surrounded by billions of tons of matter. Like Barney surrounded by boxes of donuts, it was hard to see how it could avoid gaining weight.

Finch hadn't even wanted to bother reporting the loss of the black hole to CERN management, because he was so certain there was no danger. However, with the time and man-hours spent assembling it already on the books, some kind of an explanation was needed, so his deputy project manager had fessed up. This infuriated Finch, and after several arguments, accusations, and an acrimonious row between Finch and the other scientists on his team, nearly all of them had returned to England. Finch was being detained at CERN under United Nations orders until this could all be sorted out. Several days later, one of his junior research assistants apparently decided to test the theory of gravity on her own – by walking off the roof of a tall building in London and plunging to her death. She left a note behind explaining everything, and apologizing for having helped destroy the Earth. New Scotland Yard had scrambled to keep the note away from the news media, under direct orders from the Prime Minister. It had been a very close thing.

The President appealed to Barney's patriotism, scientific integrity, and duty to humanity. The Secretary of Energy pledged to give him all the financial and technical support he needed, including unlimited access to the personnel and computing resources of the National Labs. Barski told him simply that if they didn't figure out a way to stop this, the Earth was doomed. Barney was one of the best black hole physicists in the world, and they wanted him to lead an international team in an attempt to deal with the problem.

"All right," said Barney. "I will do it under two conditions. First, I get to name the team members. I don't want a room full of government appointees, or people who are owed political favors. I've seen enough of those special commissions, and all they ever do is rehash what is already known. We will need data. Then we will need the very best high energy physicists, engineers and singularity experts on the planet to analyze the data. I know all of them, including Dr. Nicole Shelton there, whom I know by reputation. Although no one ever told me she was a naval officer and a carrier pilot." He looked at her pointedly. "I thought you were a civilian professor at Annapolis."

The lieutenant merely smiled and saluted him smartly.

Barney continued. "Second, this is going to take money. Lots and lots of money. I can't imagine at the moment how we will deal with this, but whatever we come up with is likely to be very expensive."

"If I'm going to pick up the tab, then I reserve the right to name at least one of your team members," said President Jackson. "I want you to include Lieutenant Shelton here so we have a conduit for communications. She is competent as both a physicist and a military officer, which you may find useful."

"All right," said Barney. "As long as it's just one. Besides, I was going to select her anyway"

"Fine. The lieutenant will keep me informed of your progress through Dr. Barski. Secondly, you have my word that the financial and logistical systems of the world are at your disposal. Because if we don't find a way fix this, there may not be a world."

****

Barney was in turmoil as he walked back over to the Physics Department. He wondered what he would tell Luxley. Well, at least the chairman should be happy at the prospect of unlimited funds. Even if they might be only for a limited time.

Time! How much time did they have to work on this? His head was spinning with ideas. He needed to find Devi, and get her started on some calculations.

Devi Chowdury was Barney's current doctoral candidate. She had received her MS in physics at UC Berkeley, graduating near the top of her class. Barney had agreed to serve as her major professor at the University of Maryland on the recommendation of his friend Glenn Spivey at Berkeley, who told him that she had done some outstanding work as an intern for Lawrence Berkeley National Lab. Barney's NSF project to model gravity waves from rotating black holes was well-funded, but shorthanded. He was happy to take on Devi because it was a great study for a doctoral dissertation, and he really needed some help. In turn, Devi had turned out to be an absolute wizard with orbital computer models. Barney wanted to tap her expertise to start figuring out the orbit and behavior of Finch's singularity.

Barney found Devi in the Physics Department workroom with a half dozen students, bent over her notebook computer. "Devi," Barney called to get her attention. "Please come to my office. We have a very urgent project to discuss."

"Yes, professor," she replied. "Just let me shut down and I will be right with you."

Twenty minutes later, Devi was in tears.

"Oh my goodness, professor. What a terrible thing they have done! The whole world will be destroyed. We will die – all of us. Crushed into a gravity singularity. When? In a few years? Or months, even? What are we going to do?"

"First of all, we are *not* going to panic. At least not yet," he told her with what he hoped sounded like fatherly steadiness. "We need to start figuring this out and assemble a list of possible alternatives. Giving up hope is the last thing on the agenda, not the first."

It seemed to calm her down, and she quickly regained her composure. "Yes, you are correct, of course," she said, embarrassed by her display of emotion. "I am sorry for my childish behavior."

"It's all right," said Barney. "I didn't take it real well either when I first learned about this. Finch is an arrogant bastard, and if we are going down the rabbit hole, I vote he goes first! I want you to crank some orbital mechanics through the numerical modeling program with the best data we have so far. We must try to establish where this thing is, and where it will be in the future. "

****

16

Barney knew that the next challenge would be Shelly Freeman, his wife. Shelly was intelligent and literate; she would understand the implications of this immediately. He had decided on the way out of the Dean's office that he had to tell her. The President had asked him to keep it a secret for now so they didn't panic the masses. Barney understood and agreed with that, but Shelly wasn't one of the masses. And he would need her support.

He knew from experience that he couldn't keep secrets from Shelly. She could read him like a book. The one time he had an affair with a student, a decade ago during a trip to Keck Observatory in Hawaii, she knew about it as soon as she saw his guilty face. He had never lied to her since.

Shelly and Barney owned a coffee shop near campus that they had converted from a former university chapel. The chapel had been abandoned for years after some lawsuit over the separation of church and state, and they were able to purchase it for a song. It was roomy and bright with high ceilings, and Shelly had turned it into an Internet cafe to attract students. To honor the history of the place, they named the coffee shop Holy Grounds. She held poetry readings in the former chapel every Friday, ran a sci-fi and fantasy book exchange in the back, and featured local alternative bands and folk music on the weekends, alternating sometimes with political discussion groups. The coffee was even decent. The Sierra Club had an office nearby; there was a small Lebanese restaurant next door and an artist's supply store across the street. The neighborhood was bohemian and business was good.

Barney found her in the tiny office, ordering more beans over the Internet from one of their shade-grown, sustainable small farm suppliers in

Costa Rica. He gave her a kiss, and got himself an espresso while he waited for her to finish. The shop was almost deserted this late in the afternoon.

Shelly could tell right away that something big had happened. She joined Barney at the table and asked him what it was. Barney hesitated. How do you tell someone you love that they have just been put under a death sentence? Finally, he took a deep breath and told her everything he knew.

Shelly was badly shaken. After 30 years of marriage, she understood enough astrophysics to know that if the black hole accreted the Earth, nothing would be left.

"Surely, something can be done? They wouldn't have asked for your help if there wasn't a chance."

"Shelly, we are going to try. You have to believe that. I've already gotten Devi started on the orbital calculations. They gave me a Lieutenant Nicole Shelton of the U.S. Navy to help figure things out, who also happens to be a PhD astrophysicist and one of the best in the world. But this thing is deep inside the Earth. I don't know how to get to it, or what I would do if I could. I wonder if they only met with me to be sure they were covering all their bases."

"The President of the United States does not make personal visits to a college professor's office just to cover the bases, Barney," she said sternly. "He has flunkies for that."

"I suppose you're right," he was forced to admit. "Still, Barski said they are going to start putting important things into orbit and on the moon. NASA will be spending billions to develop thousands of large passenger spacecraft, O'Neill space colonies, and a moon base. I don't think they are really counting on me."

18

"Whether they are or not, you still need to assemble a top-notch team and give it your best shot. It's not just the human race that is at risk. It is all life on Earth. Everything, including the planet itself, will be destroyed if this black hole consumes us. There is no room in O'Neill colonies or on a moon base for things like whales, elephants or redwoods. The government can't possibly save everything. Life has not been found anywhere else. If it disappears from the Earth, it may just disappear from the universe."

"But I'm not sure how to even begin to tackle this," Barney said quietly.

"Barnard Freeman, just listen to yourself. You've only known about this for a couple of hours. No one expects you to solve it quickly or easily. Assemble your team. Get the best people with the best smarts and the most outrageous ideas. Once people start talking to each other, the perfect solution might present itself. And if not, well, at least you can cross the event horizon knowing you did everything possible. But for God's sake, at least give it a chance!"

"Thanks, Shelly. I knew I could count on your support."

She smiled at him. "I don't know how much support I can be, but I will at least try to keep all of you wide awake and well-supplied with coffee."

Chapter Two: Coping Strategy

Barney was impressed to be at the White House ten days later. Devi Chowdury was overwhelmed. Working alongside Nikki Shelton, she had run hundreds of computer simulations and orbital calculations. They had modeled the probable mass of the object, the diameter of the event horizon, the gravitational gradient, and the mean free path of the still tiny black hole on its orbit inside the Earth through subatomic space. Nikki had set up multiparameter estimates in the computer to determine the probabilistic rate of mass gain for the black hole. They were starting to nail down some facts.

Barney had called in everyone he knew who might be of help to form what Barski insisted on calling a "Tiger Team." Barney simply referred to it as a "work group." A few of the experts were reluctant to commit at first, but once the situation was explained, quietly and urgently, every single person came to College Park to work on the problem. Luxley had found them a well-appointed office building in a business park off Route 1, just north of the campus and they had set up shop. Before they even got any desks and chairs, Barney had Devi and Nikki spend a ton of money on computers, including a massive, high-speed, cantankerous multiprocessor mainframe for sophisticated modeling. Devi named it Kali, after the beautiful Hindu goddess who demanded worship and was known for her foul temper. It was appropriate.

They had not done a press release. While the work wasn't exactly secret, Barney had advised his work group that a public news release would just create unnecessary panic and fear. The two dozen scientists agreed that

20

once they had a better idea of the timing and the options, they would tell the citizens of the doomed world. Until then, the masses went about their daily business none the wiser. Apparently, everyone on the team had kept his or her promise so far, and the story had not yet been leaked to the news media.

Now Barney, Devi, and Nikki, along with a few other work group scientists, were at the White House to update President Jackson and other world leaders on the crisis. Barney hoped that they might get to see the inside of the Oval Office, but instead they were hustled directly into an elevator behind the Lincoln Bedroom. The visitors entered and the elevator began moving downward, for what felt like a fair distance.

They emerged to find themselves in an arched, cavernous room. There were banks of video screens and computer terminals on virtually every square inch of wall space, several illuminated maps, and a large, ring-shaped conference table in the center. The President stood up to greet them.

"Welcome to the White House Situation Room, Dr. Freeman. If you and your party will find seats, we can get started."

"Thank you, Mr. President," Barney replied. "I thought the Situation Room was a small room outside the Oval Office."

"A cover story. This room was built by President Kennedy during the height of the Cold War, under the cover of constructing a therapeutic swimming pool in the White House basement. It has secure data feeds and input lines from all over the world, and the communications capabilities were already astounding before we completely upgraded everything two years ago. Now they are the best in the world. The existence of this room, like the similar facility under the Kremlin, was top secret for many decades. They knew about ours just like we knew about theirs, of course, but hardly anyone else ever suspected that this room existed. It was supposed to be

21

deep enough, and seal up tight enough using Polaris submarine life support technology to survive a nuclear attack on Washington, including a direct hit on the White House. From 1960's warheads, of course. With the bunker-busters out there today, no one can really hide in the basement anymore. I didn't see any reason to let good meeting space go to waste, so this room is unclassified now. We don't broadcast that it's here, but a security clearance is no longer required to enter."

****

Once everyone was settled in their chairs, President Jackson began introductions. Besides himself, the vice president and National Science Advisor Barski, luminaries from the United States government included the Secretaries of State, Treasury, Commerce, Energy and Defense, the chairman of the Joint Chiefs, the U.N. Ambassador, and various leaders of Congress. Ministers and ambassadors from many other governments, including the European Union, United Kingdom, France, Austria, Switzerland, Germany, Spain, Italy, Russia, China, India, Japan, Brazil, Argentina, Canada, Mexico, South Africa, Egypt and Australia crowded around the ring-shaped table. Dozens more were connected in by video links or conference lines. As a professor, Barney was normally quite unfazed about public speaking, but the caliber of this crowd was starting to make him nervous.

The President introduced Dr. Barnard Freeman and his team, and asked for background, an update and a status report. Here we go, thought Barney. He hoped his digital slide show didn't lock up in the middle of all this.

"Thank you, Mr. President," he said in his best lecture voice. "I will bring everyone up to date on what we know after nearly two weeks of

22

trying to gain an understanding of this phenomenon. If you have heard some of these details before, I beg your indulgence for those who have not.

"As you are all aware, a microscopic black hole created by Dr. Geoffrey Finch three weeks ago in the particle accelerator at CERN got loose during a power failure, and has descended into the interior of the Earth. This black hole, or 'singularity' as it is called by physicists, is orbiting the center of mass of the Earth-Moon system, so it is not just sitting at the exact center of the Earth. The center of mass is a point near the boundary between the inner and outer core, and the black hole appears to be completing one orbit around this location every few minutes."

"Dr. Freeman," asked the President of France over one of the video links. "How can anything orbit inside the Earth? Is the ground below our feet not composed of solid rock, and in fact, doesn't the matter that makes up the interior of the Earth become quite compressed at those great depths?"

"Yes, the Earth is solid, and it does become denser at depth, Monsieur President," Barney replied. "But the singularity is so incredibly tiny that it passes through the empty space between electrons and atomic nuclei, only occasionally colliding with something solid and adding to its mass. Every time it does this, it produces a burst of neutrinos, which we are using to track it.

"Dr. Ted Lewis from MIT came up with the idea of using existing solar neutrino detectors around the world to track the movement and activity of the black hole. Neutrinos interact very weakly with matter, so these are the only signals that can travel long distances through the Earth to let us monitor the singularity."

"How did these detectors just happen to be available for use?" asked the Russian ambassador with a hint of suspicion.

"The devices were originally designed to measure the flux of neutrinos from the sun, to determine if the nuclear fission models were correct about of how the sun produced energy," Barney replied. "The oldest one is located in the United States deep inside a gold mine in the Black Hills of South Dakota, and has been recording solar neutrinos for almost 40 years. Other detectors have been built by the Italians in the Apennines east of Rome, and by your government in the Caucasus Mountains. The Japanese operate one called Super Kamiokande in the mountains west of Tokyo, and the Canadians have the Sudbury Neutrino Observatory located in a northern Ontario mine. There is even a large neutrino detection array imbedded in the ice sheet in Antarctica. All of these detectors are buried deep underground to distinguish solar neutrinos from cosmic rays, and they can measure the direction of travel, to be sure the neutrino came from the sun. We were able to use this ability to detect neutrinos coming from the singularity inside the Earth, and because of the wide spacing of these devices around the world, we were able to triangulate the neutrino bursts quite precisely. We now have very good measurements of the position and motion of this thing.

"Dr. Nicole Shelton on our work group has been using these data to continuously track the movement of the object, and we have been able to define the orbit. I will ask her to explain it more detail." He was ready to relinquish the microphone to someone else. Barney felt like the whole proceeding was becoming just a bit overwhelming. Lecturing the American President, and fielding questions from the Russian Ambassador and the President of France, for chrissake. It certainly wasn't a normal day at the office. But for the past couple of weeks, nothing had been normal.

Nikki picked up the narrative. "Thank you, Dr. Freeman. It is important to remember that each individual neutrino burst not only allows us to track the singularity, but also represents an episode of the singularity gaining mass. The trend of the neutrino bursts indicates that they are incrementally, but steadily increasing in frequency. This means that the rate at which the singularity is gaining mass is gradually getting more rapid over time."

"Dr. Shelton," the Brazilian ambassador interrupted her. "I was a professor of political science at the Universidade de São Paulo before being appointed to the embassy. I know, of course, what a black hole is, having heard about such things in the popular literature. But I do not understand how they form or how they work. As you probably know, Dr. Finch has told several inquiries that there is nothing to worry about, and that the black hole will merely evaporate away. Others say it will consume the Earth. I'm not certain what to believe, or whom, and if we should worry about this or not. I am sure that many of my colleagues are equally perplexed." A number of other people were nodding in agreement. "Could you please explain this to us in a bit more detail? In laymen's' terms, of course..."

"Of course, Mr. Ambassador," Nikki responded. She was embarrassed for talking over their heads. As a professor, she was supposed to be able to explain things, not baffle people. Speaking in front of an audience containing so many VIPs did nothing to help her nerves. As she continued, her voice was a bit shaky. "I apologize if I lost anyone. Let us back up to the beginning."

She took a deep breath. "A black hole is one of the most startling predictions to come out of Albert Einstein's 1915 theory of general relativity. The underpinning idea of relativity is that the speed of light, designated by

25

the letter 'C,' remains constant for all observers everywhere in the universe. According to Einstein, if a glowing object is moving toward us at 99 percent of C, and we measure the speed of the light emitted from this object, it would be exactly the same as the speed of light emitted from another glowing object at rest with respect to us. Surprisingly, it would also be exactly the same for a glowing object that is moving away from us at 99 percent of C.

"This goes against our everyday experience – for example, if someone throws a ball at us from a stationary position while another person throws a ball while speeding toward us in a car, we would expect the second ball to be moving much faster due to the car's speed. But relativity says that the speed of light is always C, no matter what. Obviously, something has to give to accommodate this. Einstein determined that space must shorten and time must pass more slowly as an object's speed increases, thus preventing any object in our universe from moving faster than the speed of light, and giving the same value to C as an object at rest. He called this concept space-time, because the two are interrelated and neither is constant or unchanging. These were outlandish ideas, and a lot of folks back then, including a number of famous physicists, thought Einstein was completely off his rocker. Even today, when the GPS navigation device in your car uses practical relativity equations to automatically account for slowed-down time on fast-moving satellites, the concepts can be hard to accept." The VIP audience was all nodding thoughtfully, and appeared to be following Nikki so far.

"Okay. Well, young Albert was just getting started. He followed the general theory with the special theory of relativity, which stated that the acceleration of an object in a gravity field will also warp space-time, bending

26

light. Einstein's credibility improved significantly when the warping of space-time by gravity was actually measured by astronomers during solar eclipses in the early 20th Century. Stars in close proximity to the eclipsed sun had their apparent positions displaced exactly as he predicted, because space had been bent by the sun's gravity, warping the light paths. Einstein began to seem less like a nut and more like a genius.

"The more massive the object, the stronger the gravity, and the more it warps space-time. Nowadays, big telescopes like Keck and Hubble often capture the gravitationally-distorted images of distant galaxies as their light passes through massive galactic clusters located along our line of sight. This is called a gravity lens, and I could show you photographs of arcs of light around galaxy clusters resulting from the warping of space-time by gravity. But an object doesn't have to be as massive as a cluster of galaxies or even a star to warp space.

"Gravity is a property of mass, and dense objects have more mass packed into the same volume of space. According to Dr. Einstein, increasing the density of an object will steepen the gravitational gradient and increase the space-time warp. The highest density objects we know of occur in the center of stars. Einstein imagined stars with extremely high densities, where the gravity is so strong and the space-time warp so intense that instead of merely displacing a passing light beam by a fraction of a degree like our sun, the light paths are bent completely around the object, never reaching an observer. Einstein called such objects dark stars, because no light could escape from the gravity. He couldn't figure out how they could be created, so he didn't believe they actually existed in nature. Other physicists took up the challenge, and determined not only that these things COULD exist, but

27

discovered that they actually DID exist. Physicists refer to these super dense bodies as singularities, but in popular usage they are called black holes.

"A star like our sun emits light through what is essentially a contained thermonuclear explosion, like a giant hydrogen bomb. Hydrogen atoms in the core of the star ram into each other under intense heat and pressure, fuse into helium, and give off energy. The energy works its way to the surface of the star, and we get sunshine. The reason the sun doesn't simply fly apart from this explosion is because gravity holds everything together. The surface of the sun is defined by the balance point between the explosive forces pushing outward and gravity pulling inward. At the end of a star's life, once the nuclear fuel is used up and there is nothing left to push outward against gravity, it will collapse. How far this goes depends on the amount of mass that is left.

"Small stars like the sun will collapse into white dwarfs, composed of what is called degenerate matter, a sort of compressed atomic soup of electrons, protons, neutrons and other subatomic particles. In 1930, an Indian-American astronomer named Subrahmanyan Chandrasekhar determined that degenerate matter had limits on how much gravity it could withstand. Larger stars with a mass greater than about one and a half times that of our sun, now called the Chandrasekhar Limit will collapse violently when their fuel runs out and then explode in an event called a supernova. The collapse compresses the core of the star beyond the limits of the weak atomic force that keeps electrons and protons apart. These particles fuse together, neutralize charges and form an extremely dense ball of neutrons. The rebound of infalling matter against this incompressible ball of neutrons creates the supernova explosion.

"These objects are called neutron stars, and contain many tons of matter per cubic inch, significantly warping space-time. I could show you a photograph of one in the center of the Crab Nebula, if anyone is interested in taking a look. If we scale this up further, a larger neutron star resulting from the collapse of an even more massive parent star will warp spacetime into a singularity, creating a black hole. Modern x-ray astronomy provides evidence that thousands of these stellar mass objects are, in fact, present throughout our galaxy. We also have a massive black hole of over four million solar masses at the center of our Milky Way galaxy, known as Sagittarius A prime, which seems to be responsible for the spiral shape. Most other galaxies appear to have them as well. Geoffrey Finch created a small one in the lab.

"By all accounts, these things are strange beasts. Light emitted from the surface of such a body will never escape. Anything that falls into the black hole's gravity well, including light, will never get back out. Nobody knows what goes on in close proximity to one of these objects, because no information or data can ever be retrieved. The only thing we can observe about them is their gravity, and the last-gasp emissions of objects and gas that are sucked in.

"The mini black hole inside the Earth manufactured by Finch from his CERN experiments is extremely tiny, yet it has the same density of matter as a black hole created by a supernova. If anything falls into a black hole, the point on the fall where the infalling object reaches the speed of light is called the event horizon. We in the outside universe can observe nothing beyond that. To us, the object appears to be frozen in time, although to an observer riding on the object, it will have continued falling toward the singularity. This is one impractical method for getting objects to move faster

29

than the speed of light, which Einstein said was not possible. It is possible, but we can't observe it. The only information we can get from beyond the event horizon is to note that the gravitational field of the singularity has increased in proportion to the mass of the object that just fell in."

Nikki was suddenly shaken by the realization that one of these things actually WAS inside the Earth, and this discussion was far from academic. They might all experience what it was like to cross an event horizon very soon. She looked over at Barney, and motioned for him to continue the discussion.

"Thank you, Lieutenant Shelton," Barney said, picking up the thread. "To continue on this train of thought, remember that nothing can escape from a black hole except gravity. Stephen Hawking published some work many years ago in which he theorized that the gravitational effects of a rotating black hole on surrounding space might be a mechanism for carrying off energy. According to Hawking, a black hole will slowly evaporate over time because of Einstein's equation of matter-energy equivalence, the famous $E = MC^2$. As the spinning singularity loses energy because of the gravitational waves it emits into normal space, it should also lose mass. Until recently, this was an untestable hypothesis. Even Hawking waffled on the idea, often expressing doubts about whether or not this could actually happen. One thing Geoffrey Finch did manage to prove with his otherwise irresponsible CERN experiments is that Hawking radiation from a black hole is a real phenomenon. The super tiny black holes they were creating in the LHC were evaporating away within a fraction of a second. It was Finch's desire to experiment with a longer-lived black hole that led to the creation of the current singularity that is causing us problems."

"So what is this thing going to do to the Earth, Dr. Freeman?" the President of the Unites States asked him pointedly. "That is, if left to its own devices."

"Mr. President, I regret to report that our mathematical models show that Finch's black hole will continue to gain mass. The mass gained through random collisions with matter will be much greater than any mass lost through Hawking radiation. Each additional bit of mass it gains will strengthen the gravitational field, allowing it to accrete even more mass. The model shows that the sequence will be a geometrical progression, starting off slowly at first until it reaches an inflection point, and then proceeding rather rapidly until it consumes the Earth."

"What is this inflection point?" asked the German Chancellor.

"It is the point at which the black hole gains enough mass for its event horizon to be larger than subatomic size. When that happens, the black hole will no longer be able to pass through the empty space inside atoms. It will collide with all of the matter in its path, and gravity will pull the material into the event horizon," Barney answered. "Although it will still be tiny, the rate at which it will accrete mass will increase dramatically. If we haven't fixed the problem by then, the black hole will begin a runaway accretion that will accelerate until the entire Earth is consumed."

"The entire Earth?" the British Prime Minister was incredulous.

"Yes, Mr. Prime Minister. Nothing can stop it once it reaches a certain size and mass. Matter will continue to fall into it at an ever-increasing rate, until eventually the entire planet will collapse, implode, and fall into the singularity. The mass and gravity of the Earth will end up compressed into a mathematical point, because nothing can stop it. The event horizon of the black hole would be less than two centimeters in

31

diameter, or the size of a golf ball, and once all the remaining debris fell into it, there wouldn't be an accretion disk, or any other sign the Earth had existed. The moon will continue to orbit this mass, although from the lunar surface, it will appear to be orbiting an invisible point. The black hole will continue to follow the Earth's orbit around the sun."

"If any space aliens were to visit our solar system after such an event, they would find it to be a very strange arrangement," the Japanese Prime Minister commented.

"Indeed," Barney agreed. "This brings up an interesting idea. The observation has been made that the universe is many billions of years old, there are trillions of stars, many stars have been observed to have planets, at least some of these planets should support life, and a few of those should have evolved intelligence. Even considering the difficulties of interstellar space travel, given the probable number of advanced civilizations out there, visitors should still be arriving on our doorstep every few decades. Since they have not been showing up to the best of our knowledge, many scientists are wondering where everybody is. A few people have suggested that all technological civilizations might be doomed after advancing in scientific research to the point of developing nuclear weapons, intelligent machines, bioengineered diseases, or simply polluting their environment to the point that it destroys them. So now here is another one: Consider what might happen if most technical civilizations are inspired at some point to create a black hole in the lab. Maybe 80 to 90 percent of the time, it gets loose and swallows up their entire planet. Perhaps our efforts to find extraterrestrial civilizations should have been directed toward searching for black holes orbiting stable, sun-like stars at Earth-like distances." The room grew quiet as the implications hit everyone.

"So how long do we have?" President Jackson asked, getting back to the subject at hand. "Have you calculated this out?"

"Yes," said Barney. "My colleague, Lieutenant Shelton, has the details."

Nikki got up so speak again. "Our computer model shows that the gradually-increasing singularity mass will reach the inflection point in approximately 20 months," she answered. "After that, the runaway matter accretion will take an estimated additional four months or so. The singularity will probably begin to seriously affect the structure of the Earth within a few weeks after passing the inflection point. It will cause huge earthquakes, tsunamis and volcanic eruptions as it accretes matter along its orbit. It may also cause strong storms as it ingests air along its path through the atmosphere, and it will surely create a vortex of some kind as it passes through the oceans. Great disruption and many deaths can be expected.

"The most rapid accretion will take place in the final week to ten days, once the mass of the singularity gets large enough to have a strong gravitational attraction on other matter over large distances. It will forcefully ingest the matter around it by pulling it in through a swirling vortex, and creating tunnels for itself in the crust and mantle as it slowly continues to orbit through what is left of the Earth. By then our planet will resemble a block of Swiss cheese. Extremely hot magma from the Earth's core can be expected to follow the black hole out along these tunnels and erupt at the surface. The heat, radiation and poison gases emitted during this stage will kill anything still alive on the Earth. The terminal implosion of the planet will soon follow. The black hole will eventually stop orbiting and come to rest at the center of the Earth's mass. The shell of the planet will fall into it soon afterward. The final collapse of Earth into the singularity will be brighter and hotter than a stellar explosion, Mr. President, and probably outshine the entire galaxy for a few hours. It will kill any unprotected life in the Solar System. Please keep in mind that the 24 month timeframe is only an estimate, however, and things could develop more slowly or much more quickly. We just don't know."

A collective gasp went up from the audience. Two years...24 months. That was all they had.

"How could such a thing be allowed to happen?" the Chinese ambassador urgently asked the French ambassador.

"It was not 'allowed' Ambassador Cheng," the Frenchman replied. "A British madman with an oversized ego broke a lot of rules to make this object. Finch's reckless behavior has now threatened the entire Earth. If we are all going down the drain, he ought to go first."

"Agreed," said Ambassador Cheng.

"Thank you, Lieutenant Shelton," President Jackson's voice boomed above the murmur and hushed conversations. "We will discuss some contingencies in a moment. I have directed NASA to begin designing some large spacecraft that can transport a thousand people at a time to the moon. We may have to learn how to survive there in large numbers if we lose Earth. However, right now I'd like to ask Dr. Freeman if there is any way to stop this from happening?"

"We have some ideas, Mr. President," Barney said. The crowd quieted and listened intently. "Our work group has the best physicists in the world and we have been racking our brains for a week to come up with a plan. Thank you for mentioning the moon. It is one advantage the Earth has over other planets. The moon is such a large percentage of the Earth's mass that we are, in effect, a double planet. Dr. Shelton found that the gravity of

34

the orbiting moon is affecting the singularity, forcing its path around the center of mass of the Earth-moon system to be in the shape of an ellipse." Barney ran a Power Point animation that showed the initially circular orbit of Finch's singularity gradually elongating into an oval shaped ellipse. "Because of changing tidal forces as the moon orbits the Earth, and the Earth orbits the sun, this ellipse is getting more eccentric or narrower with each orbit. The lieutenant's data suggest that in about six months' time, the orbit will have elongated enough so that the singularity will be relatively close to the surface of the Earth at its apogee point. It ought to be reachable with a drill rig. We have a pretty good notion of where it will be, and when it will be there. If we can capture it, or somehow boost the orbit just a little bit higher, we might be able to extract this thing from the planet and put it safely into orbit."

"Just how close to the surface is relatively close?" asked the Secretary of Defense.

"About fifteen kilometers or 50,000 feet," Nikki answered him. "The deepest drilling rigs can get that deep."

"Do we have anything that can be mobilized in short order to get to the required depth?" asked the President.

"We might be able to modify something like a deep gas rig," replied the Secretary of Energy. "But the Russians have a deep drill rig that is currently operational."

"Da," said the Russian Ambassador. "In the Kola Peninsula."

"So what do you need from us in government to accomplish this?" the President asked.

"Tons of money, cut the red tape, give us unlimited logistical support, and make arrangements to borrow the Russian deep drill rig," Barney said. "Time is of the essence. And did I mention money?"

Chapter Three: Deep Drilling

The Uralmash-1500 drill rig stood stoically inside its 200-foot high derrick shelter on a rocky plain in the treeless and windy Kola Peninsula. It was the deepest drilling rig in the world, and the Americans wanted it. It had not been moved from this spot since being assembled in 1970.

The Kola Peninsula separates the Barents Sea from the White Sea above the Arctic Circle. It juts from the northern part of Scandinavia, where Finland, Sweden and Norway all meet. It belonged to Russia, mainly because it was so barren and desolate that nobody else bothered to claim it.

The Uralmash-1500 drill rig held the world depth record for drilling a hole into the Earth. It had bored down more than 40,000 feet in 1989 as part of an experiment by the old Soviet Union to explore the deep structure of the Baltic shield. None of the predicted phenomena were found in the drillhole, but all sorts of other unexpected things were. The geothermal temperature rose more quickly with depth than expected, mineral assemblages were different than predicted, and a seismic anomaly that was thought to be the contact between granitic continental crust and basaltic oceanic crust turned out instead to be a zone containing vast amounts of water that had been given off by the recrystallization of minerals under the temperatures and pressures of the great depths.

Arkady Kutuzov was the Kola site manager for the Russian Deep Geo Laboratory, which was actually little more than the barren and desolate spot on the tundra where the rig sat. He reported to a small, bureaucratic agency in Moscow with the impressive name of State Scientific Enterprise on Superdeep Drilling and Complex Investigations in the Earth's Interior.

37

Kutuzov's boss had called him the day before and announced that an official party from the Kremlin would be escorting three American scientists to visit the drill rig. The Russian government had agreed to allow the Americans to borrow and utilize the rig, and he was to cooperate fully with their wishes. They would explain when they got there.

Arkady hoped so. This was most irregular.

Dr. Ludmilla Porizskova was leading the group. She was an associate director at the State Scientific Enterprise, and Arkady's boss' boss. She was also a consummate bureaucrat, who had smoothly survived the transition from the Soviet Union bureaucracy to the Russian Federation bureaucracy without missing a beat. She had a couple of younger Russian scientists with her that Arkady did not know, plus the three American visitors in tow. The whole party entered the derrick shelter of the Uralmash-1500 through the person-sized man door, stomping snow off their boots and trying to shake off the bitter cold.

Dr. Porizskova greeted Arkady, whom she knew slightly from his occasional visits to Moscow, and introduced the others in the party. The two Russians were a geologist and an astrophysicist from the Russian Academy of Sciences, and the three Americans were Dr. Barney Freeman from the University of Maryland, Lieutenant Nicole Shelton of the U.S. Navy, and a drilling engineer named Clyde Rose from Oklahoma.

"Thank you for agreeing to meet with us, Dr. Kutuzov," Nikki said, in perfect Russian. "We have a need for this drill rig in the Virgin Islands."

****

During the course of the explanation, Arkady was by turns outraged, appalled, frightened, amazed, and finally, slightly optimistic. Yes, he assured the Americans, the Uralmash 1500 could drill as deep as

38

they needed. It had only gone 40,000 feet in past attempts, but should be able to get much deeper. The Americans said that they could intercept the singularity at a depth of about 51,000 feet. The original target depth of the Kola well was 50,000 feet, but the unusually high geothermal gradient had stopped them. It should be much cooler under Saint Croix, which was near the Puerto Rico Trench and the Lesser Antilles subduction zone, where cold crust was descending into the mantle. With a little bit of extra bracing, the rig might even go as deep as 60,000 feet.

His faint optimism evaporated when he heard their schedule. Six months. Six months to drill the deepest borehole ever attempted on the Earth.

"Dr. Shelton, do you realize that it took us 24 years to drill SG-3 down to a depth of 12 kilometers? That is the deepest hole ever, and you want to go 10,000 feet beyond that? Impossible!"

"No, it ain't impossible," Clyde Rose spoke up. His Anadarko accent was so thick the Russians had trouble understanding him. Sometimes even Barney and Nikki had trouble following what he was saying, but despite his cowpoke phrasing and homespun metaphors, he was the best deep drilling engineer on the planet. If anyone could accomplish this, it would be Clyde Rose.

"How is it not impossible?" asked Arkady. "Even if everything goes perfectly, it would still take years, and nothing ever goes perfectly."

"Well, we ain't got years. What we have is less than six months before that critter gets close to the surface under St. Croix, and we need to be ready to grab ahold of it. It took y'all so long because you were cutting drill core the entire way for science. We don't need core, just a hole. If we can get this here rig to spud within a couple weeks, and then make a thousand

39

feet of hole per day, we can get her done in two months of steady effort if we keep up that pace. It will require drilling 42 feet an hour, or about 9 inches a minute. I've drilled that fast many a time."

"How will you do that? There are always problems, especially at depth."

"I know that, my Russian friend. That is why we are going to use your rig, and modify a couple of our own Anadarko Basin deep gas rigs to work just like her. We plan to drill two parallel holes at the same time, so that if we have a problem with one hole or one rig, the other can keep going while we fix whatever broke."

"That is a very expensive way to drill."

"The President did say that money was no object. And if'n we all get sucked into that black hole, money ain't going to mean much anyhow."

****

President Jackson and his advisors had discussed contingency plans. They could build spacecraft and evacuate at least some people from the Earth. But they couldn't just go into orbit. Nikki Shelton had made it clear that the final collapse of the Earth into the singularity would create a mini-supernova that would shine thousands of times brighter than the Sun. For a few hours, it would be the brightest object in the entire galaxy. The planetary implosion was going to release an extremely intense burst of light, heat, x-rays, gamma rays and subatomic particles that would fry anyone and anything orbiting the Earth. Escaping spacecraft might be safe on the farside of the moon, by putting its bulk between them and the doomed planet. A much better location would be in orbit on the opposite side of the sun, but the NASA director wasn't sure they could get there in time.

His press secretary was again urging him to tell the public.

"Too many people know about this already, Mr. President. It is going to get out one way or another, and it would be better if the public heard it from you."

"I can't speak for the world, Jim. At least, not without a lot of other world leaders agreeing to make me the spokesperson. And what do we tell the people? We're all doomed?"

"I don't know, Mr. President. I'm not a speechwriter, but you are one of the most eloquent speakers the world stage has seen in decades. No one else can deliver this news as well as you."

"It's pretty lousy news."

"Of course it is, sir. But there is cause for hope. We are doing something – the Russian deep drill rig will be moved onsite in the next few days, and NASA is designing the huge escape spacecraft. People need to know. All of this is going to take a lot of effort and a lot of money. Both will have to come from somewhere, and I guarantee you that even now, if a nosy reporter follows the money, he or she will find a story at the end of the trail. There is no plausible deniability of something this big. If you delay going public with this for too long, Mr. President, you will be accused of orchestrating a cover-up. I know you're a big fan of fixing things quietly behind the scenes, but this problem is beyond that. Someone is going to notice the deep drilling in the Caribbean, and they will definitely notice when NASA starts laying keels for thousands of spacecraft, each the size of an ocean liner."

"Perhaps you're right, Jim. We have probably learned as much as we are going to by keeping this classified. But before we call a press conference, do you know if MI-5 has put that arrogant bastard Finch behind bars yet?"

"Yes, sir. They transferred him to England from Switzerland a few days ago, and threw him into H.M. Prison Cotswold. I think they are calling it protective custody, but in any case the Brits have assured us they'll keep him on ice for as long as necessary. He's being uncooperative as hell, and squawking about his right to submit his paper on creating the singularity to *Nature*."

"When I go public with the story, Finch will be damned glad to have Her Majesty's prison guards and probably a contingent of Royal Marines protecting his sorry ass from the vengeful masses. If there is to be any glory in all this, it will go to Barney Freeman and his team, not Dr. Geoffrey Finch. And if we don't survive, I sincerely hope that son of a bitch is the first one sucked in."

"I do believe that is a fairly common feeling among insiders these days, sir."

"All right. With Finch out of the way and progress being made, perhaps it is time to inform the world. Get the speechwriting team assembled for me, Jim. I'm going to make some phone calls, and if the other leaders agree, we'll try to figure out how to sugarcoat a very bitter pill."

****

"You are going to use aircraft?" Arkady Kutuzov was incredulous. "Nobody uses aircraft to move a drill rig!"

"We have to, my friend," said Clyde Rose. "A ship would take too long. We need to be up and drilling by next week if we're going to meet the schedule."

Although it was December on the Kola Peninsula, they caught a break with the weather. Instead of the usual howling blizzard, the air was calm and the sun was up for a few hours each day. It even warmed up to near freezing. A swarm of Russian and American drilling engineers, rig hands, welders, fitters and laborers descended on the drill site like a flock of vultures. And like vultures stripping a carcass, they were rapidly taking apart the Uralmash 1500 drill rig, placing it on pallets, and loading those pallets onto helicopters for transport to Archangelsk, the closest city with an airport. Once there, the pallets were loaded into giant American C-5 aircraft and even bigger Russian Antonovs for the journey to the Caribbean. A similar swarm of experts on the other end were prepared to take the parts off the pallets and reassemble the drill rig on the tropical island.

Another deep drill rig was being flown into St. Croix from Texas the same manner to drill the back-up hole alongside the Russian rig. In 1974, it had drilled the Bertha Rogers gas well in Oklahoma to 31,441 feet, which held the record as the deepest well in the United States for nearly 30 years. With additional bracing, heavy duty cables, winches, pumps and motors, it ought to be able to handle the drilling, and go it alone if the Uralmash 1500 was down for maintenance or repairs.

Almost like watching a sped-up time-lapse movie, the two drill rigs were assembled a short distance from the Queen Mary Highway in a sugar cane field on the volcanic plain of central St. Croix. Drilling would commence soon afterward. Nikki Shelton and the best computer modelers in the world had determined that the singularity would ascend to within 51, 284 feet of the surface under this exact spot at the apogee of an eccentric orbit in precisely 176 days.

****

43

President Jackson was not happy about this speech, but someone had to do it. He had given difficult speeches before, about the economy, wars, budgets and scandals, but nothing like this. At best, Barney Freeman's crazy plan had a snowball's chance in hell of succeeding. The odds were much better that in slightly more than two years, all life on Earth, and shortly afterward the Earth itself, would be destroyed. The G-20 world leaders and U.N. Secretary General had decided unanimously that the American President was the best person to tell everyone in the world that they were doomed. Great.

President Jackson looked into the camera lens as the speech scrolled up on the Teleprompter. He was an expert at reading it without obviously looking at it. Some people had criticized his use of the device, but he knew he always gave a better speech when he didn't have to ad-lib or search for words. This was one speech that would be a bad idea to make up as he went along, and where he most definitely wanted the facts in front of him.

"Fellow citizens of the world, I bring you grave news. For the past two months, a human-made singularity, popularly known as a 'black hole,' has been loose inside the Earth and is slowly consuming the planet. As it gains mass, the rate at which it consumes matter will increase. In approximately two years, unless we can figure out a way to stop it, this black hole will completely destroy the Earth, and all life upon it.

"I realize this is a shocking statement. World leaders have known about the black hole for only a few weeks, and we are in shock as well. It was made in a European particle accelerator by a reckless scientist, who then lost control of it. I have been chosen to speak on behalf of the leaders of all nations, to tell you that we are doing everything humanly possible to try to stop the annihilation of the Earth from this object. Hundreds of the best scientists, technicians and engineers from many countries around the world are working together at this moment to bore a hole deep into the ground to try to retrieve the singularity from the Earth. We have every hope that they will succeed. Should they fail, however, we are also making plans to try to save as many people as possible. But let me be clear. If we cannot stop the black hole and a planetary evacuation is required, we will not be able to save everyone.

"There is simply not enough time to build sufficient spaceships. By committing all of the resources and labor in the world to this task, we have calculated that a maximum of one million large spacecraft could be built in two years. If each craft was constructed to be the size of an ocean liner, and could carry a thousand passengers, we might be able to evacuate as many as one billion people. That sounds like a lot, but it is only one sixth of the population of the Earth. If we have somewhere to drop people off, say at a moon base or on Mars, we could make multiple trips and perhaps evacuate two or possibly three billion. But however you do the math, there is simply not enough time or resources to evacuate everyone and at least half of the people living on this planet will be forced to remain behind.

"I will take a few minutes to explain what a black hole is, and how this happened. Then I will describe the steps that we are taking to try to intercept this black hole on one of its orbits. I will also share with you the plans to build numerous, large spacecraft to carry as many people as possible to the farside of the moon as survivors of the human race. And then I will ask for your help. "

****

Outside of Grafton, West Virginia, in a mobile home park located off Route 50 near the Tygart Valley River, Sue Ellen Pusser was listening to

45

the President. She was working on getting Truett's lunch together for his midnight shift at the mine in the kitchen of their double-wide, and only half-watching the flat screen satellite TV in the other room. Some of what was being said suddenly registered with her, and she backed up the digital video recorder to the beginning of the speech. Sue Ellen went to get her husband. Truett was definitely going to want to hear this.

Like most people in the River View Estates mobile home park, Sue Ellen Pusser thought that the politicians in Washington were basically criminals who wasted honest people's tax money, and normally were not relevant to her daily life. Even if they were honest when they got there, like the last Christian President, the system itself corrupted them. This current fellow had been elected saying straight out that he intended to give more of their hard-earned tax dollars to shiftless, lazy, no-count poor folks for free doctor visits. Well, at least he was honest about it, but it still wasn't right. Sue Ellen had a bumper sticker on her truck that said "Voting for Free Health Care is easier than working for a living."

Sue Ellen's husband was a Pentecostal minister. Since that didn't pay real well, Truett Pusser was also a coal miner, construction laborer, and occasionally a roofer. The Pussers believed that they were living in the End Times, and they were looking forward to seeing the end of the world and the second coming of Jesus Christ. They had always believed that it would happen soon, and now the President was saying these events would transpire in two years!

"So what happened to the Rapture, Truett?" Sue Ellen asked, after they had watched the speech all the way through. "I thought all righteous Christians were supposed to be taken up to Heaven seven years before the End of Days."

"Perhaps we are sinners," he answered in his gruff, preacher's voice. "We may not be fit for Heaven. No one can presume to know the will of God. He may wish to judge us on His own time."

"Well, perhaps that is true of us," she admitted. "But there hasn't been a Rapture anywhere that I know of. Lots of our friends have given vital testimony at one time or another about accepting Jesus Christ as their personal savior. Surely, not all are unrepentant sinners, yet none have been taken in the Rapture."

"God works in His own mysterious ways." It was Truett's standard answer when the theology of the moment baffled him.

"They are trying to stop this, the President said. Can they do that? Can we allow it?" Sue Ellen looked at him with concern, desperately seeking an answer.

"If it is truly the End of Days, they won't be able to stop it," Truett answered confidently. "Forces and events set in motion by the Lord God Almighty will overwhelm any of their puny attempts to interfere."

"What if we are supposed to be the tools of God, Truett? If we know this is meant to be, and they are trying to stop it, are we not duty-bound to the Lord to intervene?"

Truett pondered for a few moments. "I must pray on this," he told Sue Ellen. "If God wants us to do something about it, He will give us a sign. In the meantime, we can discuss it with the other members of our congregation to see how they feel. If it is the consensus of the Church of the Righteous Sword in the Hand of the Lord to intervene, then so be it."

****

The first person to see President Jackson in the Oval Office after the speech was Don Martin, the National Security Advisor. He was clearly worried.

"Mr. President. Every loose wingnut on the planet is going to come off his or her threads after that speech. If people think they are doomed and have nothing to lose, it could push some marginal folks into rash acts. We have to institute some security lockdowns on federal facilities and put everyone on alert."

"Calm down, Don. The federal government is going to be far too busy over the next two years to function under a security lockdown. There are always a few nuts. We need to identify the threats and protect against them, not bar the door so people can't do their work. Set up a meeting in a day or two with the Secretary of Homeland Security, the heads of the CIA and FBI, and we will figure out how to address this."

Martin turned away, still unhappy. But he knew better than to argue with this President. Charles Godell, the Secretary of Commerce, took his place.

"So what is the plan of attack, Mr. President?"

"NASA is to design, and we must begin constructing some 350,000 spacecraft, and get them launched as quickly as possible, Charlie. By the end of this week, I want to see a logistical plan that will mobilize every industry in the United States, describe how we will complete this task, what facilities will be used, where the manpower and resources will be procured, and what kind of schedule will be followed. I also want some rough cost estimates. We have no choice but to pay the piper, although I would like to know the approximate size of the bill."

"Tony," he called to his chief of staff. "Tell the Secretary of Energy that we will be using the Nevada Test Site for the construction and launching location. It has enough open land with reasonable access for materials. And we can protect the site." He was thinking about the warnings from his National Security Advisor. "Then tell FEMA on my orders to send every available emergency housing unit they have to the Nevada Test Site," he continued. "They can coordinate with the Department of Energy on where to set them up. That place used to mobilize in decades past for nuclear weapon tests. Hopefully, somebody there still remembers how to do it. I need space for tens of thousands of construction workers and all the support workers that come with them."

He turned to the Chairman of the Joint Chiefs and the Secretary of Defense. "The active duty military, reserves and the academies are to provide crews for these space vessels, and I want the crews trained and ready. You can start with the Navy. Every ship is to return to port, and all personnel are to learn how to operate spacecraft. Ditto for the Air Force – everyone is grounded as of now from all missions except those in support of this effort, and they are to cooperate with the Navy and NASA to help design these vessels. You can also empty out the three academies and clear the desk jockeys from the Pentagon. All of our troops overseas are to come home immediately and be assigned to this project. Navy and Air Force personnel first, then fill the remaining personnel gaps with the Army and the Marines as best you can, but keep some well-armed troops in reserve to maintain order. Things might get ugly. Also, we need airtight security around the perimeter of the Nevada Test Site. No rent-a-cops – I want real soldiers armed with real bullets, and the best electronic surveillance measures available. I am totally serious that every single serviceman and woman in the United States military is to begin working on and training for this fleet as of now. If we are to have any chance of success at all, we have to get mobilized and keep moving on this project at a flat out, dead run. We have a fixed and very unforgiving deadline. This just became the nation's number one, top priority task."

"Aye, aye, sir," the admiral replied. "It sounds like you're not very confident about Professor Freeman and his team."

"They are the best in the world, Sam. But all it takes is one small screw-up or failure on their part, and they could miss the singularity, or be unable to hold onto it if they do catch it. I'd rather be pessimistic and end up with 350,000 spaceships we don't need, than to be caught flat-footed as the planet collapses beneath us with no way to get out of here. If everything works out all right, we can always use the spacecraft later on for regular old space travel."

"I thought you said in the speech that we were building a million. What happened to the others?"

"The Chinese and Japanese are going to cooperate to build another 350,000, and the Russians and European Union will be constructing a similar number. This is a global effort to face a global threat."

****

The Uralmash 1500 drill rig sat atop a borehole that extended 100 feet into the Earth. This was called the "rat hole," and was a starter bore. It was designed to get the Uralmash bit underground where it could begin grinding away at the rock and making hole.

The Russian drill rig used a downhole mud motor to turn the bit. Unlike old-fashioned oilfield rigs, which turned the entire drill string from the surface using a rotating platform called a Kelly bushing, the Russian drill pipe remained stationary, supporting the weight of the bit. Drilling mud was pumped down the center of the pipe under enormous pressure. Just before getting to the cutting head, the thin mud squeezed through a helical, turbine-like apparatus that spun the bit. It then exited through small holes in the cutting head, cooling the bit and removing rock cuttings, which were returned to the surface by the recirculating mud. Because the drill string didn't turn, it could bend, turn and even drill horizontally. The downhole assembly was steered with a gyroscope and inertial guidance system similar to those found on nuclear submarines. These mud motors had revolutionized deep drilling and directional drilling, making both more practical and less costly. The Russians had invented the downhole motor for the Kola deep well, but the Americans had refined it considerably for offshore oil drilling in deep water. With the use of a steerable downhole assembly, a rig anchored on one spot could drill toward all points of the compass, tapping into dozens of oil reservoirs without the expensive and time-consuming task of having to move the deepwater platform from place to place as they drilled.

The Uralmash 1500 used a double drill string with an inner pipe called a tremmie, which carried the mud downhole to the mud motor and bit. The mud returned to the surface with the rock cuttings by flowing through the ring-like space between the tremmie and the main drill pipe, called the annulus. This double drill string allowed the Russians to drill an open hole without setting casing, because the outer drill pipe itself acted as casing to keep the hole from collapsing. They could even change a worn-out drillbit without having to pull the entire drill pipe from the hole. The old bit could be detached and folded down to fit inside the outer drill string.

It was then pulled up to the surface on the end of the tremmie pipe for replacement and re-installation. The Russians had evolved these deep drilling designs gradually over decades of painful experience. Clyde Rose sought to adapt them posthaste to the Texas rig.

They drilled 9,265 feet deep on St. Croix the first week with the Russian rig, and 8,948 feet with the American drill. It was great progress, exceeding the 1,000 feet per day needed to meet their goal. Still, Clyde Rose and Arkady Kutuzov were not relaxing. They had not expected many problems with the solid volcanic rock of St. Croix at shallow depths. The difficulties would come when they got deeper, and perhaps hit a zone of water-filled fractures that could flood the bottom of the hole with hot, high-pressure saltwater. These geopressured brines were highly corrosive – Arkady had seen equipment made of exotic stainless steel alloys that had been lowered into such brines for only a few minutes, and returned to the surface looking as rusted as if made of cast iron. They would have to seal any troublesome fractures by pumping down cement grout under high pressure, losing time and headway. Other potential problems included pockets of deadly hydrogen sulfide gas, and the ever increasing temperature and pressure with depth. The geologic consensus was that the crust under St. Croix should not have as high of a geothermal gradient as that under the Kola Peninsula, but no one had ever drilled deeply here before, so no one really knew.

The American engineer and the Russian scientist continued to tend their drill rigs around the clock, and the holes gradually progressed deeper.

****

The day after the President's speech, Dr. Lauren Chang, the director of the National Aeronautics and Space Administration, called a meeting of all hands. Her message was terse and to the point.

"NASA has many personnel trained in science and engineering. You know better than most the potential consequences of what may happen with Finch's black hole orbiting inside the Earth. There is a high probability that this egotistical idiot's misjudgment will not have a happy ending.

"Therefore, I am ordering everyone to drop all other duties, and focus on the design elements for the large lifeboat spacecraft. Because that is what they will be, if Dr. Freeman and his team are unable to capture the singularity. We need to get the engineering done quickly. I want drawings on the table and vessels under construction within one month. The design criteria are simple. These vessels must be large, maneuverable, and comfortable for a thousand people, safe, and have enough power to get at least to the far side of the moon. Anything goes, including nuclear, as long as it will work. Use your imaginations.

"All other NASA programs are hereby suspended. This means all manned spaceflight, the International Space Station, all space science, Earth science and life science programs – everything. If they manage to tame the singularity, we can all go back to our daily routines. Until then, however, the lifeboat program is our new, single, focused priority. These ships could be the only thing that might save humanity from extinction. If we don't get them built and the black hole destroys the Earth, we're all dead. Period. It's that simple.

"We have organized teams to engineer these ships. All engineering, scientific and support personnel at NASA are assigned to these teams. We've also brought in large numbers of contractors to help with the

53

details. We need to design systems for the materials, propulsion, maneuvering, life support, air circulation, plumbing, electrical, so help me God, everything! Each ship must be able to supply air, water, food and medical care to a thousand frightened citizens who have never been in space before. Like the old World War II Liberty Ships, the lifeboat design must work, it must be something that can be constructed quickly and safely, and must perform with a zero failure rate. Then we need to build hundreds of thousands of them.

"Now, I can't ask you officially to give more than 100% of your best efforts to get these ships designed and built, but you all know what is at stake here. Unofficially, we will keep NASA operations running 24 hours a day, seven days a week until further notice, and personnel are welcome to put in as much time as they feel they safely can. We will provide access to cots, showers, laundry, and food services around the clock at strategic locations throughout Agency facilities. Please see your supervisor for details about your new duties."

Similar speeches were being given by the directors of the European Space Agency, the Russian Space Agency, Chinese Space Agency, and Japanese Space Agency.

****

The man with the plan turned out to be a balding, overweight, 30-year NASA veteran with the improbable name of Daniel R. Spaniel. For the past decade, he had been the director, chief engineer, and more often than not, the lone employee of the NASA Office for Future Manned Spaceflight.

Spaniel had spent years developing new spacecraft concepts for manned exploration of the solar system, planetary colonization, habitats in space, and even a long haul, multi-generational starship. He forwarded these faithfully to NASA upper management in the Spacecraft Engineering Directorate, only to see them filed and ignored. When he followed-up on the fate of his submissions, he was told that the designs were too large, too expensive, too difficult to engineer, or did not fit with current NASA program priorities. His most recent disappointment was the shelving of his revolutionary design for a new lunar mission spacecraft in favor of the Orion program, which was basically just an unimaginative scale-up of the old Apollo vehicle.

Dr. Daniel Spaniel was an avid science fiction fan, to the point of obsession. He knew every episode of every Star Trek series from memory, along with every Battlestar Galactica, Stargate, the Star Wars movies and nearly every other book, movie or television show that involved spaceflight. He wrote space opera novels and short stories in his spare time for fun, and had even published a few. He had tried sending in some scripts for the Stargate series that were never used. Spaniel was the ultimate scifi nerd, and his talks on futuristic spacecraft designs were extremely popular at scifi conventions. He even got to meet Samantha Carter of Stargate fame at one of these shows, and followed her around like a love-struck puppy. NASA knew a good public relations gig when they saw one, so his bosses were told to keep him working away on concept spacecraft, and encouraged him to attend scifi conventions. Although being used as a NASA public relations tool didn't especially bother Spaniel, and he enjoyed the scifi conventions, he was frustrated because the agency seemed to regard his spacecraft designs as science fiction also. Spaniel knew his engineering was a quantum leap improvement over current NASA hardware, and that his designs would work if they would only give him half a chance.

Now they needed him. The Director had called for new spacecraft ideas. Spaniel had file drawers, CD-ROM disks and jump drives full of them. Although never built or tested, the designs had been thoroughly engineered, and the theoretical performance modeled with sophisticated computer programs. They were as ready to go as anything at the agency. He put some of the most applicable designs on a jump drive and went to see his boss.

"Ben, we need to get these to Dr. Chang. I have the large spacecraft designs she is seeking."

Benjamin Silverstein was a young, aggressive manager. He was extremely image conscious, and a little bit unsure of himself. He usually humored Dr. Spaniel, because the word had come down that this guy was important to the agency outreach program. But allowing the eccentric scientist to send his far out and sometimes bizarre spacecraft designs directly to Lauren Chang? No way. She might question Ben's competence as a manager, and his ability to control his people. Such questions from the Director could hurt his career. He would have to review Spaniel's designs first before they went anywhere.

"Now hold on a minute, Dan. What is so special about these designs? I will need to review them before we can talk to the Director."

"There isn't a lot of time," Spaniel replied impatiently. "She said the designs were to be forwarded immediately. These are for big ships, Ben! Space liners that can carry thousands of people. Dr. Chang must see them."

"After I review them. Please let me have them and I will take a look now."

Reluctantly, Spaniel handed over his memory stick to Ben Silverstein, who downloaded the designs into his computer. Briefly, he wondered if such a move was wise, but Ben was his boss, and he wasn't about to do an end run around his manager. Ben told him to check back in a couple of days, and Spaniel returned to his graphics computer to make some fine adjustments to the existing designs.

The next day, Ben Silverstein decided to take a look at Dan Spaniel's ship designs. He was astounded. Silverstein had learned in college and been indoctrinated into NASA management with the belief that manned spacecraft required billions of dollars for development and decades of research. Space technology was mostly an extension of aircraft technology. Because the atmosphere had to be traversed to enter space, it had always been assumed that the basic manned spacecraft design would be some kind of modified aircraft that could enter space. This had started with the X-1 and X-15 rocket plane programs back in the 1950's, which were put on hold for the Mercury, Gemini and Apollo spacecraft designed from ballistic missiles that were needed to win the race to the moon. Still, the apex of this idea was the original space shuttle, which was little more than a glider attached to rockets, even though it was the most complex machine of its time when built.

Spaniel had dumped the aircraft-as-space-vehicle design, and gone with something completely different. His space liners were big and bold, designed to move through dangerous, hostile environments, while protecting their occupants. And like an old-style, Queen Mary-type ocean liner, the design could accommodate thousands of people in comfort. Despite the size, the designs were simple, and could be built with readily available materials. Fancy alloys were not required for hull metal when titanium steel plate would work. The re-breathing air had simple scrubbers to remove CO_2, and oxygen tanks for replenishment. The control systems

57

used metal wires, not optical cables, and the ship had lithium batteries for back-up power instead of fuel cells. Wastewater was distilled and reused. Spaniel had gotten a lot of his design ideas from the Battlestar Galactica TV series, which Ben Silverstein had never watched, and therefore didn't make the connection. Otherwise, he would have smiled at the name of the ship on the design drawings: "Pegasus."

The designs on his computer screen were good, and exactly what the agency was looking for. Silverstein decided to forward them to the Director himself, without mentioning Daniel Spaniel as the source. Of course he would fess up if she asked him about it, but why push it? There would be many laurels heaped upon the person who brought these designs forward. Ben though it might do a lot to advance his career, if he could get his name associated with these plans. In any case, Spaniel was such a flake that he probably wouldn't even notice, or care if he did. Without a trace of guilt or remorse, Silverstein wrote an e-mail and attached the plans. It was addressed to the Agency Director, the head of the Manned Spaceflight Directorate, and his immediate supervisor. He didn't even bother to include Dan Spaniel on the "cc" line. He clicked the "send" button and it was gone.

****

On board the orbiting International Space Station, the American astronauts and Russian cosmonauts were shutting it down. It was time to get off, catch the last ride home, and get to work on the lifeboats.

"*Tovarisch*," the senior cosmonaut caught the attention of the American commander just before entering the Soyuz capsule for the journey home. "Was this space station not scheduled for a boost into a higher orbit?"

"*Da,*" the American replied, in the odd "Russlish" mixed language that had evolved aboard the station. "There was supposed to be a booster bringing fuel to the maneuvering rockets next week. I guess that is canceled now, along with everything else."

"What will happen if it does not get the boost?" the Russian colonel asked, mainly to be on record for the station voice recorder, clearly knowing the answer already.

"I presume there will be a fairly spectacular re-entry burn in a few weeks as she scrapes the top of the atmosphere, and comes on down."

"A rather sad and expensive end to a useful space station," the Russian commented.

"True, but it can't be helped. We have to deal with the singularity. I suppose this will be one more item they can add onto Dr. Finch's already considerable bar tab."

****

Dr. Lauren Chang had to admit she was impressed. The design of the proposed lifeboat spaceship appeared to have started out as a submarine, except the nose tapered almost to a spire, topped by a pearl-like globe. There were three large fins near the base, equally-spaced around the perimeter of the ship. The nuclear powerplant was in the pearl, and it was placed atop the spire to keep the radiation source a safe distance away from the inhabited part of the ship. The big fins were for radiative cooling, not steering. Still, it looked like a spaceship that Edgar Rice Burroughs might have dreamed up for John Carter to fly to Barsoom, as drawn by Chesley Bonestell. It was to be built from relatively inexpensive and simple alloys of steel, titanium, and aluminum, and powered by a sodium-cooled fission reactor.

59

"What about propulsion, Ben?" Dr. Chang asked Ben Silverstein after she reviewed the details. "I don't understand how you plan to move the beastie."

"I am sorry Dr. Chang. I don't know that much about it. Dr. Spaniel will have to explain." It was the most humiliating hour of Silverstein's young life. After forwarding the plans to the Director in a way that made them look like his, Dr. Chang had called Ben to her office to discuss the technical details. Although a bit rusty after having been in administration for so long, Lauren Chang was a formidable engineering talent in her own right. It took her only a few seconds to realize that the plans had not been generated by Silverstein, nor did he have much of a clue about what was in them. She demanded to know where he had gotten the designs, and why the engineer who had actually created the designs was not in the room to help explain them.

Silverstein spluttered uncomfortably, trying to explain that he was just representing the work of one of his people who had asked that it be forwarded to the Director. Chang had dealt with credit-grabbing managers before, and decided to teach the young Mr. Silverstein a lesson. She demanded that he get the engineer who had developed the designs into her office immediately. When Daniel Spaniel arrived, she greeted him warmly and thanked him for forwarding his plans to her through his manager. She told him that these designs were an important breakthrough. Spaniel fairly glowed.

Then, as she reviewed the plans with the two men, Lauren Chang deliberately directed every complex and difficult technical question solely to Ben Silverstein. He was unable to answer any but the simplest, and was forced to refer almost every question over to Dr. Spaniel, who answered with aplomb. Silverstein came across looking like an idiot, which was Chang's exact point. In this context, he WAS an idiot. Managers should let the technical people who understand the work talk about technical issues. Supervisors look best in reflected light.

Dan Spaniel was answering the propulsion question. "It became obvious early-on in the research that the best propulsion system for a ship this large is nuclear-electric. I came up with a compact, liquid sodium reactor to generate the electricity, and also to thermalize the fuel before sending it down the electromagnetic propulsionway. The drive design starts with hydrogen fuel being bombarded with fast neutrons, which causes the atomic nuclei to ionize, 'thermalize,' and accelerate to high speeds. Powerful electromagnetic fields then move the ionized atoms faster and in a uniform direction, ejecting them out the rear of the ship as a high-speed beam of ionized matter. It is a nuclear ion drive, and is far more efficient per kilogram of fuel than a chemical rocket. They did tests on nuclear drives of a much simpler design out at the Nevada Test Site back in the 1960's, and some of the results were astounding. I think this drive will perform much better with many additional years of electronics, materials and nuclear research behind it."

"Dr. Chang," said Silverstein, as the subject finally moved onto something he knew about, "We must discuss the launching facilities for getting these ships into orbit."

"You can't just take off using this fancy ion drive?"

"Well, yes we could," Spaniel answered. "It can provide nearly enough thrust by itself, and with some secondary boosters, she would fly, all right. However, the process of bombarding hydrogen with high-speed

61

neutrons to turn it into energetic plasma creates tritium, which is moderately radioactive."

"We think it would be a wise policy to restrict the use of the ion drive until the ship is outside the atmosphere," Silverstein said.

"I see," replied Chang. "Well, I suppose dusting the southwestern U.S. with a cloud of radioactive rocket exhaust after every launch would not win the space program many friends. However, if we are launching everything that will fly because the world is coming to an end, I don't think we need to worry about niceties. We can start off launching them cleanly, but if this turns into a mass exodus at the end of days, we will need to be more concerned with just getting every ship off the ground. What do we need for clean launches, and how can we set them up to launch dirty?"

"The simplest option for getting this ship above the atmosphere," Spaniel said, "is what NASA for many years has derisively called a 'big, dumb booster.' This is essentially an enormous steel cylinder the size of a city water tank, with a divider and a rocket nozzle, filled up on one side with liquid oxygen and the other with fuel, like liquefied natural gas. The booster is big, ugly, cheap, and easy to build, uses common materials, and can be reused, but it is also expendable if necessary. You put the spaceship on top of the tank, light it off and away you go. We could even attach a ring of air-breathing jet engines around the rim of the tank to provide extra boost in the atmosphere. The whole assembly gets up to sub-orbital altitude, where the big, dumb booster runs out of fuel, separates, and falls back to Earth, to be recovered and reused. The main part of the ship coasts clear, and uses its ion drive to exit the last wisps of atmosphere, boosting into orbit. It should be high enough at this point that any radioactive hydrogen ions will be trapped in the Van Allen belts."

"I see. All right, that sounds workable. How do we launch the ships directly?"

Silverstein spoke up. "If we can't use the big, dumb booster for launch, we can strap three STS-size solid rocket boosters onto the fuselage at the base of the fins. Those combined with the ion drive should get the ship to orbit. However, we would be forced to expend the SRBs about three quarters of the way there, and they won't be reusable."

"That's quite all right, Mr. Silverstein. If it comes down to launching the ships directly, there won't be a need for reusable boosters. Everyone will be getting out of Dodge, for good."

****

"Well, Flavio, what do you think of all this? Can it be done?"

Flavio Belladonna, the Deputy Director of NASA slowly shook his head. "Dr. Chang, one can't simply take an ocean liner and fly it into space. There would still be some development work necessary to create such a thing." At Chang's request, he had listened in on her meeting with Silverstein and Spaniel surreptitiously via the intercom. She had wanted Ben Silverstein to think he was one-on-one with the director, but she also wanted a second set of ears on the conversation. Flavio had rather spectacular ears, and she trusted his insights.

"I think Dr. Spaniel has done a fantastic job of designing a large spacecraft by blending and adapting existing submarine technology, large aircraft technology, and materials technology. Believe me; he has worked out most of the details. It doesn't require a lot of research for us to determine if it will work and how to build it. The design uses standard materials and off-the-shelf parts. Almost everything needed already exists, and merely has to be procured. So can it be built?"

"Yes, Madame Director, I think it can. But there will be significant resistance among many of the engineers at NASA to embark on such a radical change..."

"Flavio let me be absolutely clear on this." Lauren Chang raised her voice slightly and her face flushed. It was obviously a sore point. The Deputy Director wisely decided to shut up and pay attention to his boss.

"I have heard enough excuses from NASA engineers about why we can't put large numbers of people into space," she continued. "It is hogwash. Dan Spaniel did this engineering years ago, and the big dumb booster concept, or 'heavy lift vehicle' for the official name, has been around for decades. This agency could have moved ahead with a High Frontier, post-Apollo space program back in the 1970's when O'Neill first proposed it. The technology was there. If we had a large population already living in space, it wouldn't be such a life and death situation now for humanity. Here we are, stuck on one planet, and it is in mortal danger. I know that Barney Freeman and his people are going to do their best to tame the singularity, but if they fail and we have to evacuate Earth, there had better be ships. I'm talking about big ships, and lots of them. We also need somewhere for those ships to go.

"I want you to dust off the old lunar base plans, update them and get a team ready for construction. Adapt Earth construction techniques and equipment for the moon. We don't have time to design anything from scratch. The first new big ship out of the gate should be a construction vessel to carry loads of equipment and engineers to the moon. The sooner we start building habitation up there, the sooner we can start moving people off the Earth. This is life and death, Flavio. The longer we delay, the more people will be left behind to die.

"We are incredibly fortunate that Dr. Spaniel had these designs readily available, and was able to simply hand us the blueprints. His efforts to work out the engineering details saved us months of development time, which can be spent on construction instead. You see, Flavio, money isn't the limiting factor here. It is time. For each day we delay, the black hole ingests a little more of our planet and grows a little more massive. Those days are lost, and we can never get them back.

"The end of the world is approaching, and we don't have time for debates. Developing and constructing a space liner capable of carrying a thousand or more people is now the top NASA priority, and building hundreds of thousands of them is the top priority of the U.S. military and every other government agency. If you cannot stare down the troops and impose this change of program direction on the NASA bureaucracy, or if you are not capable of making this project a reality within a very short time frame, please tell me now, and I will find someone who can. We must build it, test it, perfect it, and send the plans to every other space agency on the planet to get them building similar designs. If we fail, the entire human race is doomed in less than two years. If we succeed, at least a sixth and perhaps as much as half of humanity will survive. This is the single most important engineering task anyone in history has ever attempted. I do not wish to hear any more reasons about why this can't be done. Got it?"

"Yes, Madame Director." Belladonna remained silent for a few moments.

"Well?"

"The NASA engineers will be difficult. I know them. They will try to overdesign it, using excessively strong materials, exotic electronics and making everything triple-redundant. After losing the crews of Apollo 1,

65

Challenger, and Columbia, the original safety awareness at NASA has evolved into a culture that rewards the overly cautious, the timid, meek, and the risk-averse. So much for the Right Stuff. Then we wonder why there are no bold leaders stepping out from among the ranks."

"So how will you handle them, Flavio?" Chang asked, pressing.

His response was a simple shrug, "They have to be made afraid."

"What do you mean?" Chang looked at him with surprise.

"They have to understand that this is a matter of life and death, as you say," Belladonna replied. "However, I intend that this should be THEIR life and their death as well. We will motivate them to build a moon base and 350,000 large spacecraft in 18 months by allowing them to build one more. The last lifeboat craft will be designated for NASA technical staff and their families. They don't get to start it until all the others are underway. I will simply tell them that if they want to have a chance to live, they had best get cracking."

Chapter Four: Preparations

After four weeks of drilling, the two holes on St. Croix had reached a depth of 25,000 feet. This was deeper than most deep oil and gas drillholes, but they were only halfway. As the onsite supervisor, Clyde Rose was called the "tool pusher." Arkady was the driller. The crew of American, Canadian, British, Russian, Dutch and Saudi drill rig workers was known as "roughnecks."

Several fracture zones had been encountered, which resulted in lost circulation of the drilling mud. Instead of returning up the annulus carrying the drill cuttings, the pressurized mud had disappeared into the downhole fracture systems, becoming lost to the formation. Sometimes they could power through by simply adding more mud up top to replace that lost to the fractures. This would not be considered good practice in normal drilling operations, where cement grout would be injected into the fractures, allowed to harden, and then drilled through. However, this was not a normal drilling operation, and anything that could be done to keep them on schedule was fair game. Sometimes, though, if the fracture systems were too severe, they had no choice but to stop and grout. These episodes saw Clyde and Arkady beside themselves with impatience, pacing nervously around the drill pad and constantly checking their watches to see if the grout had cured enough to resume drilling. During these times, most of the rig crew hid out in their trailers, drinking coffee and keeping out of the bosses' way.

The news media were having a field day. Reporters and camera operators were all over the Virgin Islands, trying to get images of the drill rigs, interview workers, and most importantly, hoping to corner Arkady or

Clyde for a progress update. They got in the way, and got underfoot. Sooner or later, somebody was going to get hurt or worse in the dangerous location of a drill rig.

After a reporter tried to walk across the apparently dry surface of a pit filled with drilling mud, and went in waist-deep, losing his expensive commercial camera in the process, Clyde and Arkady decided that something needed to be done. They discussed the media problem with Barney, who took it to President Jackson. Despite the preoccupation in Washington with getting the spacecraft construction started, within two days, the perimeter of the drill site had been fenced with 6-foot high chain link, and the only entrance was through a gate staffed around the clock by armed guards. The President sent some White House media staffers down to help. They organized a press briefing every morning for Clyde and Arkady to report progress and answer questions. Every worker on the rig was told to refer any and all media inquiries to the morning briefing. It soon became routine.

Lieutenant Nicole Shelton arrived on-site a few weeks later to track the singularity, monitor drilling progress, and oversee a team of scientists from Los Alamos, Sandia, and Lawrence Livermore National Laboratories who were constructing the electromagnetic cage to catch Finch's black hole. Nikki caused quite a sensation among the rig crew the first day she showed up, wearing a low cut spaghetti-strap top, khaki shorts, and running shoes.

The crews had been working 12-hour shifts and sleeping in trailers on the site. Most of them had not seen a woman in weeks, except for the elderly ladies who served up food in the chow trailer. Nikki's appearance in the doghouse where drilling operations were centered nearly caused everything to come to a halt. Everyone on the crew was trying to get a look, coming into the doghouse trailer on any flimsy excuse to sneak a peek. Arkady, who was in the middle of calculating the timing for the next bit changeout, got annoyed and kicked them all out. Clyde walked her around the drill pad and explained the operation. After a roughneck got a finger jammed in a pulley because he was watching Nikki instead of what he was doing, Arkady asked Clyde to get her off the site.

Clyde ushered her back inside the doghouse, under the gaze of dozens of roughnecks who had better things to do. He wasn't quite sure how to broach this subject, but he had to say something.

"Nikki, you are an attractive young woman, and a distraction to the rig crew."

"Well, I can't help how I look, Clyde. I'm not interested in any of them."

"That's not the point. They are interested in you, and when you show up dressed that way, they pay far more attention to you than to what they are doing. A drill rig is an extremely dangerous place, where being distracted can get someone killed."

"What is wrong with how I'm dressed? It's just shorts and a top, for crying out loud. Everything important is under cover. I'm certainly legal, and everybody in the Virgin Islands dresses this way. I'm not wearing dress blues to work around greasy machinery. And we are in the tropics, you know."

"I know that, but it's causing a problem here. These guys have been living on this rig for a month. It is a natural reaction."

"Now you listen here, Clyde Rose," Nikki said angrily. "I have just as much right to be on this rig as anyone else. I'm down here to do a job, not seek out romance. And I'm sure as hell not doing a strip tease act! It is 95 degrees in the shade and I refuse to wear a burka. If these boys forgot what a woman looks like and can't keep from hurting themselves because I'm walking around on their precious drill rig, then maybe you'd better get another crew composed of gentlemen, instead of a bunch of leering perverts. The first one I catch staring at my tits is going to get beaned with a pipe wrench!" Her voice was loud enough to carry above the sound of the machinery, and several of the roughnecks heard her. The word began to pass quietly to back off on the new girl.

"All right, Nikki. Take it easy." Clyde had not expected quite so intense of a reaction. In his previous experience with her, he had pegged her as somewhat timid. However, this issue obviously struck a nerve. Still, she needed to dress properly for her own safety, as well as the safety of the roughnecks. Even if they were leering perverts.

"This is one of the best drill crews on the planet. They are gentlemen, at least within limits. I think everyone just forgot their manners today, and I will have a little discussion with all three shifts about how we treat colleagues, especially female colleagues, on this rig. But I also want you to understand that there are safety standards on a drill rig, which include a dress code. Before I can allow you back on-site, you will need to be wearing long pants, a shirt that covers your shoulders and upper arms, safety glasses, steel-toed boots and a hard hat. Go into Christiansted and find the supply store for sugar cane workers. They will have all the stuff you need."

"I have a battle dress uniform, combat boots and other safety gear that will meet all those requirements," Nikki said in disgust. "But if I dress out in that, I'll look just like one of those roughnecks."

"That's the idea," Clyde replied quietly.

****

People in the world were beginning to react to the singularity in bizarre ways. It had started slowly, but as the enormity of what the President of the United States had told them began to sink in, citizens got quietly hysterical. Early on, people began buying things they had always wanted but could never afford, putting themselves into immense debt. If the world was going to end in two years, who cared? The vacation resorts and cruise ships began to fill up, as did hotels in fun cities like Las Vegas, Orlando, Monte Carlo, Amsterdam and Bangkok. Luxury goods flew off the store shelves. Expensive wine, brandy and liquor were sold out within weeks. Premium cigars were unobtainable at any price. Tobacco use was up, along with alcohol, prostitution and most illegal drugs. People were spending money like there was no tomorrow, which was, of course, a fairly high probability within two years.

After a few months, nearly all of the world's material and labor resources were being diverted to the construction of the lifeboats, leaving precious little else for other goods. Many things were simply no longer being manufactured. Prices shot up as demand exceeded supply. The value of goods and services changed overnight, as whole national economies were redirected toward lifeboat construction. Buying luxury goods or taking expensive vacations became viewed as a waste of resources and a waste of time, both of which could be better spent on lifeboat construction.

The labor market was turned on its ear by the lifeboat program. A host of formerly wealthy occupations found themselves to be irrelevant to the construction of spacecraft. It was the kiss of death in the job market. Attorneys, investment bankers, hedge fund managers, stockbrokers, sports

71

figures, movie stars, musicians, real estate moguls, insurance executives, and many others were unwanted, unneeded and unemployed. Many were living off their savings. On the other hand, engineers, scientists, miners, mill workers, truck drivers, sheet metal workers, welders, pipefitters and electricians were in huge demand and commanding fantastic salaries. The stock market crashed and burned as capital was pulled out to finance the lifeboats, and nobody knew what anything was worth anymore. The national governments of most major nations controlled nearly all available funds, and used the cash flow to build spacecraft. Although the Earth itself had not yet imploded, the world economy certainly had.

There were almost no new marriages, because of the uncertainty. Couples stopped having children. Many existing marriages were strained or failing as people decided to have affairs with as many partners as they could in two years. No sense in putting off that office romance, or summer fling – it was now or never. Teenage sex, which had always used the imminent end of the world as an excuse, reached epidemic proportions now that there was bona fide evidence, and from no less than the President.

Crime was up. Robbery and burglary followed close on the heels of all the new consumerism. Why bother with credit card debt when you can just steal it? More disturbingly, murders, especially revenge murders, were at an all-time high. People were starting to think that since they had nothing to lose, why not kill that loudmouth neighbor? Or someone who practiced a religion you didn't like? The most prison time you would serve was likely to be less than two years anyway. It was a great opportunity to rid yourself of the money-hungry ex-wife, the cheating husband, or the demanding boss. Gun sales jumped as everyone tried to defend themselves from everyone else. Millions of people worldwide died within the first few months.

In response, world governments put forth intense efforts to calm down their citizens. They pleaded that lifeboats were being built, and there needed to be a least a few sane people left to ride as passengers. Economies were hurriedly restructured around the need to build spaceships. Workers without the proper construction skills were assigned other tasks, in factories manufacturing spacecraft parts, growing and processing food and other supplies for the ships, or preparing documents, records, family histories and other records for the shipboard archives. But little could be done to stop the panic. Many people got religion, and attendance at churches, mosques, synagogues and temples swelled to record numbers. Most religious leaders appealed for calm, and for hope. Still, none of the various patriarchs, rabbis, archbishops, priests, ministers, ayatollahs, and mullahs, the Dalai Lama, the Pope or any other religious leader really had an answer. Some preachers took advantage of the situation by scaring the hell out of everyone with portents of doom, the last judgment and impending Armageddon. Attendance in their churches went even higher.

A very contentious debate was going on inside the United Nations and out of public view as to how the lifeboats should be filled. The initial discussions were agreeable, as everyone recognized that the population in the vessels should be restricted to young adults of breeding age, and children. Except for maybe a few hundred senior military and civilian leaders to guide the fleet, there was no point in sending geezers into space, because they wouldn't be much help in expanding the human population. For the purposes of this discussion, a geezer was defined as anyone over 35.

The make-up of the rest of the people to be assigned to lifeboats was the problem. Some countries, like the United States, thought the passenger lists ought to be filled by the countries that were building the lifeboats. According to this version of the math, North America would get to send 350 million people, with Europe and Asia sending similar numbers. The logic was that the countries making the effort and spending the money should get to put their people on their ships. Most of the poorer nations of the world rejected this notion, saying the passengers on the ships ought to be selected in proportion with the population of the world. In their version of math, although the United States was building a third of the ships, its citizens would make up only 5% of the total passengers, in proportion to their world population. India, on the other hand, would supply a fifth of the people on board the ships, and a quarter would be Chinese. The debate was becoming intractable, and might end up being settled by military force as the final departure day neared.

No one was even sure if the lifeboat fleet and moon colony could survive the final collapse of the Earth into a black hole. The ships would be landed near the colony on the far side of the moon, putting its bulk between them and the deadly imploding planet, but the intensity of the final few hours was difficult to predict. Matter crossing the event horizon of a black hole gets squeezed together very violently, emitting high-energy radiation in the process as hard x-rays and gamma rays. Collapsing neutron stars were known to create "gamma ray bursters," with super intense radiation directed outward in a beam that could be detected nearly across the universe. For about half a day, the final accretion of the imploding Earth would shine more brightly than the entire galaxy, sending gamma ray bursts toward the North Star and the Southern Cross. No one knew if the bulk of the moon would be enough to shield the ships from this intense radiation, or if the people inside them would still get a lethal dose. They really should be on the other side of the sun, using its much greater bulk for shielding, and the greater distance to decrease the intensity of any possible radiation exposure. Although the ships were designed to handle such a mission, there simply wouldn't be enough time to get there before the final collapse.

****

Despite her preoccupation with astrophysics and multi-body orbital computer models, U.S. Navy Lieutenant Nicole Marie Shelton was far from a typical physics nerd. At 28, she was slender, athletic and pretty, in top physical condition with pale skin, short brown hair and dark eyes. Her family in Ohio was successful Mennonite farmers, who were proud of her success, even though most of them didn't have a clue what she actually did beyond the vague knowledge that she flew airplanes. Nikki explained during rare family get-togethers that the physics work was her passion these days, and she did it as an attempt to seek a better understanding of God by learning the rules under which His universe operated. That went over quite well with the Mennonites, who were generally more flexible and open to interpretation than other conservative Christian groups. A bit of self-discovery combined with a God quest was understandable to many.

Nikki was sitting in the Uralmash doghouse with Clyde, going over the gyroscopic compass data to determine the exact location of the bottom of the hole. It was important that this drillhole end up in the precise geographical location as the black hole orbit when they reached total depth if they expected to have any chance at all of capturing Finch's singularity. The national lab people were going to be arriving next week to start

75

assembling and testing the electromagnetic cage. It had to be placed perfectly.

Nikki was now clad in part of her BDU, or Battle Dress Uniform. She wore tropic camouflage trousers, an olive drab tee shirt, and a pair of black, steel-toed combat boots. Her orange hard hat sat on a nearby desk with her safety glasses, which looked like fashionable shades. Only the small ANSI sticker on the lens gave them away.

There was a knock on the trailer door, and a man entered.

"Hello, Clyde," he said with a British accent, shaking the engineers hand. "How have you been, mate?"

"Fine, Dud, just fine." Clyde responded. Nikki looked up from her work, as it was obviously someone Clyde knew.

"Oh, let me introduce you," Clyde said, remembering Nikki. "Dr. Nicole Shelton, this is Dr. Dudley Gardner of the British Geological Survey, out of Tortola. Dud visits us on occasion to check the borehole geology and monitor progress as we drill. Dud, Nikki is a Navy physicist assisting Barney Freeman with the orbital calculations of the singularity we soon hope to intercept."

"Very pleased to meet you, Dr. Shelton," he said warmly, shaking her hand.

"Oh, thank you...I mean, uh, pleased to meet you as well," she replied, a bit flustered. He was a rather handsome, middle-aged man, in a rough-cut, James Bond-ish sort of way. She noticed he had sea green eyes and close cropped iron grey hair. "Please, just call me Nikki."

"Certainly, Nikki. I'm known as Dud, even though I've been going off for years."

76

She smiled at what must have been a very old and well-worn joke. Dudley Gardner went on to explain that although his official station was the British Geological Survey headquarters in Nottingham, England, he had been on an extended field assignment in the British Virgin Islands for years because of his expertise on Caribbean volcanoes. He was apparently the nearest available expert on St. Croix geology, so his government had pressed him into service to help with the drilling. He spent a lot of time in his office on Tortola working through data analysis and reports. He only needed to visit the field site about once a week.

He asked her what she was doing, and seemed fascinated by the gyroscopic compass data. She found him interesting and easy to talk to.

Arkady came into the doghouse just then. "Clyde, we have to stop and grout again. It's another fracture zone. I lost circulation and I don't think we're going to be able to power through this one."

"How much mud did you lose?" Dud asked.

"At least a thousand liters before I decided to stop," Arkady replied. He turned to Dud. "Say, Mister Geologist, do you have any idea when we might get through these damned fracture zones and into more solid rock?"

"Hopefully, pretty soon. The seismic reflection data showed an attenuating layer between 20,000 and 25,000 feet, which has been interpreted as fractures. The returns suggested solid rock below it. You should be almost there."

"Well, we're obviously not there yet," Clyde said with some sarcasm. He picked up his radio and called his crew chiefs. "Billy Bob and Mohammed, get set up for another grout injection."

They replied with brief affirmatives, and Nikki thought they sounded tired.

"Great," said Arkady. "We are going to be down for at least another four hours placing grout and waiting for it to cure. All I want to do is DRILL!" He and Clyde left the trailer to organize the grouting.

Dud turned to Nikki. "Well, that looks like one party we are not invited to."

"I wouldn't want to attend anyway," she replied. "It sounds like a grouch festival."

"The boys are definitely getting frustrated. Nobody has ever tried to do this before under such time pressure. Things get a bit tense, but I am confident they will get it done."

"I'm glad one of us is. I'm starting to wonder."

"Hey, I have an idea. How about if I pack up my cuttings samples, which I can't analyze until I get back to Tortola anyway, and take you into town for dinner and a drink? We can chat about this drilling program, and why I think it is going to be successful."

Despite her initial instinct to resist such an obvious come-on, Nikki found him attractive and funny. Besides, it would beat having dinner with Clyde and Arkady, who talked shop incessantly and never seemed to wind down about the drilling. It also occurred to Nikki that she hadn't been on an actual date in several years, and with the possible end of the world approaching, perhaps she ought to take advantage of one last fling before going out in a flash of gamma rays.

"Okay, Dr. Dudley Gardner of the British Geological Survey. You have yourself a date with Lieutenant Nicole Shelton, United States Navy astrophysicist."

"You're an officer? Oh crap...I thought you were a civilian employee."

"Really?" she replied. "Which part of the uniform did you miss?" She twirled her dogtags above the olive drab shirt collar.

"Oh." Dud seemed a bit taken aback. "Not very observant for a big-time scientist, am I? No wonder I've been out here for ten years studying the same damn volcano. Do you have a ship?"

"Nope. Only a supersonic jet fighter that I fly off of aircraft carriers. I also skydive for fun."

His eyes widened with respect, and then he laughed. "You're just another bloody nutter," he said.

"Come on, Dudley. Haven't you heard that crazy women are more fun?"

"Yeah," he replied, with a wink. "If you can survive it."

With that, they were off.

****

The International Space Station was coming down. It had been parked in a low orbit several months earlier as modules and supplies were boosted up to it on the last, few remaining U.S. shuttle flights, and by unmanned Russian Progress supply rockets staged on Energia boosters. All this stuff was easier to deliver to the ISS in low orbit, and the final configuration of the space station had been completed. The plan was to fuel the navigation rockets as the last step, and move it up to a higher, safer orbit.

But the Progress that was supposed to bring up fuel for the rockets never arrived because of the singularity crisis, and now everyone in every world space agency had bigger things to worry about than the fate of the ISS. So it drifted along in low Earth orbit, abandoned and unwatched, gradually scraping the outer fringes of the Earth's atmosphere, slowing down and dipping ever lower. It wouldn't be long before it made a final, fatal plunge, and returned to the planet from which it was made.

****

The first manned spacecraft since the 1970s landed in a crater on the moon. Unlike the Apollo landers, however, this one was huge, larger than an ocean liner and crammed with equipment. It had landed on the moon's farside, the hemisphere never seen from Earth because the moon's rotation was tidally locked to the Earth's.

The craft disgorged a number of men in spacesuits, which set about measuring and marking a construction site on a dark lava flow filling the crater. Other space-suited figures unloaded and assembled a large machine from inside the ship. The machine was a long, tapered cylinder with a blunt head. The head was a convex dish studded with cutting wheels that looked like extremely substantial pizza slicers. The rim of the dish had evenly-spaced, square openings big enough for a man's head, and lined on one side with carbide teeth. It was the business end of a tunnel boring machine. When pressed up against a wall of rock and turned, the pizza cutter wheels would spall the rock off the wall in small chunks. The toothed openings on the rim scooped these up and dropped them into a hopper, which fed a conveyor belt that transported the cut material out of the tunnel.

The engineers from the spacecraft set about drilling and blasting a sloping box cut in the lava flow. The explosives were soundless on the

80

airless moon, although they could feel the vibrations through the ground. Modified D-10 bulldozers with radiative cooling fins that carried their own oxygen supply for the diesel engines picked up the blasted rock and piled it onto berms on either side of the cut. Eventually, the tunnel boring machine was brought forward, and began eating its way into the newly created cliff face. The excavation proceeded at a rapid pace, creating several hundred feet of tunnel every 24 hours.

Moon Base Alpha was going to be home for a billion people from Earth, if Barney Freeman and his crew failed to tame the singularity. The unimaginative name was the best the U.N. bureaucracy could come up with. A foothold on the moon was needed before the evacuation of Earth could begin. The men worked frantically, because the sooner this habitat was available, the sooner they could start bringing people up. The leaders at the U.N. had done the math, and realized that the lifeboat ships under construction were not limited to one trip, as long as there was a destination at the other end where they could unload. The plans for Earth's evacuation now included the construction of a lunar base as a place to start moving people out of harm's way. There were still limits, but they might be able to save another billion people.

****

Truett Pusser was holding a Sabbath evening service at his Pentecostal Church of the Righteous Sword in the Hand of the Lord. There was to be snake handling. People would be giving vital testimony and speaking in tongues. Truett would do some fire and brimstone preaching. Just like Neil Diamond's song about Brother Love's traveling salvation show, which was one of Sue Ellen's favorites. Good old-time religion. It made him proud to be an American!

81

Most Christian churches held their weekly services on Sunday morning, but Truitt's Pentecostal church believed that the true Sabbath was the Jewish Sabbath day of Saturday, which was the one practiced by the Lord Jesus Christ, who was, after all, Jewish until he died on the cross. Also, the only time they could get the space was on Saturday night, so it worked out. Since the small Pentecostal congregation in Grafton was unable to afford their own church building, they met in the basement of the Valley Baptist Church. The pastor was the manager of the Quick Mart where Sue Ellen worked as a cashier, and he allowed Truitt's congregation use the basement for free, but only on Saturdays. They had to clean up after themselves and could leave no trace that they had been there on Saturday night when the Holy Roller Baptists arrived on Sunday morning. Truitt hoped to increase the size of his congregation and budget to the point where he could obtain his own church building someday, but for now, this would have to do.

He also did not know that the church basement wasn't quite free – Sue Ellen had an arrangement with her manager that involved regular episodes of oral pleasuring and occasional bouts of genuine down and dirty sex, but she didn't see any other way they could afford a place to hold weekly services. She told herself that she was doing it for the sake of Truitt and the pastorate, and besides, what he didn't know wouldn't hurt him. Sue Ellen was good at keeping secrets.

They were helping Jimmy Byner bring cages of snakes into the basement from his van when a glow in the western sky caught Truett's attention. He wasn't one to normally stargaze, but this was a bright light low on the horizon that appeared to be moving slowly upward.

"Jimmy, do you see that?" Truett asked. "Sue Ellen, come look at this!"

Jimmy Byner was a big, slow country boy. "Shoo, Truett. What is that?" He squinted into the western sky, where a trace of sunset remained.

"Call me Reverend, you idjit. No one is ever going to believe we are a real congregation if you don't address me as Reverend."

"Sorry, Truitt. I mean Reverend Truitt. Er, Reverend Pusser."

Sue Ellen came out of the van with another cat carrier full of snakes, and joined them to look at the bright point of light. It was gradually rising into the sky, and glowing brighter by the second. Truett could barely make out a shape, and had a moment of intuition.

"Sue Ellen, this is important. Get everyone out here. Quick!"

She ran into the church and ushered the two dozen people of their small congregation outside in less than a minute. The object was still there, and had grown brighter. It appeared to be in flames.

Truett and his congregation watched in awe as the brilliant light climbed toward the zenith in the clear, moonless sky. Pieces of it appeared to be breaking off, and all of it seemed to be burning. The object continued to grow in size and brightness as it moved overhead.

The ISS had been configured with most of the modules joined head to tail in a line. A central module, dubbed Unity, was shaped like a plus sign, and allowed additional modules, mainly laboratories, to be added at right angles to the main length of the space station, giving it a cross or "T" shape. As the ISS began its re-entry burn, fragile structures, like the solar panels, radio antennas and sun shielding were ripped away by the thinnest traces of atmosphere. The strong Unity module kept the main body of the

83

space station intact. As the ISS fell deeper into the atmosphere, the structure began to glow from the heat, and then to produce a long, incandescent trail as material was ablated off by friction with the air. In moments, the entire space station was engulfed in glowing plasma.

The Reverend Truett Pusser and his congregation looked up into the indigo evening sky to witness a small, bright, flaming Christian cross traverse the sky from west to east, leaving behind incandescent orange embers and a long, glowing smoke trail. He dropped to his knees in supplication. Sue Ellen dropped to her knees beside him, as did Jimmy Byner and the rest of the congregation.

This was it! This was the sign, clear and unmistakable. The flaming cross could only mean that the One, True God wanted the Church of the Righteous Sword in the Hand of the Lord to stop those who would interfere with the End Times. The Word could not have been spoken any more plainly.

After the object had disappeared over the horizon, they ushered everyone back inside. Truett addressed his frightened congregation.

"Fellow Christians," he said. "We have just been shown a sign from the Lord. There can be no doubt about it – you all witnessed it right here with Sue Ellen and myself. We prayed to the Lord when we first heard about the black hole, and asked if He wanted our help to stop these government people from doing the Devil's work by interfering with the End Times. The Lord did not answer us immediately, as is His right, but bided His time and provided an answer tonight, when all of you could bear witness. His will is clear. We must prepare a holy warrior to go to the Virgin Islands, and we must stop this blasphemy."

Indifferent about whether or not it was truly a Sign from God, the charred remains of the International Space Station slammed into the Atlantic Ocean several hundred miles west of the Azores, and sank into the deep, pelagic waters.

****

Nikki and Dud climbed out on the rocks at Peterborg on St. Thomas, and watched the waves funnel in. It was their third date. Although Dud was two decades older than Nikki, his years of outdoor work, including hiking, climbing and SCUBA diving, had kept him in remarkable shape. Nikki could barely keep up with him on the hike along the Peterborg peninsula.

She had taken him skydiving in Puerto Rico that morning. He had never done anything as crazy or outlandish as jumping out of an airplane before. Nikki was an accomplished military and sport parachutist, and outfitted Dud in a jumpsuit, helmet, goggles and boots. She then strapped him into a tandem harness that she also attached to herself. The small airplane took them to an altitude of 15,000 feet, and with Dud holding on tightly, Nikki walked out onto the wing brace and jumped. They fell toward the Earth, with the plane growing ever smaller above them. After 5,000 feet of free fall, Nikki opened the main chute and slowed them with a jerk. Hanging from the shrouds, they descended slowly in a broad, lazy spiral. The view was breathtaking. No matter how often she did this, Nikki still got an adrenaline rush every time. She figured Dud's adrenaline levels must be off the chart. The ground gradually came up to meet them, and Nikki landed on her feet with a graceful running motion, simultaneously dumping the air out of the steerable parachute so it collapsed. Dud was unable to keep his legs under him, however, and fell over sideways, taking Nikki down with him. They rolled in the soft grass of the target area, and Nikki popped the quick release on the harness of the parachute so they wouldn't get tangled in the shroud lines. She also released the tandem harness, and Dud sat up, flushed and breathless. On many levels and in many ways, he was impressed.

Nikki was still a little wound up from the parachute jump as they sat side-by-side in a cleft between two massive andesite columns on the narrow, rocky peninsula of Peterborg, shaded from the afternoon sun. Dud put his arm around Nikki's shoulders, and they quietly watched the ocean. It was a deep azure blue, flecked with white foam from beating against the rocks. Several small tidal pools on a flat, rocky plateau below them were filled with clear seawater, though which they could see numerous urchins, anemones, snails and starfish. The waves funneled in between the rock walls and crashed against the rocks at the base of the cliffs. About every third one was high enough to add water to the tide pools.

Dud had been a perfect gentleman on all three dates so far. Nikki was hoping he'd be a little less of a gentleman by the time they finished up today, because she was getting horny.

He had shaken hands with her warmly after their first dinner date on St. Croix. Their second date on Tortola had been spent on his small sailboat traveling out to the island of Jost van Dyke. They had a lovely mid-day brunch at a small resort where he knew the owner, and spent the afternoon snorkeling on the reefs before heading back at dusk. Nikki thought something might spark on that date, and although he kissed her goodnight before putting her aboard the last ferry, she had to head back to St. Croix, and there simply wasn't time.

This date might be different, she thought. There wasn't any rush to get back, and she could even spend the night with Dud if she wanted. The thought of that created a tingle in her bare thighs.

The scientists and techs from the national labs were busy assembling and testing the singularity capture cage on St. Croix. Nikki had filled them in on the singularity orbit, the timeline, and the capture deadline. Arkady and Clyde gave them status updates on the drilling, which had improved as Dud promised once they got to the bottom of the fractured zone, and was back on schedule. The lab people knew what they needed to do, and Nikki was in the way. She was a theoretical physicist, and couldn't help much with mechanical parts, electronics, wiring diagrams or electrical devices. But the capture cage was her responsibility, and she fretted over it like a mother hen. She was driving everybody nuts, and word got back to Barney in College Park. He told her to get off the island for a few days to let the lab people work. So here she was with several days off, on St. Thomas with Dud. She needed him to take her mind off the capture cage, and she wanted him to make love to her.

When she was younger, Nikki had always been timid about showing affection. Her parents were strict, and her dour, domineering father would book no backtalk, debate or discussion on anything. His word was the law, and he terrified Nikki. The old man was about as far from warm and fuzzy as someone could get and still remain human. She dreaded the consequences of crossing him. Her mousy mother backed him up 100 percent, and would not listen to nor allow any criticism of her husband. Both parents doted on Nikki's older brother Stuart, who could do no wrong in their eyes. Only Nikki knew what a conniving bastard and a creep he really was. But if she tried to tell her parents about some of the stunts Stuart

87

had pulled, they wouldn't believe her, and her brother would exact a timely and painful revenge on his own terms later. So she learned to survive by being quiet, timid, and shy. She lost herself in her books and studies, and eventually developed the ultimate camouflage by becoming a part of the background, unnoticed. She escaped into the Naval Academy right out of high school and stayed in Annapolis as much as possible, rarely visiting Ohio. Most of her colleagues thought she was cold and distant.

While this strategy may have been necessary for childhood survival, it was not exactly a great approach for meeting men. At 28, she was quite inexperienced at sex. Not a virgin, certainly – her first time had been after the high school prom, when her moderately drunken date started coming onto her and making a pass. Nikki was afraid to stand up to him and tell him no, and he interpreted her hesitation as agreement. She lost her virginity sprawled across the top of the dryer in the laundry room of her friend Rachel's house. After this somewhat painful and less than romantic start to her lovemaking career, she had been involved in only two other encounters over the last ten years, both with fellow officers. She hadn't actually felt anything either time. Well, maybe a little bit once, but it was over so quickly that she couldn't be sure. Timid little Nikki just couldn't seem to please anyone, including herself.

Many things seemed to have changed with the appearance of the singularity, including Lieutenant Nicole Shelton. She now found herself thrust into a role as a major player in a desperate scheme to save planet Earth from complete destruction. Heady stuff. She had the resources of entire nations at her beck and call. There were huge responsibilities, critical deadlines, and difficult management decisions to make. Being timid wasn't going to cut it. Once she found her voice to speak to the President and other heads of state at the initial White House briefing, she began to feel more confident in herself, and more assertive. She carried out her added responsibilities with a firm hand, expressed opinions, and made her point of view known. Strength built on strength, and today's Nikki Shelton was a much stronger and bolder version than the previous model of only a few months ago. Saving the world did that to you.

Nikki decided she needed to be a little more assertive with Dud, because he was definitely not picking up on the subtle hints. They were the only ones out there on the rocks amid the waves of Peterborg. The place was wild, with splintered black columns and slabs of frozen lava smoothed off by the waves. The salt spray, wind, and surge of the deep blue ocean were constant and unrelenting. It was romantic and adventurous. What the hell. Nikki turned to Dud and kissed him fiercely, while undoing the strings holding her bikini top. She let it fall away. He reacted with surprise at first, and then smiled and took her in his arms.

Nikki found Dud to be a passionate and caring lover. He recognized her inexperience, and caressed, kissed, licked and stroked her in ways and in places that brought her to the edge of ecstasy. She had no idea such a thing was possible. Dud held her there for what seemed like hours, and then gently brought her to a forceful and satisfying release. It was her first real orgasm, and she was grateful that she had the chance to experience such a wonder before the world ended. He invited her to climb on top of him so she could control the rate of penetration and the pace of movement. She did so gingerly, and they gently made love among the rocks and the waves. Nikki had a second orgasm that set Dud off at the same time, and they rode the crest of ecstasy together. She had never felt more empowered in her life.

Peter Hassenberg from Los Alamos National Laboratory was responsible for building the singularity cage. The actual construction of the device had been done at Los Alamos by an army of technicians and machinists, using the best machine shops in the world crammed with the best equipment and people.

The facilities were a relic from the Cold War, when they had been built at great expense to turn lumps of plutonium and other radioactive metals into useful shapes for nuclear weapons. A weapons scientist could come up with a concept, drop off a set of drawings at the shop on his way home, and the thing, whatever it was, would be fabricated overnight and ready for testing by the next morning. Impressive service, but not cheap. Still, national security was not to be compromised by pinching pennies, and having machinists available around the clock was considered a small price to pay to defend the nation against the evil Soviet Empire.

The machine shop had reduced their staff and kept normal business hours these days, but they were still the best in the world at turning something from a design drawing into reality. Hassenberg had his team of engineers draft up the design months ago when this crazy scheme was hatched. The singularity cage was constructed and tested at the lab, and then trucked down to Sandia in Albuquerque, where the electronics were added. From Sandia, the equipment was taken to nearby Kirtland AFB, and loaded onto a C17 military transport for St. Croix. Once on the island, Hassenberg and two dozen technicians labored around the clock to re-assemble and test the device, making sure it and its controllers were ready for deployment into the super deep drillhole.

According to Nikki's continually-updated orbital calculations, the singularity was due to make an appearance in the bottom of Clyde and Arkady's main drillhole in another ten days. The parallel borehole drilled by the American rig was halted a thousand feet above the target depth, and the rig idled. They were going to concentrate all available manpower on the Russian rig to capture the singularity, but the American rig could be called back into service if they ran into problems. The Russian hole still needed to be deepened by an additional thousand feet, and then widened out at the bottom to give them some elbow room in which to work. The actual capture was all going to be done remotely in a complicated and carefully timed ballet.

Arkady and Clyde were working to finish the deep drilling. The carbide tricone bit was chewing steadily downward through hard, brittle rock at more than twenty feet per hour. The cutting action of the bit was percussive, which spalled off flakes of rock instead of grinding it to dust. The harder the rock, the better it worked. The downhole mud motor appeared to be operating fine under the ambient pressure and temperature, and they were getting a thousand feet of hole drilled between bit changes. With ten days to go, the bottom of the hole was at 50,650 feet. Although they were ahead of schedule, no one was relaxing. There was still time for a lot of things to go wrong. Nikki's latest orbital calculations told them they singularity would be intercepted at a depth of 51, 530 feet, give or take a couple of feet.

The plan was to drill the borehole down to 52,000 feet in the next three to four days, and then widen the bottom thousand feet by reaming the 12-inch diameter borehole into a 60-inch diameter shaft. The five-foot wide shaft would give the Los Alamos and Sandia scientists some room to

91

maneuver the capture cage to nab the singularity. Fortunately, since it would be at the apogee of a highly elliptical orbit, the singularity should be moving at a relative snail's pace when it entered the chamber deep below the surface, giving them a better chance of catching it. Still, there was little room for error.

****

Five days later, they were ready. The well was completed and the capture shaft reamed out. All the muds and fluids had been cleared, and the borehole contained nothing but air. The complicated singularity capture cage was successfully assembled and tested, and then the whole works had been carefully folded and lowered down into the deep subsurface chamber. Figuring out how to get the four-foot square, cubical cage down a 12-inch wellbore had been a major challenge of the whole operation. NASA helped solve the problem by providing a little high tech they had developed for folding up satellite parts during launch for later deployment in orbit. Still, it was a miracle that everything had worked and there hadn't been any major delays or problems. Nikki began to feel just a little more optimistic, and began to wonder if this whole crazy scheme might actually be possible. Dud's unfailing confidence didn't hurt. Now all they had to do was wait a few more days for the singularity to show up.

The capture cage was designed to zap the singularity with a strong, negative electrical charge, and then hold it inside the cage using a complex grouping of magnetic dipoles. The magnets were made of a newly developed, superconducting ceramic that worked at high-temperatures – in this case, chilled by liquid nitrogen instead of the much colder liquid helium. Keeping the magnets cooled to liquid nitrogen temperatures at the bottom of a 50,000 foot drillhole was another difficult technical issue that Nikki

92

thought they would never solve. Still, they managed it by using insulated tubing and rapid circulation through a line run down from the surface.

One issue no one had yet figured out was how they were going to extract a captured black hole from deep underground to the surface. Barney had told Nikki that a team at Livermore was working on that issue, and would have something soon. As long as her group on St. Croix captured the singularity and held onto it for a few days or weeks, a much smaller Livermore cage should be ready that would allow them to engulf and extract the black hole from the larger capture cage, and retrieve it up the 12-inch diameter well bore.

****

In the mountains of Afghanistan, the war against the occupiers had not been going well. Commander Nazir had lost many men and supplies to the hated American drone aircraft. The unmanned Predators had attacked them day and night, firing air to ground missiles, or simply broadcasting their locations to American and Afghan government troops, who hit them with mortars and sniper fire. Nazir had to keep his mujahedeen holed up in the mountains. They moved cautiously from cave to cave, unable to regroup, mount a counterattack, or even to resupply food and water from a nearby village. As soon as they came out from under cover, they were spotted and attacked.

Then Allah intervened. First, they were joined by a young French convert named Phillipe who claimed to be able to tap into the radio frequencies used to control the drones. He was not able to affect the weapons or flight controls, at least not yet, but he was able to tap into the video feeds through a satellite Internet connection. They could observe in real time what the American soldiers controlling the craft back in Nevada

93

were seeing, and tell when a Predator was watching them. Several times now, before a drone aircraft could launch missiles, Nazir had been able to order his fighters to take cover. The men disappeared like rainwater onto the desert sands behind rocks and into caves and tunnels, leaving the stunned Americans with little more than a scenic view of barren hills on their computer screens. Phillipe worked continuously to improve his hacking skills, with the goal of gaining actual control of the drones, and crashing them.

The second miracle occurred when the singularity escaped into the Earth. Truly, Allah desired the complete annihilation of corrupt Western civilization. Apparently, the entire world had to be destroyed to achieve it, so widespread was their evil influence. Although it would also mean the end of Islamic civilization, such was the Will of God. No one could argue with that. In the end, they would all enter Paradise knowing that they had won the final victory over the infidels.

Commander Nazir experienced an additional minor miracle after the American President told the world about the singularity and the possible imminent destruction of humanity. All of the American troops hunting him and his men suddenly disappeared. Almost overnight. They packed up their helicopters, drones and jet fighters and left the country. Nazir learned later that all the American soldiers had been ordered to assist with the lifeboat program. He laughed, as if escaping the Will of God could be as easy as flying into space and hiding on the far side of the moon. Did they not think that Allah, the Supreme Being of the entire universe, could reach behind the moon and swat them like flies? Fools! Still, it removed the American soldiers with their hated drones, and without their support, the Afghan government troops were easily defeated, intimidated and driven off.

With a bit of breathing space, Nazir was able to start rebuilding the strength of his mujahedeen army.

They had a new focus now. If the infidels were somehow successful in taming the singularity and saving the planet, it would fall onto Nazir and his mujahedeen to implement the Will of God and remove all traces of Western civilization from the world. To accomplish this, they needed bigger weapons than the RPGs and improvised explosive devices they were currently using. Much bigger. They needed nukes. Nazir realized that while the entire planet was waiting breathlessly and focusing on the events unfolding in the Caribbean, it should be fairly easy to obtain such a weapon. No one would be watching his sources. He needed to get to a telephone.

Insh'Allah! Praise God!

****

After his first tandem jump with Nikki, Dud surprised her by signing up for skydiving lessons on Tortola. He went twice a week for a month to get certified for solo free fall, and he enjoyed it so much that he told Nikki he wished the lessons were more frequent.

In return, Nikki enrolled in a SCUBA class. Although she enjoyed snorkeling just fine, she wanted the freedom to go beneath the waves and explore the deeper ocean with Dud. She learned how to check the gear, don and doff equipment, and monitor air supply, pressure and temperature. She learned about dangerous sea creatures and how to deal with encounters. They taught her how to buddy breathe, purge water out of a facemask, and ascend safely, never outrunning her bubbles. She understood the causes of the bends, nitrogen narcosis and the need to decompress after a deep dive.

Nikki enjoyed the weekly class on Tortola. Of course, meeting up with Dud after the lessons, and spending the night at his small villa didn't hurt, either. The sex was wonderful, in the hot tub, on the beach in the surf with waves breaking over them, under the waterfall in the stream, in a quiet place in the jungle, on chaise lounges out in the back garden, and sometimes even in a regular bed. Dud was a careful teacher, and Nikki a fast learner.

He had been through a nasty divorce a decade earlier, which was why he was in the British Virgin Islands. Dud never did learn exactly what triggered the split, but he had been spending a lot of time in the Azores doing field work on the volcanoes. He came home after an extended field trip and found the wife and the furnishings gone, with a notice from her solicitor tacked onto the door of his empty flat. The ex-wife had nicked him for nearly everything she could, including the furniture, car, dog, pots and pans, dishes, towels, sheets, house plants and even the bloody damned ice cube trays out of the freezer. There hadn't been any children, so at least he was spared that, but she was vindictive and spiteful. She had taken up with a banker, who Dud described to Nikki as a gray, dull, soulless little man. His ex-wife defended her new lover by saying "at least he comes home every night." Dud couldn't argue with that. So he got out, got away. Ran away, perhaps, he confessed to Nikki. The Caribbean was almost as far as he could get from Nottingham and still be on U.K. soil. Thankfully, the British Empire hadn't given up ALL the colonies! The whole affair had put him off women for years, and this romance with Nikki was his first serious relationship in quite some time.

Nikki worked hard at staying out of the way on St. Croix, while remaining in the loop. As the pace of activity increased, the scrutiny of the news media increased, and the attention of the politicians increased. She did

96

press conferences and gave regular progress reports to Barney Freeman in College Park. She also gave occasional briefings directly to President Jackson, whom she had come to know and like. The President made it clear that he felt the one person who would be responsible on the ground for the success of this venture was Lieutenant Nicole Shelton. Perfect, she thought, because that same person will also be responsible in the event of a failure. No pressure. Still, she thought, we will all learn together soon enough if this was going to work.

****

The Empire Iron Mine in the upper peninsula of Michigan was a hub of activity. Dormant for many years after the collapse of the American steel industry, it had been limping along on life support for the past decade, supplying a trickle of iron ore to the flood of raw materials fueling the booming Chinese economy. This huge, open pit mine, and many others like it had supplied the steel that built America, won the Second World War, rebuilt Europe and Japan, and provided material for the post-war consumer glut of appliances, automobiles, freeways and machines. For years, the iron mines lay nearly abandoned and forlorn, scattered across the northern Wisconsin and Michigan countryside like gigantic craters, named Empire, Tilden, Groveland and Republic.

Now, steel from the banded iron formations of Earth was needed for a million spaceships, each vessel the size of an old-style ocean liner. It would be alloyed with titanium, and used to make the strong keels and support ribs, decks and bulkheads, all sheathed in lighter aluminum. Steel was also needed for the big, dumb boosters, the launching gantry and the cradle infrastructure to hold the ships on top of the boosters. Steel was critical for the tools needed to dig, refine, cast, stamp, clamp, weld and construct the gigantic spacecraft.

The iron ore was blasted from the walls of the pits, crushed, then ground to powder by rod and ball mills, and separated by floatation tanks. The heavy iron oxide sank to the bottom of the tanks, while the lighter silica floated off. The iron was mixed with clay, formed into half inch spheres and baked in an oven. The resulting ore pellets, called taconite, were loaded onto railcars and taken to the docks at Marquette, where they were placed on ships. An endless stream of ore boats, many brought out of retirement, left Marquette for the steel mills of Milwaukee, Gary, Cleveland, Erie and Buffalo. Ore on railcars was taken to Pittsburgh, Youngstown, Sharon, Warren, Allentown, and Bethlehem. Even the shipbuilding yard at Sparrows Point in Baltimore was pressed into service. Every steel mill in the United States, whether brand new, or old and tired, was running full blast for the lifeboat project.

Bauxite mines in Arkansas produced aluminum, copper came from Arizona and Utah, and titanium was mined in Nevada. Lead, zinc, and tin were frantically dug up in the Tri-State mining district in Missouri, Kansas and Oklahoma, which hadn't seen this much action in nearly a century. Dozens of other metals and materials were extracted, refined and shipped to Nevada for the lifeboats. Mines that had long been abandoned as uneconomic were re-opened to produce rare metals like molybdenum, chromium, vanadium and rare earth elements needed for steel alloys. The definition of what was profitable changed under desperate circumstances.

In addition to the geological ore deposits, materials for the lifeboats were being gleaned from every source imaginable. Groups of citizens throughout the land dug through garbage dumps, rubbish heaps, trash pits and landfills seeking steel, aluminum, and copper. Plastic was collected for spaceship interior wall finishes and furnishings. People donated old clothing to supply the fibers for fabric seat covers and bunks. These recycling efforts supplied nearly a quarter of the raw material stream, competing against giant, yellow Electra-Haul mine trucks, 800-foot long ore freighters, and trains extending many miles across the countryside to get minerals, metals and plastics to the shipwrights. All around the world, many others did the same. They did it because the fate of the human race was at stake. If a significant percentage of the population did not get safely off the planet, it would be the end of humanity. Everyone helped, and did what they could. But no one knew if it would be enough.

Chapter Five: Capture

It was almost Capture Day, or C-Day, and everything was ready. After months of preparation, and a few last minute glitches, they were prepared to capture and tame the singularity. Barney Freeman had arrived a few weeks earlier, and was personally overseeing the operations on St. Croix. He had brought his wife Shelly, grad student Devi Chowdury and most of the singularity work group with him, and they had taken over the Sugar Bay Resort on St. Thomas. Shelly Freeman figured that in the worst case scenario, at least she would get one final, all-expenses paid vacation at a five-star tropical hotel before the world ended. She spent her days under a palm tree on the beach or down by the pool, reading and ordering brightly colored boat drinks complete with paper umbrellas.

The singularity now massed a bit more than two metric tons, about as much as a large sport-utility vehicle. The rate at which it was gaining mass was continuing to increase. Barney asked Peter Hassenberg to check and recheck the engineering calculations to make sure the capture cage was strong enough to stop and hold this much mass. The extra mass also complicated the logistics of the retrieval cage as well. The object itself was still far smaller than a subatomic particle, but the small retrieval cage would have to be capable of hauling a weight equivalent to a Chevy Suburban up a ten mile-deep borehole.

They still hadn't figured out how to dispose of the singularity if they were successful at capturing it. Barney thought that launching it into deep space with enough velocity to escape the solar system should render it harmless. It would take millions of years to reach another star system, and it was still small enough that it should evaporate away well before then. However, at the moment all personnel at NASA and every other space agency in the world were working frantically on the lifeboat project, and Barney had decided to wait until they actually had the singularity in a cage before approaching the engineers to ask about a launch vehicle. NASA could probably assemble something out of existing hardware to carry it far enough. In the meantime, it could sit in the cage until a rocket was ready.

****

The press swarmed over them like ants on a jar of honey. This was arguably the most important story in human history, in that they were either going to save the world or destroy it. Every tidbit of information coming from the drill site was a scoop, and the scientists and engineers were scrutinized like movie stars. Every move they made, and every step they took was a matter for public record. Barney Freeman was quoted famously as saying that he couldn't even take a crap without somebody writing it up.

The media quickly found Shelly Freeman, and she entertained a phalanx of reporters at poolside every day. Because she was not a scientist, they felt less intimidated talking to her, and all manner of things got discussed. They asked the usual, predictable questions about Barney – what kind of a man was he, how had they met, what kind of marriage they had, what she did to cope, *etcetera ad nauseum*. Since there wasn't any real news coming from the drill rig, the conversations turned mundane, philosophical, gossipy, opinionated and dramatic, all by turns. Shelly answered what questions she could and deflected the rest. She was accessible and pleasant, and they liked her.

They didn't like Barney nearly so much. His daily press briefings were dry, technical affairs, with information passed along about the depth of the hole, progress on the cage construction, refined singularity orbital calculations, and other dull, science stuff. Barney refused to answer many personal questions, claiming that the press briefing was supposed to focus on technical progress, not personalities. It didn't really matter, because the reporters would just pose the same questions to Shelly by the pool the following day, and get answers.

Clyde Rose never seemed to want to talk about much except his grandchildren. It was clear that he was working on capturing the singularity for their sakes, and it was a touching human interest story. They found his daughter and grandkids in Piedmont, Oklahoma, just outside Oklahoma City, and did an interview. The daughter was sweet, the kids were cute, but after a week of it, nobody cared anymore. Except for Clyde, who kept on talking about them. By week three, most of the reporters lost interest.

Arkady Kutuzov enjoyed nothing more than an opportunity to lecture the media about Russian politics. He would go off on rants about the bureaucracy in Moscow, the incompetent idiots they had appointed to run the provinces, the corruption, bribes and larceny, organized crime, the lack of state control, and on and on. Most of the reporters began to glaze over by the afternoon of the second day – they didn't know most of the players, who were obscure Politbureau hacks or unknown provincial officials. They also didn't know what he was talking about half the time. Arkady simply assumed that everyone was familiar with the issues, and forged ahead without giving any background. After hearing each and every rant delivered with equal degrees of sincerity, urgency and importance, they had a hard time telling which way was up.

102

Nicole Shelton, on the other hand, was a gold mine. She was young and attractive, which immediately got a lot of attention. She was also smart, and she flew fighter jets, which made her incredibly exciting. She became a media darling after her first interview. The press quickly learned that she was dating Dud, and hounded him as well. There were endless requests for interviews, comments and opinions, and photographers followed them around like *paparazzi* chasing movie stars. Nikki and Dud were good sports about it, and cooperated with the reporters and photographers as best they could.

The reporters didn't know that Nikki and Dud had been briefed by the new White House press secretary herself a few weeks earlier. Dana Tatton had warned them that this would happen, and asked them to cooperate. She told them that the media feeding frenzy would only get worse if the reporters and photographers didn't have something to send back to their editors. Nikki and Dud were the perfect couple to act as decoys so the reporters had a story. It would take some of the heat off the rest of the scientists and engineers who were frantically trying to get work done. Nikki started to object, saying that her work was just as important. Ms. Tatton responded by telling her the request came directly from the President, and played a video on her laptop to prove it.

No stranger to the media spotlight himself, President Jackson expressed sympathy, but told Nikki and Dud that their jobs were basically finished. The drillhole was located at the best estimated position to intercept the singularity, but if Nikki's orbital calculations were off, well, there wasn't anything they could do about it now. Constantly recalculating orbital parameters at this late date wasn't going to help anyone, and she was to stand down. Likewise, Dud's geological expertise was no longer needed

103

because they were done drilling, and the world was grateful to him for his hard work. Dud snorted. The President went on to make it clear that having the media run amok near the drill site could cause mishaps, injuries and delays, possibly even resulting in missing the singularity interception. Given the delicate nature of the task, the President could not allow this, and he was ordering Nikki and requesting Dud to fill their appointed roles as media targets.

Dana Tatton told them afterward that as C-Day got nearer, the President would be sending some NASA media handlers down to take control of the situation. They were experts at media outreach during space launches, and could deal with the press during the lead-up to the actual capture event. After hearing this explanation, Nikki and Dud agreed to do the best they could, and became instant celebrities.

Nikki was surprised to find that most reporters considered scientists to be very odd or unusual. Almost none of the mainstream journalists had a clue about what an astrophysicist did, nor why anyone would want to pursue such a profession. Their ideas about scientists had been shaped by egomaniacs like Geoffrey Finch, or serious, focused types like Barney Freeman. Worst of all, what many of them knew about scientists came from Hollywood movie portrayals. Great Scott! thought Nikki, remembering the zany Doc Brown character from the "Back to the Future" movies.

Nikki and Dud set about trying to show the world that scientists were human. They took a couple of reporters out island-hopping on Dud's boat, stopping off to snorkel at favorite spots, and putting in for food and drinks at various marinas where Dud knew the owners and they owed him a favor. They talked about their experiences, dreams and aspirations. Dud

104

touched on how painful his divorce had been. Nikki opened up a little about her strict father and overcoming her shyness to speak in front of large groups. In the end, the reporters decided they were just regular people who happened to make a living as scientists. Nikki even allowed a few photographs to be taken of herself in a bikini, which she was certain would end up in the supermarket tabloids, and scandalize her straitlaced family.

****

Despite their best efforts to control the media circus, there was one serious incident that occurred on live TV. It caused an immense dust-up, and severely disrupted the project. An assertive young reporter from Atlanta named Jessica Pierce was on the drill site, with full press credentials and a camera crew. The energetic Ms. Pierce had gotten permission from Clyde and Arkady after hours of wheedling to set up on the drill rig platform itself. She intended to present a report about how the capture of the rogue black hole would save the world. Of course, the story had been done endlessly by now, but Jessica's angle was to stand on the actual drill rig with the wellhead of the 50,000-foot deep drillhole behind her as a backdrop. Since the drilling had been completed and the capture cage lowered into the hole, there would be virtually no activity on the rig floor for several days until they actually attempted to capture the singularity.

Clyde and Arkady talked with Barney about it, because despite her outward appearance as a creature of sweetness and light, Ms. Pierce could be quite a dragon when she got her claws hooked into someone. After deciding that the camera crew wouldn't interfere with any ongoing operations, and that there wasn't really anything up there they could harm, Barney thought it would be all right as long as they had an escort. Clyde and Arkady agreed, mostly because they wanted to be rid of her. Barney

105

cautioned them to keep her away from the wellhead, and to monitor for hydrogen sulfide while they were on the platform.

Jessica Pierce was told that she would have access. Clyde gave her and the camera crew a thorough safety briefing, telling them she could stand on the edge of the rig platform, but she was NOT to touch anything. Most importantly, she was to stay away from the wellhead on top of the casing to the 50,000 foot borehole. Clyde impressed on them that poison gas from deep within the Earth could belch out of the well without warning, and even though the eight-foot tall valve on the wellhead was shut and they were monitoring emissions from the well, the TV people still needed to stay back. Jessica spent a lot of time during the briefing on her Blackberry texting with her producer in Atlanta, and missed the part about the poison gases. Clyde assigned Pedro, one of the rig hands, to act as their escort on the platform.

Jessica privately decided to ignore the restrictions, because her viewers would be thrilled at the sight of a hole in the ground that was over ten miles deep. The crew set up near the center of the platform, positioning their star reporter a few feet from the massive valve on top of the casing. It was clearly visible in the shot over her right shoulder. Pedro had not been present for the safety briefing, but he knew the wellhead was usually off limits. He started to protest, but Jessica assured him that Clyde had given her full access to anywhere on the platform. Unsure, Pedro decided to leave them alone for a few minutes while he went and checked with Clyde. It probably saved his life.

Gases in the fractured bedrock had been escaping from the hole intermittently since it was drilled. Because of the requirement for speed, there had not been time to set protective steel pipe or casing in the well to seal it off from fluids in the rock. The well was completed "open hole" with

106

bare rock walls exposed virtually the entire way down. Clyde had made sure that fractures and gassy zones in the rock formations were grouted off to stabilize the well, but as the borehole dried out and the rock walls sagged inward, the grout cracked and sometimes fell out of the fractures it was supposed to be plugging. Small volumes of high pressure gas could then escape from the formation and vent uphole.

On the day that Jessica Pierce got permission to do her story from the platform of the drill rig, an especially large piece of grout at a depth of 32,000 feet was in the process of working loose. This was not holding back a small volume of gas, but was blocking instead an extensive fracture system filled with high pressure hydrogen sulfide. This gas is known for its "rotten egg" smell, and can be quite deadly in small quantities. In the way that bad fortunes sometime accumulate from a series of small errors, a group of geochemists from the University of Florida had collected gas samples earlier that day, running a video camera down the well during their sampling. No one had noticed anything amiss, but they had stopped at 30,000 feet. The problem grout was 2,000 feet deeper. A small ballast weight had come loose from the line once they stopped, and fell to the bottom of the well, bouncing off walls as it went. It hit the weakened grout at 32,000 feet dead center, creating dozens of small cracks. The Florida group then neglected to completely shut the wellhead valve when they were finished. Jessica Pierce was standing next to a gas chamber that was primed and ready.

As Jessica began her feature story on the live newscast, the large piece of grout in the well began to give way. Small bits fell from the fracture like crumbling plaster, and continued their journey downward nearly 20,000 feet to the bottom of the borehole. Hydrogen sulfide gas began seeping out of the fracture system, slowly at first, but increasing in volume as more and

107

more grout was blown out of the crack by the enormous pressure of the escaping gas.

At the surface, the wellhead orifice began making a whistling sound, and Ms. Pierce noticed an offensive odor in the air. She wrinkled her pert nose slightly and apologized to her viewers, explaining that a foul smell was coming from the well. A moment later, despite the continued whistling sound from the wellhead, she mentioned that the odor was gone, apparently dissipated.

Jessica was not aware that a potent side effect of hydrogen sulfide gas on the human body is to deaden the sense of smell. Oil and gas drillers know that the rotten egg smell of hydrogen sulfide is a warning of danger, and if the odor disappears suddenly, it is time to run like hell. A hand-held H_2S monitor left behind by Pedro suddenly went off, distracting Jessica. She ignored the alarm, not wanting it to ruin her feature piece, especially after all the trouble she had gone through to set it up. So she gamely continued on with the story, although appearing a bit woozy and unsteady to her viewers. Her cameraman Bart had difficulty maintaining the shot, first losing focus and then the horizon.

Upwind and behind Jessica, in full view of the camera, Pedro returned to the platform, dramatically jumping onto the wellhead and turning the wheel to close the giant valve. Another alarm went off in the doghouse, the whooping sound clearly discernible to viewers. Seconds later, Jessica Pierce stopped in mid-sentence. Her eyes rolled up into her head, and she collapsed onto the rig platform in a heap. Bart slid forward an instant later, with his still-operational camera landing upright on the floor of the drill rig. It was all shown worldwide on live TV. The camera came to rest focused on the pretty, freshly dead face of the reporter, in a macabre,

108

frozen close-up. The network cut the feed in seconds, but it was on long enough for the video to be captured and spread far and wide over the web.

The death of Jessica Pierce on live TV was a public relations disaster for the drilling program. Questions were raised immediately about why she was allowed into such a dangerous location, and why there had been no warning of the gas release until just seconds before she and the cameraman succumbed. The other media on site hounded Barney, Clyde, and Arkady for more details. Many of the reporters went after Nikki.

They handled it as best they could, explaining that a degree of judgment was involved, and the fact that no large releases of hydrogen sulfide had been noted during the entire drilling operation up until now. It was also made clear that Ms. Pierce was told specifically to keep her distance from the wellhead, but she chose to ignore this restriction and died two feet in front of it. The singularity capture crew was shorthanded and busy, and Pedro had his hands full trying to babysit her. It had been bad luck that the valve was left open and bad timing that Ms. Pierce had been on the rig floor when the release occurred. No other media would be permitted up there or anywhere else on the rig structure, and in fact, Barney insisted that henceforth the daily briefing in an offsite conference room would be the only source for information. They were due to make the capture attempt in two more days, and he could not allow any more distractions.

Dana Tatton arrived on St. Croix the following day with a White House press team, and took the briefing in hand. She had answers, fact sheets on hydrogen sulfide, descriptions of standard drill rig practices and other information that kept the media busy and explained the situation. Nikki breathed a sigh of relief, and went back to reviewing her orbital

109

calculations. Ms. Pierce and Bart the cameraman were given heroes' burials in Atlanta. The late reporter was only 25 years old.

****

Two days later, as if in payback for all the bad luck encountered in the previous few weeks, the singularity capture itself went better than expected. They got the electrostatic cage deployed and fully charged, with the locking charge ready to go. Numerous sensitive instruments were watching for the singularity to emerge from the rock walls at the bottom of the cavity, with computer programs running to achieve the microsecond timing necessary for the capture.

Despite what President Jackson had told her, Nikki was in a secret panic that she had made some foolish error, and frantically double-checked her orbital parameters to make sure no additional, last minute corrections were needed. While she was absolutely certain that Finch's black hole would arrive as predicted, it soothed her nerves to rerun the calculations. She checked everything again and again, umpteen thousand times. Devi worked with her when she could.

At the appointed moment, the downhole television monitoring cameras showed something like a tiny, intensely bright star emerge from the wall of the excavated chamber, traveling upward and diagonally at a rather stately speed. The pinprick of bluish-white light moved within range of the capture cage, where it was zapped in a millisecond by a lightning bolt containing twenty amperes of electrons, delivered at over a million volts. The black hole absorbed the jolt, which would have instantly killed an elephant, and took on a strong negative charge.

A microsecond later, an electronic switch controlled by a very fast computer at the surface sent a powerful current flowing at nearly lightspeed

110

down a superconducting cable into the borehole. The current ran into and through the cage structure in a complex, predetermined manner, stripping electrons and rendering it strongly positive. The negatively-charged singularity was drawn into the positively charged cage like a moth to a floodlight.

Guided by the computer, electrical fields played around the cage in a choreographed series of dances to first counteract the orbital motion of the object, and then freeze it in place. After a few minor overcorrections, and a bit of a wobble east to west, the complex electromagnetic fields eventually slowed the black hole and stopped it, balancing the singularity in space with uniform forces of equal pull. It hung between competing fields of force, held tightly as if roped into place and secured with bungee cords. As long as the power stayed on, the black hole would stay put. Despite all the difficulties and setbacks, they had done it.

Arkady detailed a couple of men and two soldiers to look after the site generator. It had to be kept operating at all costs. Clyde had the rest of the crew prep the back-up jenny, just in case.

****

Before announcing the successful taming of the singularity to the news media, Barney called Washington. He got Karl Barski on the phone.

"I need to speak to the President."

"You don't have that kind of access," the Presidential Science Advisor told him. "Give me the information and I will pass it along."

"I have access for this," Barney replied, irritated. "You know what we're doing down here, Karl. He told me that he wanted to hear the outcome directly. So be a good soldier and hook me up."

"All right, give me a minute." Now Barski was irritated.

Barney could hear through the satellite phone connection that Barski was having a discussion with someone about entering the Oval Office, probably Tony Amato, the President's notoriously prickly Chief of Staff. Eventually, the door opened and after another muffled conversation, the President spoke into the phone.

"All right, Dr. Freeman, this is Jackson. You have my attention. What is the situation?"

"Three words, Mr. President. We have it."

"Well, here are two words back: Thank God!"

****

But God was not thankful for the efforts of Dr. Barnard Freeman, at least as far as the Reverend Truett Pusser and the congregation of the Church of the Righteous Sword in the Hand of the Lord were concerned. For a week after the capture, most of the world celebrated the reprieve from a death sentence in endless street parties and drunken revelry. Barney Freeman was their hero. Truett thought the frivolity was shameful, and that Barney was surely an agent of the Devil. He gave his congregation a fiery sermon on the Sabbath following the announcement that the singularity had been captured.

"It is wrong, I say to you, that mere men should attempt to thwart the will of the Lord. The all-powerful and all-knowing Lord God Jehovah made it clear to us, by the sign of the burning cross, that these are indeed the End Times. We believe... in fact, we KNOW that the Lord has sent this so-called singularity to destroy the Earth in preparation for the Second Coming of Jesus Christ. Nevertheless, God gave all humans the free will to choose between good and evil. Satan has influenced certain individuals to interfere with the plans of the Lord, and these actions have been allowed by God so far. But be forewarned that the Day of Judgment is at hand.

"The members of this congregation shall defend the plans of the Lord, and not allow a group of secular humanists to attempt a derailment of the Second Coming of Christ! The black hole has been captured, but it still lies ten miles beneath the Earth. So far, they have found no way to bring it to the surface. They expect it will take weeks to develop a vessel that can carry the black hole upward, and during this time we must act. We shall overcome the Evil One, and find our destiny as an instrument of a righteous Lord God Almighty. We will send a true believer to the island where this beast is being caged, and set it free to perform the work of the Lord. Such is the will of God! Amen."

The congregation thundered their approval. Everyone came forward to contribute money and ideas for the fight to undo this monumental wrong.

****

Jimmy Byner had never been to the Caribbean before. In fact, he'd never been any farther south than Fort Bragg and Fayetteville in South Carolina during a brief stint in the Army. Jimmy had washed out of the military after two years with a medical disability, but not before learning a little bit about explosives. One of the lessons he learned the hard way was that a blasting cap only looks like a small firecracker, and having one go off in your hand will do major damage. In a way he was grateful for the accident because it was responsible for his medical discharge, but the hand hurt like hell most of the time. Still, it had gotten him a ticket back to Grafton.

Jimmy changed planes in Fort Lauderdale on his way to St. Croix. Truitt had impressed upon him the need to travel clean of anything that might raise the suspicions of TSA or any of the gate agents. Jimmy had wanted to try getting some C-4 down to the Virgin Islands to use against the singularity cage, but Truitt – no, dammit "Reverend Pusser" had told him he needed to think on his feet and improvise something out of the available materials already there. Jimmy was not at all confident in this course of action. The Army had taught him to follow orders, not improvise. He didn't do well at improvising.

The aircraft was half empty as they headed out over the ocean. Jimmy had never seen so much water before, and he fretted about what might happen if the plane was to be caught up and teleported to somewhere within the Bermuda Triangle by aliens. Jimmy watched a lot of television, and he was sure that almost half of the planes and boats that tried to cross this area disappeared without a trace. If the Earth was destroyed by the black hole, would the Bermuda Triangle be doomed as well? Or did it exist outside of their universe, like another dimension, or somewhere? He only knew one thing for sure – Truitt would be royally pissed off if this plane disappeared. The congregation had forked over a lot of hard earned money to send him down here, and couldn't afford to send another. He HAD to succeed, and with the help of Our Lord Jesus, he would.

Whether through the help of God or just the inaccuracy of most legends, Jimmy's plane managed to survive the flight through the Bermuda Triangle, and landed without incident at Cyril King Airport on St. Thomas. Relieved that he had gotten through the Bermuda Triangle safely, Jimmy collected his luggage and found a taxi that would take him to the town of Charlotte Amalie, where he would board a ferry for St. Croix.

The taxi was a van, with 5 other people headed for the same destination. Jimmy was initially alarmed because the driver was barreling down the wrong side of the road, but he eventually noticed that everyone else was driving on the left as well. He wondered if it was like England or something. Maybe Sue Ellen and Truett should have studied this place a bit more before sending him down here. He was doing the Lord's work, but if Jimmy had learned anything in the military, it was that any and all surprises are a cause for worry. Surprises got you killed.

The taxi driver had a fundamentalist preacher jabbering on the radio, which he turned up full blast for all to hear. The elderly couple seated in the back simply removed their hearing aids and rode in blissful silence. The three Dutch tourists in the bench seat held on and endured it. Jimmy was sitting up front and listening raptly, nodding and agreeing with nearly every point the preacher was making. It was all fire and brimstone, and the Second Coming of Christ, and Jimmy thought the radio preacher sounded just like Truett, except with a Caribbean accent.

When they reached the Charlotte Amalie docks, all the passengers piled out except Jimmy. He had an hour to wait for his ferry, and asked the taxi driver if he could stay and listen to the radio preacher for a little longer. He felt a kinship with the overtly-religious driver, and almost told him his intentions, but checked himself in time. Truett had impressed upon him that the success of the mission depended on Jimmy being the only person in the Virgin Islands who knew what was being planned. If anyone else found out, it could get to the FBI, and he would be stopped.

The driver was a large, good-natured man with dreadlocks and a heavy West Indies accent. Although Jimmy could barely understand him, they talked about the Second Coming and joined together in fellowship for a prayer. By the time Jimmy Byner got on the ferry and headed toward St. Croix, he was more convinced than ever that he was doing the right thing. He would need to find fireworks for a blasting cap, fertilizer, diesel fuel, and a few other supplies, some of which could be hard to obtain, but he would not give up. Jimmy was determined to stop this blasphemy against the Lord at all costs.

Chapter Six: The Loss

Nikki Shelton was camping with Dud Gardner at Cinnamon Bay on St. John. After all the stress and excitement of capturing the singularity, Dud had suggested that the two of them get away for a week of R&R. Nikki had some leave coming, and she decided she'd rather spend it with Dud than anywhere else in the world.

The Cinnamon Bay campground had gorgeous campsites near the beach. A few were bare, but most were equipped with tents, cots, cook stoves, lanterns and other camping necessities. The resort recognized that people generally came to the Virgin Islands by boat or by aircraft, and couldn't lug a lot of camping gear along, so they supplied almost everything but the food. Many sites had permanent screen cottages for accommodations, which were a lot like sleeping on somebody's screened-in back porch. These had concrete floors, cement block walls, and a solid wooden roof, plus real beds, electric lights and fans. For "camping," they were pretty luxurious.

It was virtually impossible to secure a spot at Cinnamon Bay in the winter unless reservations were made far in advance, but the place was practically deserted in summer. The manager was an old pal of Dud's, who was able to find them a screen house at a dirt cheap rate.

Nikki and Dud had been at the campground for most of a week, hiking into the hills, snorkeling on the reef, kayaking the bay, and sailing a small catamaran they had rented. The days were glorious and sunny; the nights velvet and passionate. Nikki was falling deeply in love with Dud, and scheming to find ways to stay in the Caribbean past the end of the singularity project. Now that she could consider a possible future beyond the imminent end of the world, there might actually be something to plan for. She was trying to figure out a way to get out of Annapolis and posted to Key West Naval Air Station. It wasn't exactly Tortola, but it was a hell of a lot closer than Maryland.

She thought Dud might feel the same way. Neither of them had uttered the "L" word specifically in context yet, but it was working its way into their vocabulary. "I love the way you do that." "I love snorkeling here." "I really love how that bikini looks on you." And so on. It was just a matter of time.

They had taken a safari into Cruz Bay to get some supplies. The safaris were unique Virgin Island taxis, constructed on St. Thomas out of large pickup trucks, with rows of open bench seats welded onto the cargo bed like so many church pews. There was a roof of metal and plastic, or sometimes a canvas awning on a metal frame above the passenger seats for protection from rain and sun. Each safari could haul a dozen people or more, and there were hundreds of them all over the Virgin Islands. It was the simplest way to get around. Every vehicle was unique, and was the pride and joy of its owner. They were often loaded down with customized details, decorations and designs that could sometimes be quite ornate. The driver sat closed up in the truck cab, so there wasn't usually much conversation.

Cruz Bay was the main town on St. John, containing the headquarters for the national park, the ferry terminal, and the only real stores to obtain supplies. The whole island of St. John was a bit off the beaten path – the big cruise ships came into Charlotte Amalie or Havensight on St. Thomas, which also hosted the international airport. It required an

118

extra ferry ride to reach the adjacent islands of St. John or St. Croix, and many people didn't bother. Most of the tourists were content to remain on the more commercially-developed island of St. Thomas, wandering through the cut-rate jewelry stores and tony boutiques built into the ancient brick sugar warehouses along the Danish streets of Charlotte Amalie. In fact, very few debarking cruise ship passengers even bothered to leave the vicinity of the factory stores and outlet malls right at the Havensight docks, which were dwarfed by the towering ships. That was fine with most of the residents of St. John and St. Croix.

Like most resort areas, the Virgin Islands had a love-hate relationship with the tourists. The visitors drove the economy, bringing in much needed dollars and jobs. On the other hand, they also crowded the islands' beaches, streets, and shops. Many of the visitors were spoiled, rude, and expected to be waited on hand and foot. The locals who worked at the resorts were forced to put up with it, be nice to people who didn't always deserve it, and provide service with a smile. It ensured that the tips would keep coming, but it slowly ate away at your soul. No wonder the Brits called them bloody tourists!

Nikki and Dud went into the Starfish Market in Cruz Bay that afternoon to get some coffee, fresh vegetables, and maybe a steak to celebrate their last few days of camping. Nikki never ceased to be amazed at the food prices down here, which were easily double those of a mainland supermarket in Maryland. Even the specialty shops and gourmet markets around Washington weren't this expensive. Oh, well. The options were pretty clear-cut: you could either pay the price, or go hungry.

119

Nikki overheard some people in the front of the store jabbering with the cashier about the big explosion on St. Croix today. She stopped cold, and felt the bottom fall out of her stomach. WHAT big explosion?

Dud was in another aisle trying to find cereal or something. Nikki went up to the front of the store to listen to the conversation. The man relating the tale was a local, and she had a hard time understanding some of his words through a heavy West Indies accent.

"No, lissen, mon. Him be driving a church bus. Doan know where he got it, but from what was left, it look like a local church. He done drove dat ting right through the project fence when dey stop for lunch. Guards was shootin at him da whole time, and he be bloody but he doan care. He drive dat bus right into the drill rig. Boom! Dey have a big explosion. Police say bus was packed with explosives. Suicide bomber. Lots of people die, drill tower falls over. And dat black hole ting that was eating the Earth – she escapes! Now we back where we was, except worse, because all the science people who know how to fix this are dead or hurt."

Nikki staggered backward, and nearly fell. Dud caught her from behind. "Easy, Nikki, just take it easy."

"You heard?" She turned to face him.

"Yes. At least, I heard enough. We have to get back there, as quickly as possible."

"Who could do such a thing?" she whispered. "And why?"

****

They left the market empty handed, and made their way down to the ferry terminal in a daze. A quick check showed that the fastest they could get to St. Croix commercially would be in four hours on two different ferries. And that was assuming everything ran on time, which it rarely did.

"Come on," Dud said, taking Nikki by the elbow. "Let's go back to Cinnamon Bay, get our stuff and get a boat. Henry the manager there has a fast boat he will probably let me borrow in an emergency. We should be able to get down to St. Croix in an hour."

Thirty minutes later, they were rounding the Cinnamon Bay reef, and heading for St. Croix. The boat was a cigarette class, with a small cabin, big engine, high freeboard, and lots of speed. Dud put it up on plane and let her rip at 50 knots. His friend Henry had gotten the boat through a DEA acquaintance in Miami, who instructed him on how to bid for it at auction. The vessel had been impounded by the DEA as evidence in a drug dealer arrest, and with her former captain now convicted and doing 30 years to life, Henry had bought the fancy boat for a song. As soon as he heard about what happened on St. Croix, he insisted that they take the boat. He gave Dud the keys and told him to just put some gas in it when he brought it back. Cigarette boats were not noted for their fuel economy.

"Okay, here is the plan," Dud said from the pilot seat once they were underway. "I will take you down to St. Croix, find out what is going on, and get you situated. Then I'll bring Henry back his boat, take the ferry from Cruz Bay to Tortola, and get my own boat. I'll come back to St. Croix and see what I can do." He looked around at Nikki.

She was sitting near the stern in tears, crying like a child. He throttled back, locked the helm, and took her in his arms. She began to wail uncontrollably, and Dud hugged her tightly for a few moments, letting her work through it. While he had been talking to Henry about the boat, she

121

had been frantically making phone calls. She finally got in touch with Peter Hassenberg, who filled her in on the details.

The attack had occurred around noon. The powerful bomb killed Clyde Rose, Devi Chowdhury, and 10 additional members of the crew outright. Nikki knew each and every one of them, and hearing each name from Peter was a blow to her heart. The Uralmash 1500 drill rig derrick had toppled onto and crushed the research trailer, showering Arkady Kutuzov with broken glass and pinning Barney Freeman under tons of steel. Both were alive but seriously injured and in hospital, along with dozens of others. Barney had a spinal injury, a broken arm and multiple lacerations. They didn't think he would ever walk again. Shelly had gotten there already on an Air Force helicopter from St. Thomas and was with him. Arkady had lost an eye, and might lose the other one. The security contractor was working to keep the media away from the site. The police were sorting through the wreckage, trying to preserve evidence. President Jackson had mobilized the FBI and the Bureau of Alcohol, Tobacco and Firearms. Agents were on their way. And finally, worst of all, the singularity had gotten loose, and fallen back into the Earth. They didn't know where it was or have any information about the orbit.

It was all too much for Nikki, and the reality of it washed over her like a tidal wave. All that work for nothing. The frantic calculations, weeks of desperate drilling, and building the capture cage with a computer clever enough to capture the singularity. Successfully taming the singularity had been followed by a huge, global sigh of relief. And for what? So some nut with a bus bomb could destroy it all? Clyde had been doing this for his grandchildren's future. Barney and Arkady had been trying to save the world. Devi had been nothing more than a young, conscientious grad student, for God's sake. Why had they been repaid with death and injury? What kind of cold, unfeeling bastards were out there, anyway? She sobbed in Dud's arms. Eventually, she began to get control of herself.

"You're going to have to step up for this Lieutenant," he told her presently. "There is no one else with the experience or background. Clyde is gone, Barney is a cripple and Arkady is nearly blind. You are the only one who can put this right, Nikki."

"Me?" she said. "How the hell am I supposed to put this right? I'm an assistant professor of astrophysics at the Naval Academy. I have five scientific publications to my name, very little breakthrough original research, and zero Nobel Prizes. There are lots of other people on the committee who are more qualified, Dud. I can't take this on...I made a few decisions and gave some directions on the project when necessary, but I was never anything more than Barney's assistant."

"Stop it," he said. "A woman who lands jet fighters on aircraft carriers and parachutes out of airplanes is not my idea of timid. Don't sell yourself short. You have bigger balls than most men, Nikki, although I, for one, am glad they are only virtual." He got a brief smile out of her, and continued.

"Barney thought of you as his second in command, not his assistant. There is a difference. You were the *de facto* number two on this project in the eyes of everyone from the President of the United States down to the ladies washing dishes in the chow hall. Now that Barney is out of action, you are the only one who can step up and take the controls. No one else on that committee has the breadth of experience that you do with all aspects of this problem. You know I'm right, and you'll do it because it is your duty. I have seen you, Nikki. When the chips are down and you are

123

faced with a do or die choice, you always take it on. And you do the right thing and make the best decisions possible. It is a real talent, and one of the reasons why I love you."

Time paused for a moment as what he said sank in.

"Did you just say...?"

"Yes, Nikki. There are many things I love about you, but mostly, I just love you. I have fallen for you completely and totally. There. It's been said. I will do everything I can to help you tame the singularity, but ultimately, you are going to have to take charge. I believe in you, love. Like it or not, you are the expert, and the best hope we have."

"Dudley, I love you, too. And telling me that was possibly the single greatest thing you could have done to support me on this." She kissed him deeply.

Moments later, she dried her tears, and he throttled up the engines on a heading for St. Croix.

****

It was several days before the FBI reconstructed what had happened. The explosion had been caused by a suicide bomber driving a church bus, exactly as reported by the rumors in the Starfish Market. The bus had been packed with drums of ammonium nitrate fertilizer soaked in fuel oil, an explosive known as ANFO. Each canister was primed with one of the loud aerial reports removed from a skyrocket firework. These were wired together so that all the bomber had to do was insert a plug into the cigarette lighter socket on the bus, and all the fuses would light. Each aerial report would impart enough of a shock wave to its drum of ANFO to cause it to detonate. Timing wasn't important - once a single ANFO canister

124

exploded, it would set off its neighbors, and the whole bus would go up in a millisecond. It was improvised and rather ingenious, and the FBI concluded that someone trained in demolition had constructed it.

What was left of the bomber was identified as one James Earl (Jimmy) Byner of Grafton, West Virginia. They quickly learned that he had spent time in the Army at Fort Bragg where he learned demolition, which at least answered that question. However, what he was doing in the Virgin Islands with a bus full of explosives remained a mystery for another half day, until some FBI inquires on the ground in Grafton learned about Jimmy's connection to the Church of the Righteous Sword in the Hand of the Lord, and to its pastor, the Reverend Truett Pusser. Disturbingly, no one in federal law enforcement had ever heard previously of Jimmy Byner and his poetically named church.

The FBI maintained watch lists for all manner of groups thought to be capable of potentially criminal acts, terror and mayhem, including one list that was known informally within the bureau as the orange list, spelled ARNJ, for "armed religious nut jobs." It contained the names of all sorts of organized fundamentalist Christian militia members, Islamic jihadists, militant Zionists, and independent crazies who were prepared to join with Jesus Christ, Allah or Yahweh to fight the armies of Satan, purify the Aryan race, hasten the coming of Armageddon, defeat the Anti-Christ once he, she or it was identified, defend the fortress of Zion for God's Chosen People, defeat the infidel Crusaders and occupying Semites once and for all, take on the rag heads, and blow up the world in order to save it. There was even a militant Buddhist group seeking to free Tibet using nonviolence. The details of this list made for some entertaining reading, but Jimmy Byner had not been on it. He and the Reverend Pusser were unknown quantities, which

125

created a great deal of concern within the FBI. Like all law enforcement agencies everywhere, they really hated surprises.

Truett and Sue Ellen were brought to Pittsburgh for questioning. It didn't take long for the agents to hear about the vision of the flaming cross, which was quickly identified as the re-entering International Space Station. Truett insisted that it was a sign from heaven to his congregation sent by the One, True God, demanding that the Church of the Righteous Sword in the Hand of the Lord stop those who would attempt to interfere with the End Times. Thus, had Jimmy Byner been enabled to go to St. Croix, get use of a local church bus, and load it with explosives made from locally-obtained fertilizer, fuel oil, and fireworks, following a recipe that Sue Ellen had found on the Internet. Jimmy was instructed to drive the bus off the Queen Mary Highway, crash through the fence and onto the drill site, and detonate the explosives as close to the rig as possible. Truett was pleased that the plan had succeeded, and Jimmy was surely in the pinnacle of heaven reserved for martyrs. Truett and Sue Ellen were headed for the pinnacle of federal prison, but neither one cared what the FBI did with them. They were secure in the knowledge that the End Times would continue to approach, and no prison would hold them for long, because very soon the Last Trump would sound and free everyone.

The FBI agents passed all this information along to their managers, who consulted in turn with their superiors on ways to avoid any similar attacks. The FBI was concerned about the possibility of a copycat attempt on whatever singularity capture technique was tried next. The more worrisome scenario was a broader attack on another, much more visible target – the lifeboat manufacturing. The spaceships were critically important, especially now that the captured singularity had been lost in the explosion. Work on the vessels had resumed with even greater intensity than before. The scientists might remount another capture attempt, but it could be a longer shot than the first try. Getting a breeding population of people off the planet and behind the moon was the only way to ensure the survival of humanity.

With President Jackson weighing in at one point, it was finally decided that the best way to handle the religious terrorism incident was to shine a lot of daylight on it. They came up with a media plan to let the people of the world know what kind of nutty visionaries were out there, and to ask everyone to be vigilant. They simply couldn't afford another disaster.

****

The meeting had not started well. Dr. Nicole Shelton had called together Barney's singularity working group in College Park for a discussion on what to do next. Many of the senior scientists in the room were obviously leery about her ability to lead. Barney had cajoled them into joining the team through the force of his personality, long-time acquaintance, or an appeal to their egos. Most of these people had been in charge of large research programs for years, and several were now questioning Nikki's leadership credentials. She responded that it was Barney Freeman's desire that she lead the project, and his decision was supported at the highest levels. Nikki's temper was beginning to flare.

She was about to tell several of them where they could stuff their abundant publication records when Dr. Karl Barski, the Presidential Science Advisor, came into the room. He was out of breath and a bit rushed.

"Hello, everybody. Hi, Nikki. Sorry I'm late. We had a little trouble with traffic on the Beltway."

"Even in a White House motorcade?" asked Nikki.

127

"Dr. Barski," Leon Hammermesh from Harvard interrupted. "What is the status of Barney Freeman, and when will he be back to lead this effort? Dr. Shelton claims that she has been asked to fill in, but surely, the situation is temporary."

"Leon, I'm afraid Barney will not be rejoining us for quite some time. He has had multiple surgeries, stem cell nerve replacement, and is in physical therapy to try to rehabilitate his legs. It was decided that he should withdraw from the singularity project, so he named Dr. Shelton to lead the group."

"You mean that young lady over there? Her degree is less than five years old; she is an assistant professor with no graduate students and a minimal research record. She is hardly qualified to be the second in line. Why, I doubt she has even a dozen publications to her name." He sniffed derisively. "Barney must have been delirious from the pain medication. What bonehead agreed to that decision?"

"I did," said the President of the United States, as he entered the room. "And if you don't like it, Dr. Hammermesh, you and your oversized ego are welcome to leave. Along with anyone else in this room that might be struggling with the concept that Dr. Shelton is now leading this project. I would like to remind all of you that she was the one who came up with the original plan to capture the singularity at a depth reachable by deep drilling technology based on her orbital calculations. I don't know what the hell the rest of you so-called geniuses were doing to contribute to the solution to this problem, but this lowly Navy lieutenant you are treating like some kind of washerwoman is the only scientist in the room who produced concrete results. I like results.

128

"I will also remind you that Dr. Shelton has been involved in this project since day one as my special representative, and she knows all the players and all the moves. That is more than I can say about the rest of you. Dr. Freeman asked that she be put in charge, and I agree. In the big picture view, if we don't fix this problem in the few short months we have left, there isn't going to be any human race left to admire your research accomplishments and publications record. You'll all just be dead, along with almost everybody else. So I suggest we end this discussion and get to work. Any questions?"

The tension in the room deflated rapidly. No one could face off with President Jackson when it came to a game of put up or shut up. He had dealt with overstuffed egos for years, first in academia as a law professor, and then in politics with both Congress and prickly foreign leaders. He also had a considerable ego of his own, having been duly elected (twice, in fact) to the office of the President of the United States; nobody in the room came close to trumping him in terms of who was actually important.

"All right," the President said, clearly considering the matter to be closed. "Dr. Shelton, please tell us the next step."

"Thank you, Mr. President." Nikki was feeling much relieved by his clear and unequivocal support. The senior scientists in the room might be arrogant bastards, but they were nothing compared to the President. He would need to keep them in line, because she was about to lay a big egg. "I don't think anyone will be happy with this plan, but I can't find any possible way to avoid it. If we want to try again to tame the singularity, then we are going to need the help of Dr. Geoffrey Finch."

****

129

"Bloody hell," said Dr. Leon Hammermesh hours later, after the discussion had wound down. "Having to work with that bastard just pops my cork!"

"Now Leon," said Dr. Nellie Meade from Sandia, who had known him for years. "You know you shouldn't get your blood pressure up."

"Screw that, Nellie. I need a drink." He slumped down glumly behind the table.

"Come on, Leon. You've worked with worse than Finch back in the days of nuclear testing," said Dr. Ted Lewis, another old colleague from Los Alamos who now taught at MIT. Lewis was actually a rare Doctor-Doctor, because he possessed two PhD's. He had gotten his original degree in nuclear engineering, but in order to develop the instrumentation that was required to make the proper measurements for his experiments, he had to learn so much about electrical engineering that he ended up with a doctorate in that subject as well. Everyone in the room was brilliant in their field, but Lewis beat them all.

"I know I've worked with worse," Hammermesh replied. "Hell, half of those boys Oppenheimer brought on were as bad as Finch. But the fate of the world wasn't at stake."

"Yes it was, Leon," Lewis retorted. "Or did you forget that it was the Cold War and we had tens of thousands of nuclear warheads aimed at the Soviet Union, with a similar number aimed back at us? The whole planet could have been turned into a cinder in about 90 minutes. I was one of Oppie's boys, and I can tell you that we thought the work we were doing back then was damned important. So stop crying in your beer, and let's figure out how to get Finch to cooperate. We need to save the world once again, and after all, his ass is on the line too."

****

For some reason, probably because The End of The World as We Know It was fast approaching, Nikki had decided to ask Dudley about his thoughts on God. She knew he wasn't a particularly religious person and didn't go to church, but she wondered how he might square up the successful terrorist attack on the drill rig and the imminent death of everyone on Earth with a just and caring God. Even though she wasn't especially religious either, she was struggling with this in the context of what remained of her Anabaptist faith. She wondered if he might have some insights.

They were having coffee at a small cafe on the roof of the Torpedo Factory in Alexandria. It boasted a sweeping view of the Potomac River and the monuments of Washington, D.C. The Torpedo Factory had actually manufactured real submarine munitions during World War II, but it now housed a cooperative of artist galleries, natural shops and cafes. Dud was in Washington to de-brief Congress with his account of what they had found after reaching St. Croix. He looked at her oddly across the table. Nikki wondered if he was an atheist, and would tell her that the universe operated by random numbers.

"I've gone in circles with these ideas for many years, Nikki. As a scientist, I finally decided to look at the whole issue of God scientifically, and found to my surprise that it was quite comforting."

"Really?" she replied, suspicious that he was pulling her leg. "I didn't think it was possible to quantify God through science."

"Einstein once stated that his sense of God was his sense of wonder at the universe, and I figured that was a good place to start," Dud said seriously. "Look, if we begin with what we know, some basic truths emerge.

131

The first thing we know is that the universe had a beginning. It wasn't always here. Sometime between 13 and 14 billion years ago, there was a creation event. We have ironclad proof from the movement of galaxies and the cosmic background radiation that everything in the current universe began expanding from a point source at Time Zero, and has been expanding outward ever since. The British steady-state cosmologist Sir Fred Hoyle derisively termed this initial event the Big Bang, and the term caught on in the popular literature, much to his annoyance. Whatever it is called, it demonstrates that the universe had an origin. That is a huge deal. We can't say scientifically what caused the creation event, or what might have occurred before it. But we know it happened, and logic suggests that it was triggered by something, or perhaps by someone.

"The second thing we know is that the universe operates by a set of rules that appear to be the same everywhere. Water freezes at zero degrees Celsius on Earth, on Mars, on a hypothetical planet circling Antares, and on the far side of the Virgo Galaxy. The universe operates in a predictable and logical manner by adhering to this set of rules. When you study the science in detail, you realize that the engineering is very, very good. Quite a bit better than is has to be, in many cases. Protons are stable for 10^{50} years, which is probably five times longer than the expected life of the universe. Gravity is just strong enough to trigger nuclear reactions in the core of a star and hold it together against them, but not strong enough to crush the star so long as it is burning. This creates an exact balance of force that gives most stars an incredibly stable thermal output for most of their lifetimes. There are dozens more examples, but the point is that whoever or whatever set up all these rules was a superb, careful, and very conservative engineer.

132

"The third thing we know is that the rules under which the universe operates are favorable to life. Not just life on Earth, but anywhere. There are many examples of these life rules, but my favorite is ice. Almost every material in nature increases in density as it cools down, and most make the transition from liquid to solid by getting ever denser. If you throw a hunk of scrap iron into a cauldron of molten iron, it will sink. Solid candle wax sinks into melted wax, and so on. The most significant exception is water. If you place solid water into the liquid, it floats." He pointed at the ice in his water glass.

"Water is at its densest just before freezing," Dud continued. "As it freezes, the molecules lock into crystalline bonds that space them farther apart than when they were liquid. As a result, ice is only 90% as dense as liquid water, and it floats. This is hugely important to life on Earth, most of which has lived in the oceans throughout the history of the planet. If ice sank, the oceans would have filled up with solidified water long ago, and the only liquid water would be a melted surface layer a few dozen feet deep at most. The summer sun could melt it down a little ways farther, but ice at the bottom of the ocean would never have melted. The oceans are so deep that sunlight can't penetrate more than a few hundred feet. So with a minor adjustment, our engineer makes ice float, and the oceans below the floating ice stay liquid year around. Life thrives in the water and everyone is happy. Now understand that this is not totally necessary for life to exist. Creatures could have lived in puddles. But it makes everything much more pleasant.

"All these things speak to me of the presence of a creator. Some of your cosmology folks will argue the only reason that we find the universe is friendly to life is because we are here to make the observation. If it wasn't compatible, we wouldn't be here and no one would ever know. True, but

133

that logic is circular and doesn't really explain anything. Others invoke an infinite number of parallel universes, and say life in our universe is the result of a bunch of random coincidences, just one of many possibilities, and there are a trillion similar universes with no life. I've always thought that the multiverse theory was little more than a complicated way to get some mathematical equations to balance, and it is extremely messy in terms of both the energy and space needed. It reminds me of the ancient Greek explanation for celestial motion, with the sun, moon and planets all circling the Earth on crystal spheres, including small epicycle spheres to explain the retrograde motion of the planets. Like the multiverse, it was inelegant and clumsy, but it did explain the observations. We also know that it was dead wrong. Hopefully, someone will come along one day and redo the multiverse math properly, and find that we only need the one universe. Even if there are multiple universes, having a new one kick off every time a subatomic particle does a quantum jump just does not sit well with me.

"The simplest, most logical explanation for life in the universe, following Occam's razor and all the other rules of philosophical simplification, is that the universe was created, designed, engineered and assembled by a creator to be favorable for life. Whether or not the word creator should be spelled with an upper case C is a different discussion."

"Wow," was Nikki's reply. She absolutely had not expected such an involved and obviously long-thought-about explanation out of Dudley Gardner. "So are you a believer in intelligent design?"

"Not in the way it has been promoted by fundamentalist Christians," Dud said. "They try to show the direct hand of God in every creature, mineral, and landscape feature. I prefer to take a step back and say that geological processes, nuclear physics, and biological evolution all

134

operate on their own within parameters defined by a set of rules. It is how the rules are set up, and by whom that lead to my definition of intelligent design."

"So where in the rules does it say that the Earth should be destroyed by a black hole?" asked Nikki, with a quaver in her voice.

Dud reached across the table and held her hand. "One of the rules seems to be that humans have a free will, and that includes the ability to do good as well as evil. I don't believe in the devil, because I think people are perfectly capable of doing all sorts of nasty, cruel, mean, and despicable things without the need to blame it on the intervention of a fallen angel. This singularity is not the fault of any god or devil. The blame falls squarely on the head of Dr. Geoffrey Finch and his overinflated ego."

"What of those who died? Clyde Rose was only trying to save the world for his grandkids. There wasn't any reason for him or Devi or any of the other crew members to be killed in the explosion."

"True, as far as we know. But just because we don't see a reason for why things happen, it doesn't mean there isn't one, Nikki. Death is a part of life. If no one died, nothing would ever change and the most advanced life form on Earth would still be pond scum."

"So do you have an opinion of death in your scientific religious philosophy?"

"Just this. Einstein showed that matter and energy in the universe are equivalent. Matter and energy can be transformed from one form to another, such as heat to light, and can even be transformed into each other, such as uranium into an atomic fireball, but never destroyed. Thus, I believe that the matter and energy that make up a living being are not destroyed at death, but transformed. Despite the theories of Crick, I'm

135

pretty sure that I am more than just a bunch of organic molecules animated by chemical reactions. If life was that simple, we would have created it in the lab years ago. I think it takes a spark of life force or life energy, what might be called a soul if you wish to animate living beings. So Clyde, Devi, and the others were not destroyed; their souls were merely transformed by death into another form of energy. Enough actual scientific evidence for life after death has been gathered that I believe this transformation takes place."

"What kind of evidence?" Nikki asked, curious.

"Documentation of ghosts, for one. I know a lot of the photographs and sound recordings are faked, but not all of them. There are enough genuine, solid pieces of evidence out there to prove ghosts exist. The second thing is near-death experiences, where people report leaving their bodies and floating up to the ceiling. After being revived, they describe objects and events they couldn't possibly have witnessed if they were just an inert lump of electrically-charged chemicals tucked into an operating table. These two lines of evidence are pretty convincing, especially when you consider that if there was no life after death, we would have no evidence at all."

"I'd like to believe it wasn't for nothing," Nikki said. She pounded the table in frustration, causing the coffee in their cups to slosh dangerously. "We had caged the black hole and we were ready to get it off the planet when the Reverend Truett Pusser took it away from us with his hillbilly army of one. How could God let us get so close and then allow it all to come to ruin? What hope do we have of being successful on another try?"

"There was a reason, Nikki. Maybe the original plan was flawed in a way we didn't know. Perhaps it could have led to an even bigger disaster, like the having the black hole fall into the sun, for instance. That would definitely have been the end for us, because we couldn't possibly extract it

136

from there. I don't know why Jimmy Byner was allowed to succeed, but perhaps God was telling you to try something else."

"I can't!" The frustration and stress brought tears to her eyes. "They won't let me. None of those big shots on the committee will support any of my ideas. They argue every point and judge every decision. The world is ending and they are playing politics! I'm scared, Dud. I literally have been given the responsibility to save the planet, and I can't do it alone."

"You are the best hope we have, Nikki," Dud spoke gently. "You're not doing this alone. You have my support, the support of the President and other world leaders, and the support of many, many others. Forget about those egotistical bastards on the committee. The President was right; you were the one who came up with the deep drilling idea when none of them had anything. I don't care what credentials they have. If you have a plan, you should just move on it. The President gave you the authority. Screw the rest of the committee."

"What makes you so sure I have a plan?" Nikki challenged him.

"Because you have calculations for the new orbit of the singularity and soon it will be emerging from the ground at apogee. If I were Nikki Shelton, I'd be thinking about ways to re-capture the singularity out of the air from its new orbit using something mobile, like a rocket or a fighter jet."

"Okay," Nikki confessed. "You got me there, because that's exactly what I've been thinking."

"Uh huh. I knew it. See, I'm starting to learn how you think. But I still don't understand why you decided that you needed to bring in the much maligned and dastardly rotten Dr. Finch to work on the problem," Dud said. "There must be a reason why you would put yourself through

137

this. What does that odious egomaniac have to offer you that no one else on the committee can supply?"

Nikki smiled slowly. Her secret was out. "The ability to manufacture another black hole."

Chapter Seven: Rebuilding

"Another black hole?" Dr. Leon Hammermesh was incredulous. "Are you nuts? Why the hell do we need another black hole? The one we already have is doing a fine job of destroying the Earth!"

Nikki's reply was calm and measured, even though she felt like throwing a brick at him. "We need another black hole, Dr. Hammermesh, in order to intercept the one that was lost on St. Croix and shove it into orbit away from the Earth."

"Couldn't we use a ball of neutronium instead?" asked Nellie Meade from Sandia. "Black holes are just so dangerous."

"That is true, Dr. Meade," Nikki said. "But neutronium by its very nature won't hold an electrical charge. We'd have no way to control it. The event horizon of a spinning black hole, on the other hand, can be charged up with electricity and controlled with electromagnetic fields. The intercept trajectory is going to have to be precise if we hope to hit the target and give it the correct velocity."

"Perhaps you should explain the plan in more detail, Dr. Shelton," said a polite British voice from the back of the room. "It might answer a lot of questions." Most of the committee turned around to look at the speaker, Dr. Geoffrey Finch.

"Certainly, Dr. Finch," replied Nikki, thinking how polite the famous egotist seemed next to the abrupt rudeness of Leon Hammermesh. Still, he made her uncomfortable in a way the brash and bold Hammermesh did not. "We need to go to CERN and build another black hole, quickly.

The mass should be as large as possible, as long as we can still handle it. We spin it and get a bunch of electrons stuck in the event horizon to give it a strong negative charge. Then we put it in an electromagnetic cage and bring it to New Zealand."

"For what purpose?" Hammermesh interrupted. "I don't see where you are going with this."

Finch broke in. "The black hole lost from St. Croix is now in a very eccentric orbit, and massing about 5 kilotons. Tidal forces from the sun and moon are again making the ellipse increasingly narrow, and bringing the apogee part of the orbit above the surface of the Earth. By the middle of next month, the alignment of gravity from both the sun and moon will bring the high point of the orbit approximately 2 kilometers or 7,000 feet into the atmosphere about 100 km east of the South Island of New Zealand. This is well within the altitude range of drone aircraft."

"Can't we intercept it any sooner?" asked Dr. Ted Lewis from MIT.

Nikki used her new-found assertiveness to snatch the narrative thread back from Finch. "We want a collision between the new black hole and the old one to give it enough momentum to escape the Earth. We propose to fly the second black hole on a drone, like a Predator, and as Finch's black hole is slowly arcing over on the crest of its orbit, we intercept it with the Predator. The drone launches the most powerful missile it can carry with the new black hole in the nose cone, and the two black holes collide. There will be a bright flash and lots of radiation, which is why we do this with an unmanned aircraft above a deserted part of the Pacific Ocean. The blast shouldn't harm anyone, but we'll get people in New Zealand to take cover just in case. Because Finch's black hole will be moving slowly at the top of its parabolic arc, the momentum transferred from the

140

rapidly moving second black hole should be adequate to accelerate the combined mass up to escape velocity. It will fall into the Earth one last time, follow a hyperbolic arc around the center of mass at perigee, and then go into a much higher and nearly circular orbit. Once it is out of the atmosphere, we can intercept it with a spacecraft and park it at the L1 position between the Earth and Moon. Put up a flashing neon warning sign and we're done."

"And you believe this will work?" asked an incredulous Dr. Leon Hammermesh.

"No, Leon," said Geoffrey Finch. "We know it will work. The mathematics show it will work. I worked out all the details with the help of Dr. Shelton, and I am convinced it will work."

"Prove it," Hammermesh replied.

"Certainly," said Finch. "If I could just have a laptop and projector..."

"Now just wait just a minute, both of you," Nikki interrupted angrily. "First of all, this was my idea, and I will not allow Dr. Finch to hijack it. I want to point out that I was the one who painstakingly worked out the mathematical details over two sleepless nights with a minor amount of help from Dr. Finch, and I have the bags under my eyes to prove it. Secondly, the proof is in the orbital computer models, which are mine, and which Dr. Finch is not competent to run, despite what he might think. I have prepared a demonstration."

"Once again, your ego is getting you into trouble, Geoff," said Ted Lewis.

"Oh, what do you know?" Finch replied rhetorically.

"He has two PhD's and you only have one," Hammermesh said. "Therefore, according to your way of rating things, he is at least twice as smart as you, and knows plenty."

Unable to deliver a pithy response to that, Finch wisely decided to shut up. Nikki could not believe how brazen and arrogant he had been about trying to claim credit for her idea, and found herself disliking the man more and more each minute.

The computer model was elegant in its simplicity. Nikki ran the orbital simulations from the beginning. When Finch first lost the singularity from CERN, it had been affected by residual magnetism from the nearby superconducting magnets of the LHC. While not strong enough to stop it, the magnetic forces gave the black hole a bit of forward momentum as it exited the lab. This meant that it did not fall straight down into the Earth, but rather followed a parabolic arc down to the center of gravity, where it took up an elliptical orbit. The gravity of the sun and moon needed many months to stretch the orbit on the long axis of the ellipse, eventually allowing the black hole to approach close enough to the surface of the Earth for the capture attempt at St. Croix. That operation changed the orbital dynamics considerably, because being held in the drill rig cage had made the singularity motionless with respect to the Earth.

As luck would have it, Jimmy Byner drove his magic bus onto the drill site location at almost precisely high noon. When the explosion released the black hole from the drill cage, it went nearly straight down past the Earth's center of mass, continued almost the same distance upward on the other side, and then down again, oscillating through the Earth in a narrow elliptical orbit with a period of 64 minutes that was gradually lengthening. The important thing about this new orbit was that it was lined up almost perfectly at right angles to the gravitational force of the sun. So each trip upward had a little extra solar gravity giving it a boost, and each trip back down had a little solar gravity assist to slow. When the new or full moon path lined up with the orbital axis, the boost increased. The end result was that the combined gravity of the sun and moon were stretching the apogee point of the orbit ever farther from the Earth's center of mass, so that the black hole was close to breaking through the surface of the Earth every hour at the high point of the orbit. In about a month, it ought to be getting high enough in remote areas that they could get a drone under it and get it off the planet.

In the meantime, however, the singularity would be appearing above the surface of the planet almost hourly, and not every place was going to be unpopulated. NASA needed to track the apogee of every single orbit, and humans were going to have to get out of the way. The black hole had accreted enough mass that the gravity field was beginning to pull other particles into it along the slower parts of its orbit. Nikki realized that they had better get the public relations people on this pronto, or some folks were going to be freaking out when a star came up out of their front lawn.

****

Captain Joseph Goodfriend, United States Navy, was confused. As former commander of the aircraft carrier USS Theodore Roosevelt, his ship had been called into port months earlier to turn over her crew for the effort to finish, fit, test, and man the many escape spacecraft being constructed in Nevada. The Roosevelt was tied up in mothballs at the San Diego pier, and all her aircraft had been flown off to Nellis Air Force Base, where they were being used for Nevada Test Site security, ferrying personnel around, or

143

bringing in supplies. There was nobody on board except a small crew of contractor security guards.

Goodfriend himself had been training at the Nevada Test Site to command one of the spacecraft when some new orders arrived for him on the secure printer. The cover page stated that they came from the Secretary of the Navy herself. She claimed to be merely passing on orders directly from the Commander in Chief. According to this document, President Jackson wanted him to reassemble his crew, along with a full complement of fighter jets and two U.S. Air Force Reaper drones, and make best possible speed to the South Pacific Ocean off the coast of New Zealand within 30 days. The document concluded by stating that additional information would be forthcoming. He double-checked the authentication codes, and it was the real deal.

The captain had been running through spaceflight orbital simulations with his executive officer and a couple of electronics technicians. They were on a lunch break when Goodfriend read the orders. The executive officer usually went to the chow hall for lunch, but today she was in the next room reviewing the exercise.

"Marino, get in here!" Goodfriend shouted to the XO.

Commander Helen Marino came into the simulation chamber from the observation room. Goodfriend thrust the orders at her, and waited impatiently as she read them.

Marino was as surprised as he was. "Uh, sir, this is an unexpected development. With all due respect, are they serious?"

"It seems like it. The authentication codes check out. How quickly can we get ourselves and our people back aboard?"

"We can do that fairly quickly, sir. But a more relevant question might be about what kind of shape the old boy is in. We did a pretty good job of putting him in mothballs, and it could take awhile to get the Teddy fired back up. Once we do, the sailing time at full speed is going to be at least two weeks, assuming we don't run into any weather. We need to start this operation right now if we expect to have any hope of success."

"I agree, Commander. As I said, these orders appear to be the genuine article and we will treat them as such. I suggest we start by getting ourselves and all the logistical and tactical commanders back aboard the Roosevelt, and they can help us plan the rest of this operation. Most of our former crew is right here at the Test Site, and we might be able to round up everybody and be at sea in less than a week. Maybe. It's a tall order, Helen, and while I'm not one to question the wisdom of the chain of command, I wish I knew why they wanted us to get old Teddy shipshape in such a hurry and scoot halfway around the world."

"I can only guess that it has something to do with the black hole, Captain. I can't imagine any other reason why we would be put back to sea, given everything else going on these days. We may have just become part of the second capture attempt."

"Well, as T.R. himself would have said, bully to that."

****

The President of the United States was not looking forward to this discussion, but they had to figure things out. The lunar base was ready to accept colonists and they needed to start sending ships in the next few weeks. This couldn't all wait until the last minute, although he knew there would be a good deal of that anyway.

President Jackson was meeting at the United Nations with other world leaders. They were going to attempt to determine a fair and equitable way for people to be assigned places on the million ships that were being constructed. The most massive construction project in the history of humanity had room for about two billion people on the ships and in the colonies. It sounded like a lot, but no matter how they planned the evacuation, it was less than a third of the total world population. Who got to go, and who didn't?

After hours of fruitless discussion about ways of assigning population quotas to different nations, the Prime Minister of India spoke. She was a small, dark woman in a beautiful silk sari.

"The only fair way to do this is through a lottery," she said.

"What kind of a lottery?" asked the President of Nigeria.

"Numbers," replied the diminutive Indian P.M., who had been a professor of mathematics at the University of Bangalore before entering politics at the urging of her late husband. "We take everyone in the world who is eligible to evacuate, and randomly assign them a number. Perhaps we need only to go as high as 100. We assign different numbers to uniform groups of people, equally sized and diversified so that selecting a certain amount would fill the available ships. For example, suppose we determine that eight groups of people would be the correct amount to fill the available seats on the ships. So we then select eight numbers in the lottery. The people holding those numbers get to go; whereas everyone else must stay behind."

"I like your idea, but how do we ensure an equitable distribution of opportunity?" President Jackson asked. "Any system I would be willing to support must be fair to everyone, and resistant to fraud, corruption, bullying or favoritism."

"The simplest thing," replied the Indian P.M., "Is to pre-screen all the applicants to make sure that only those who are eligible to go are in the evacuation pool. We have already discussed this – it sounds harsh, but we can only afford to evacuate people who can propagate the human race. Therefore, it must be a breeding population under 35 years old, without disabilities, chronic diseases, or genetic damage. I believe we are all agreed on this."

"Well, it could still be debated," said the British Prime Minister, who had advocated giving preferential spacecraft berths to the engineers and scientists needed for rebuilding human civilization, without any kind of genetic screening or age restrictions. "But if all of the others are agreed, then it would be pointless for me to continue the discussion."

"Thank you, Mr. Conyers," the Indian P.M. said. "If I may continue to respond to President Jackson's concerns, I have given this a good deal of thought. All able-bodied evacuees would be assigned a number, which would be chosen at random. When we select groups for boarding the ships, only those with the so-called winning number would come forward."

"Too easy to cheat," said the Chinese Premier. "Each person should be identified by biometrics, such as fingerprints or retinal scans, when they are assigned a number. That way, no one can substitute themselves for an actual lottery winner. Once those numbers are picked, it would be very tempting for some people to steal the identity of a winner and go in their place."

"How would anyone do that?" asked the Indian Prime Minister.

147

The Russian President answered. "If someone had enough money, and was in a life or death situation, they would find a way. My Chinese colleague is right. We must make sure that those who win a place aboard the evacuation fleet can be positively identified."

"Collecting detailed biometrics on each, individual, eligible person would produce an enormous amount of data," the Japanese Prime Minister said. "There must be several billion qualified people in the evacuation pool. Where could so much information be stored?"

"One of the U.S. national lab supercomputers should be able to handle that much data," said President Jackson. "These are kept in highly secured locations, and access is very limited. If we do this correctly, we can enter the biometrics and assigned numbers of everyone into a large database. No one will even know in advance what number they have. Then we will choose random numbers in a lottery, and the persons selected will be notified only then, and told to board within days. There won't be much time for any hanky-panky behind the scenes."

"Those who commit such hanky-panky, as you call it, are often very clever," said the Russian President. "I suggest that each winner be given a biometrically-encoded ticket that only they can use to board the ships."

The discussion continued for hours as the exhaustive details were worked out. In the end, the plan was formalized into a U.N. resolution that passed unanimously. They all agreed that a system had been developed that was not only fair, but air-tight and most importantly, fraud proof.

As professional politicians, they should have known there was no such thing.

****

The singularity had not broken through the surface of the Earth yet, but would soon do so. The models showed that only a few orbits early on would have segments above the surface, but these would increase in frequency as tides from the sun and moon worked to draw the singularity out of the Earth. Nikki assembled a small team of NASA people to analyze the neutrino data and monitor the orbital changes. It was important to warn people in advance if the black hole was going to show up in their neighborhood. Most of the predicted orbital segments above the surface of the Earth were located over the oceans or uninhabited parts of continents. There was still a surprising amount of unoccupied space left on the Earth. For the smaller number of orbits that would actually bring the singularity through a populated area, Nikki felt that it was the duty of her group to inform the residents.

The first of these was located in southwestern United States. The computer model predicted that in less than a week, the singularity would rise from the northern Arizona desert near Meteor Crater, arc westward over California as the Earth turned beneath the orbital plane, and drop back below the planetary surface in the San Bernardino Mountains near Big Bear Lake. Nikki intended to meet it.

Dozens of weird religious cults had sprung up all over southern California in response to the singularity. One group was planning an elaborate Wiccan worship ceremony to welcome the black hole and herald the dawn of a new era for the human race. Some of the affiliated members believed that humans would transcend the collapse of Earth into a black hole in a new-age manner, and humanity would be reborn to flourish in another universe. They tended to be a little sparse on the details of how all this was supposed to happen, but that didn't seem to faze any of the starry-

149

eyed new members. A cult obsessed with human sexuality was certain that unleashing sexual energy would hold back the end of the world. They held elaborate orgies to this end, and were usually exhausted. Another group was attempting to stay falling-down, stinking drunk, and stoned out of their gourds for the duration, until scientists either fixed the problem or the world ended, whichever came first. Nikki thought their approach made about as much sense as anything. Still others were excitedly planning for the end of the world, anticipating the final trump, the four horsemen and the whole dramatic apocalyptic cataclysm word-for-word as predicted in Revelations. Their fantasies tended to be bloody, violent and contain gory details that said more about the psychology of the group than it did about their religious dogma. Other religions were trying to invoke divine intervention to drive the black hole away.

Big fights usually broke out whenever any of these cults got within striking distance of each other. Local and state police were trying to keep the different groups separated, but the orbital track was not long enough for everyone to spread out. Thousands of cult members, and tens of millions of regular people were expected to journey to locations beneath the trajectory of the black hole as it crossed from Arizona to California. There they would observe it, worship it, throw things at it, pray at it, moon it, or have orgasms under it. One guy was even planning to shoot it with a sniper rifle to try kicking it off the planet. Near-riot conditions were anticipated. Wondering why this first appearance just HAD to be in kooky Southern California, of all places, Nikki decided to see it from a jet.

She had been logging the monthly minimum flight hours needed to maintain her pilot qualification using aircraft borrowed from the Key West Naval Air Station when she was in the Caribbean and from Patuxent Naval

Air Station near the District of Columbia when she was in College Park. Nikki was qualified to fly both the F/A-18 Hornet, and the F-16 Fighting Falcon. She preferred the Hornet, which was a larger and more forgiving aircraft, to the small and skittish Falcon.

The Navy airplane that had been assigned to her when she qualified as a pilot, known as her "tail number" was now flying escort duty out of Nellis AFB for the Nevada Test Site. It was the wrong aircraft for chasing the singularity anyway – an older model, single-seat Hornet equipped as a fighter interceptor. She needed the faster, heavier F/A-18 Super Hornet, equipped for surveillance, precision photography, and sustained supersonic flight. Nikki called Karl Barski and told him what she had in mind. Barski called someone at the Pentagon, and a few hours later, Lieutenant Nicole Shelton, USN, was informed that an aircraft meeting her requirements would be made available at Edwards Air Force Base. She was ordered to proceed there posthaste, where she would fly it to meet the singularity. The Air Force had a Gulfstream jet at Andrews fueled and ready that she could take to California.

Nikki made it clear to Barski that this was to be an observational flight only. She would try to intercept and then pace the singularity as it rose and fell in an arc above the Earth. Instruments onboard the aircraft would record volumes of data on parameters such as the black hole's velocity, mass, charge, radiation emissions, and any tiny irregularities in its orbit. The data would be used to plan the attempt to try changing the trajectory of the black hole a few weeks later over an isolated spot of Pacific Ocean.

Ramming a second black hole into the first one to boost it to escape velocity was expected to release both a shock wave and radiation emission

151

equivalent to a twenty megaton hydrogen bomb. That was the main reason the interception of the singularity on this first orbital pass over the suburbs of Los Angeles would be for observational purposes only. Even if they had the second black hole ready, colliding with it on this orbit could kill millions.

****

Nikki and Dud arrived at Edwards in the late afternoon sunlight. The flat salt pan of Rogers Dry Lake stretched away to the east, notched into a vee in the Mojave Desert between the Tehachapi and San Gabriel Mountains. Autumn was the peak of the dry season in the high desert, and the sage, yucca and other plants looked parched and dead. Once the late winter rains came through, all the "dead" vegetation would green-up in a matter of days, and flower a few weeks later.

Nikki had decided to bring Dud along to help with the observations. His job would be to sit in the rear seat of the jet while she flew the plane, and keep all the instruments turned on and trained on the singularity. Barski had initially objected to her idea of taking a foreign national up in a high performance jet aircraft, which seemed a bit ludicrous to Nikki, considering the circumstances. Even if he wanted to, what avionics secrets could Dud possibly steal that weren't already being shared among the dozens of nations pouring the latest and most sophisticated aerospace technology into the escape lifeboats? Nikki patiently explained that Dud was a qualified geophysicist who could run all the instruments, and if he didn't go, who did they expect her to take instead? Since none of the military personnel who were even remotely qualified could be spared from the lifeboat work, Barski relented.

After checking over the aircraft, gear and instruments that would be needed for the singularity interception, Nikki and Dud got a rental car

152

and headed down to Barstow for a meal and a room. Like most military facilities in the country, Edwards was practically deserted. There were no ready dorm rooms, no food, no beer, no entertainment, and not much else. There wasn't even a tower crew –Nikki would be taking off and landing under visual flight rules. The crew that brought her aircraft in from Nellis had basically handed her the keys and high-tailed it out of there. Work on the lifeboats consumed the military these days. She suspected the real reason they wanted her to launch from Edwards was to keep her away from Nellis and out from underfoot.

They booked a room in a very 1950s-looking motel in Barstow, and headed over to the Hollywood Diner for some food. It was an institution on the freeway between Los Angeles and Las Vegas, and a favorite stopover. The owner had worked as an extra in the movie industry for years, and the restaurant was decorated with an incredible assortment of Hollywood memorabilia, most of it signed by the personalities represented. After dinner, Nikki and Dud returned to the motel and sat on lounge chairs near the darkened pool. They were almost the only guests, and had the courtyard to themselves.

"Nikki, are you sure I can do this tomorrow? I'm a bit nervous about trying to track a black hole on instruments whilst hurtling through the sky faster than a shout," Dud said.

"It's easy, baby," she replied with confidence. "You won't even feel us break the sound barrier, except that the flight will smooth out after we exceed Mach one."

"That's awfully damn fast." Dud was clearly still worried.

"Well, the Earth rotates at about 1,000 miles per hour," Nikki said. "If we don't go supersonic, we'll never be able to catch up and keep pace with the black hole. I am eager to get some solid data on this thing. All we have is a history of neutrino bursts. The national lab people were able to collect some mass and charge data while it was 50,000 feet underground in a cage, but we have never been able to get close enough for any serious information collection."

"How will we see it? We won't get sucked in, will we?" asked Dud, suddenly alarmed.

"No, it is nowhere near massive enough to worry about that. If I hit it with the airplane, it would probably go right through it without even making a hole. The accretion disk was smaller than a poppy seed on St. Croix, but it was luminous because it had trapped a few subatomic particles that were spiraling toward the event horizon. It ought to be a little bigger and even brighter tomorrow. We shouldn't have any trouble spotting it visually, but we'll be tracking it with radiation monitors and heat sensors as well."

"Okay, good. I don't want to get accreted any sooner than necessary."

They lost themselves in each other for the remainder of the cool desert night in the anonymous motel room in Barstow. After giving Nikki three powerful orgasms, Dud finally rolled over and slept. She had lain awake for another hour, worrying about the mission. Although it should be simple and straightforward, sometimes things went wrong. The fact that this was a dry run for the much more difficult mission that would follow a few weeks later over the South Pacific left her absolutely terrified.

****

The disaster on St. Croix caused by Jimmy Byner was by now well-known around the world. Nearly everyone was appalled at the destruction,

154

and disappointed that an apparent victory over the rogue black hole had been turned into a defeat through the actions of some religious fanatics. A few people, however, admired what Jimmy Byner had accomplished. Some believed that the Reverend Truett Pusser and his Church of the Righteous Sword in the Hand of the Lord had set the world back onto the course God had determined for it. These individuals were convinced that any other attempts by misguided scientists to stop the inevitable Last Judgment from approaching should be met with similar actions.

As such, President Jackson had ordered preparations for the South Pacific intercept mission to be made at the highest level of secrecy. It was strictly "need-to-know," and the only people who knew the full plan were the President of the United States, National Science Advisor Dr. Karl Barski, and Navy Lieutenant Dr. Nicole Shelton, who would actually fly the mission.

But word gets out.

Although Captain Joseph Goodfriend and Commander Helen Marino of the United States Navy had top secret clearances and told no one about the details of their orders, when an aircraft carrier the size of the USS Theodore Roosevelt prepares to leave port, people notice. Especially when it is the only thing leaving port. The Coronado Navy Base and nearby city of San Diego were awash in what the security people call "incidental information." This included items such as crew members returning to the ship, deliveries of large quantities of supplies, aircraft coming back aboard, and the rushed nature of preparations for this voyage. People noticed the arrival of two unmanned drones, which were rarely flown off carriers. Certain members of the military, who belonged to fundamentalist churches that shared beliefs similar to the Church of the Righteous Sword in the Hand of the Lord were troubled by these preparations, and talked to their ministers. Many suspected that the Roosevelt was being readied for a black hole intercept mission, following the same chain of logic that Commander Marino had used to figure it out. Given the devotion of resources and frantic pace of the military to fit out and crew the lifeboat spacecraft, no one could imagine any other reason for the giant carrier to go back out to sea.

Chief Warrant Officer Ibrahim Mohammed was a deeply religious man. As a career Navy NCO, he did not have to put up with taunts and criticism of his Islamic faith, and he was able to say his daily prayers toward Mecca from the privacy of his cabin. Lower rank and younger Muslims had a much more difficult time of it. He felt sorry for them, but made no move to interfere. Those who would follow the Prophet had to learn in their own way, in their own time, how to deal with all the threats faced by Muslims in America. The increase in Christian fundamentalism with the potential end of the world at hand made things all the more difficult for those of other faiths.

Chief Mohammed and his crew had been ordered to return to the engine room of the USS Theodore Roosevelt, and bring her reactors back online. Commander Marino made it clear that they needed to be underway in 72 hours. This was the bare minimum necessary to heat up the reactors and make enough steam for the turbines that turned the propellers and moved the giant ship. Mohammed privately wondered what the rush was all about, but couldn't ask. It had been made clear that the mission was secret, and the details were "need to know" only. Under the strict need to know rules, he was only allowed to ask the XO how far they were going, to make sure he had enough fissile material on hand for the reactor. She told him to plan for 7,000 miles each way, and then in an uncharacteristic spill, mentioned that their destination was off the coast of New Zealand.

Mohammed had been concerned that he might be participating in a military exercise that went directly against the will of Allah. It was obvious that the black hole had been sent by God to swallow the Earth, and all her children. He did not have any qualms about working on the lifeboat project...after all, Allah had allowed and even helped Noah to escape the flood, but did not stop it from happening. However, escape was one thing. Participating in an attempt to thwart God's will was something altogether different.

He had discussed this at some length with the imam in his San Diego mosque. The clergyman was sympathetic, suggesting to the chief that attempts to intercept the black hole and stop the destruction of the Earth were the work of nonbelievers and infidels. The imam advised Mohammed that it was his duty as a Muslim to try to stop this, thus leaving him even more troubled. He had taken an oath when he joined the Navy to defend the constitution of the United States against all enemies, foreign or domestic. Stopping a naval vessel from carrying out a mission definitely went against this oath.

It would be easy to do – Mohammed worked as the engineering chief in the engine room of a nuclear-powered aircraft carrier. One bad command line to the computers that ran the reactor, or the improper closure of a valve or electrical switch would kick-in safety protocols and fail-safes, reducing the speed of the big ship to dead slow or stop until the problem was identified and fixed. It was apparent from Commander Marino's briefing that making any headway at less than the Roosevelt's top speed of 40 knots might cause the mission to fail if they were late for the event they

157

were trying to intercept. But an action along these lines was unthinkable to the chief. He took great pride in the powerful, finely-tuned engines and the speed they imparted to the ship. Sabotaging them to slow down was out of the question.

The imam finally asked Chief Mohammed if he could say where the ship was bound. The chief didn't know at the time. The clergyman assured him that some of his Muslim brothers could be mobilized at the destination to interfere with whatever the infidels had in mind. No one would get hurt, he promised, because the warriors would find a simple way to stop the non-believers in their foolish mission, and allow the will of Allah to proceed.

Two days later, with a head of steam from the fully powered reactors, the USS Theodore Roosevelt left the harbor at San Diego. The old boy was far from battle ready, carrying only a skeleton crew for engines, navigation and minimal flight operations. It was all Captain Goodfriend was allowed. The lifeboat project still took precedence, even over a black hole intercept attempt, and the personnel simply could not be spared.

As the carrier sailed past downtown San Diego on its way to open sea, Chief Ibrahim Mohammed walked out on the flight deck with his cell phone. He dialed the mosque, and when the imam answered, the chief spoke just four words.

"New Zealand. Eight days."

Satisfied that he had done his duty as a good Muslim, but still troubled, he returned to the engine room. As the big ship headed out to sea at flank speed, Chief Mohammed could not shake the feeling that he had somehow betrayed a trust. Not with the nation, and not even with the Navy. But perhaps with some of his fellow sailors. He did not know what

158

the imam might be planning, but if anyone got hurt or killed on this mission because of the information he had given out, there would be hell to pay.

****

After finishing her preflight checklist and inspection, Nikki taxied the F/A-18 to the end of the runway in preparation for takeoff. Since there was no one in the tower at Edwards, and no other active aircraft on the tarmac, they could leave whenever they wanted to. So she clicked on the intercom, and asked her back seater if he was ready.

Dud replied that he was, with a noticeable quaver in his voice, as Nikki lined the nose up with the centerline of the runway.

"I'll bet you never had a girlfriend before who could do this," she told Dud.

"No. Hot sports cars were about the most extreme until I met you," he said. "They were pretty fast, but not supersonic fast."

"We won't be going supersonic until later in the flight. However, I do intend to use afterburners to get us upstairs quickly, so hold on to your nickers, fella."

Nikki pushed the throttles forward, and the twin engines spooled up. She released the brakes, and the jet began moving down the runway with increasing acceleration. Just as it reached takeoff speed and cleared the runway, she kicked in the afterburners. The jet accelerated like a missile, roaring upward almost vertically into the sky. As the g-forces rose, Dud felt as if a large, friendly, but very heavy elephant was sitting on his chest. Within seconds, they were crossing the outer marker of the field at a height of 20,000 feet, and Nikki called the FAA air traffic control center at Los Angeles to let them know her altitude, speed and bearing. They had spotted

159

her transponder on radar, were aware of her flight plan, and had re-routed all civilian traffic out of the area to keep commercial flights away from the singularity. Nikki reached 40,000 feet, cut back to cruising speed, and headed for Arizona.

As she passed the southern tip of Nevada, the Nellis AFB control tower called to check in on her.

"Special Navy flight one zero niner, this is Nellis control tower. Do you read?"

"Roger, Nellis. Loud and clear. This is Lieutenant Nicole Shelton, USN with Mr. Dudley Gardner of the British Geological Survey in the back seat. We are heading to Meteor Crater to first intercept and then pace the singularity from there to Big Bear Lake in the San Bernardino Mountains. Over."

"Roger, Lieutenant Shelton. We have your flight plan on record and recognize your call sign as 'Athena.' Please confirm."

"Affirmative, Nellis. Over." She was glad that Dud was seated behind her and couldn't see the expression on her face. The call sign reminded her of flight school, and how much of a science geek she had seemed to her squad mates.

"Roger that, Athena. All commercial traffic has been cleared for 100 miles on either side of the projected singularity orbit. You should have a clear theater of operations. Do you have sufficient fuel for your planned routing?"

"Affirmative, Nellis. We should get there about twenty minutes before the singularity appears, and we will loiter in slow orbits at three five thousand while waiting for it. Once we spot it, we will give chase at

160

supersonic speeds. I am planning the pursuit to be about 340 nautical miles on a heading of 262 at five zero thousand feet. We will probably exceed Mach one across most of our planned routing. I currently have full wing tanks, which I will use to top off internal tanks and drop before engaging in the pursuit. I expect to be down to about 2,000 pounds of fuel by the time we reach San Berdoo, but this should be sufficient reserves to get back to Edwards, which is nearby."

"Roger, Athena. Ground stations have been notified to expect a series of sonic booms this morning as you transit. We have launched a C-135 tanker with two F-22 Raptors under orders from the Pentagon. They are presently cruising outside the 100 mile protected zone. Let us know if you need mid-air refueling and we will vector the tanker in to your course. One of the Raptors will keep the no-fly zone clear, and the other will rendezvous with you at Meteor Crater and act as your wingman."

"Negative, Nellis. I don't really need a wingman for this mission. It's scientific observations only."

A different voice came over the radio. "Belay that, sailor. This is Commander Young. You are under orders to fly with a wingman, lieutenant. We want you to watch the singularity and make sure you stay with it. The wingman will watch out for everything else in your airspace."

"Aye, aye, Commander. I will comply. Thank you for your help. Hopefully, we will get some good data and make all this effort worthwhile."

The original radio voice returned. "Good luck and good hunting, Athena. Nellis out."

"So how did you come up with Athena as nickname?" Dud asked later.

161

"It's not a nickname, it's a call sign," she explained. "You don't make them up yourself. Your squad mates bestow them upon you based on your personality. I was quite the science geek as an undergrad at Annapolis, and even more so when I went to Johns Hopkins for a Ph.D. in astrophysics. Some of the Neanderthals who fly Navy jets decided to name me after the Greek goddess of science."

"Well, it is appropriate. You are pretty damned smart."

"Yeah, well being smart isn't always an asset. It never helped my social life very much."

"You just need to hang around with more advanced subspecies than Neanderthals who appreciate your intelligence," Dud said. "Like me."

They flew over the Painted Desert of northern Arizona to the town of Winslow. Interstate 40 and Meteor Crater were visible below them. Nikki took it slow and easy to conserve fuel while they waited for the singularity to appear. She was going to need a lot of gas for the chase, because the F/A-18 had to use afterburners to fly faster than Mach one.

The F-22 from Nellis, piloted by one Air Force Major William "Ridge" Runner showed up a few minutes later. The two pilots chatted for awhile to get logistics squared away, while Dud watched the ground. Once Ridge figured out which direction Athena was going to fly to chase the black hole, he could position himself to pace her, while avoiding her jet wash, supersonic shock wave, and other assorted hazards.

As a geologist, Dud couldn't have been more fascinated with the view. He had never been over this part of the southwestern United States before in daylight. Red sandstone cliff faces bordered the edges of mesas that were stacked like giant staircases. Black lava flows from volcanic cinder cones meandered for miles across the desert landscape. Rivers and dry

162

washes carved fantastic canyons into the plateau, with each curve incised deeply into the flat sedimentary bedrock. Most fascinating of all was the Meteor Crater itself. Dud was surprised that from the air, it actually had a rather square outline, instead of being the circular structure he expected. A quick search using the aircraft's Internet connection turned up an article explaining that the natural orthogonal jointing in the sedimentary rock making up the plateau surface was responsible for the crater's angular shape.

According to the orbital models, the black hole would rise from the desert floor just west of the crater rim. They were on time, in position, and Nikki was receiving regular reports from the neutrino detector teams who were tracking the singularity. It was on its way.

A few minutes later, Dud spotted a brilliant flash of light below them and to the west. He thought at first that it was a reflection of sunlight off a car window or other smooth surface, but the light persisted and got brighter. Through his dark glasses, he saw a miniature sun rising rapidly off the desert floor.

"Nikki, Nikki – there it is! Below us and to the left."

"I see it," she responded. "Which way is it moving? We have to get behind it."

"The automated theodolite is plotting the course. Just as predicted – it is moving upward and westward in a parabolic arc. The vertical speed is slowing, but the westward speed is constant at around 900 miles per hour."

"Right," said Nikki. "The rising movement is the orbit, slowing as the object approaches apogee. The westward movement is due to the rotation of the Earth. How high does the model predict it will go?"

163

"According to the update we just got, it should reach the top of the arc at 60,000 feet, and then keel over and fall back into the Earth. Get closer and stay with it so I can collect some data."

"Right. Let me contact our wingman." She keyed her mike to the outside frequency. "Ridge, this is Athena. Do you copy?"

"Affirmative, Athena. I see it below. State your flight plan."

"We are moving toward it now. After it rises above three five zero, we will begin to chase it from below and behind. Once it passes apogee, we will stay above it. We need to pace it to get data. The chase will get to supersonic speeds quickly."

"Roger that. I will stay off your starboard wingtip and drop back when you reach Mach zero point nine. We can regroup after going through the transition."

"Thank you, Ridge. It is nice to not be alone up here."

"Hey," Dud said over the intercom. "What am I, chopped liver?"

"I was talking about aircraft. You are merely a lowly crew member. Get back to work, swabbie."

"British sailors were called limeys, not swabbies. Had to suck on the citrus fruit to avoid scurvy. Not that I was ever a tar in Her Majesty's Navy."

"Right, landlubber."

"Yes and flying supersonic aircraft off the decks of ships is just crazy. I can't imagine how any of you people do this for a living."

"The takeoff is the easy part," Nikki replied. "It's the landing that is hard to do without crashing."

"Now she tells me."

Dud checked the altimetry and azimuth data on the rising singularity. "Nikki, our instrumentation is showing the black hole approaching 35,000 feet already. We'd better get going."

Nikki stopped joshing. "Okay, Dudley, make sure all your straps are tight. We are about to break the sound barrier just like Chuck Yeager did right near here sixty years ago. Even though this is routine stuff nowadays, I still get a little tense when that Mach scale climbs up near one. So hang on."

With that, she dropped external tanks, lit the afterburners, and the F/A-18 took off after the singularity.

Dud was focused on keeping the instruments trained on it as the jet climbed and accelerated. He barely noticed when the aircraft passed through Mach One. There was a bit of shaking, followed by remarkably smooth flight afterwards.

Nikki kept the aircraft behind the singularity. They were chasing after a meteor at a thousand miles per hour. The black hole rocketed to the west as the Earth rotated beneath it, and climbed slowly through the atmosphere. It began dimming somewhat as it reached higher altitudes. Nikki expected this, because there was less air to fall into the accretion disk. It would brighten up again when it returned to the dense lower atmosphere and re-entered the surface of the Earth.

Dud watched the data pour in. They were collecting 360 position measurements per minute, which were being fed to the modeling team in real time to fine-tune a precise orbit. The radiation monitors were telling them the size of the accretion disk and the rate at which the black hole was gaining mass. The radiative energy output was being monitored in radio waves, microwaves, infrared, visible light, ultraviolet and x-rays. All of

165

these wavelengths were being emitted by atoms falling into the accretion disk and accelerating to the speed of light at the event horizon. The levels of ionizing radiation were a bit on the high side, and he asked Nikki to drop back a few hundred meters to increase their distance from the singularity.

They had reached 60,000 feet, which was the predicted apogee for this orbit. The singularity hung there for a few seconds, like a newly risen sun. Dud wondered what the show looked like from the ground, where millions of people were undoubtedly watching. He planned to view it on the newscasts when they got back. Except for contrails from the two aircraft, the sky was cloudless and the air clear, with hundreds of miles of visibility. The black hole was nearly as bright as the sun, and should have been easy to spot from the ground, even though it was broad daylight. In any case, the view was certainly spectacular from up here. Dud rechecked the cameras and instruments for the umpteenth time.

From the apogee point above the Colorado River, the singularity started dropping downward across the Mojave Desert toward the San Bernardino Mountains. Nikki continued in hot pursuit, staying above and behind as it fell to Earth. "Ridge" Runner was holding position off their right wingtip, a mile or so away. His more advanced Raptor didn't need afterburners to fly supersonic, and he was able to pace them easily.

They flew over Twentynine Palms and down the Lucerne Valley toward the mountains and Big Bear. The solar observatory at Big Bear Lake was going to attempt to get some spectroscopic and photographic data on the black hole. The red shift on the spectrograph would indicate how fast air molecules were moving in the accretion disk, which could in turn provide better estimates of the singularity's mass. Although the singularity itself was still far smaller than the diameter of an atom, the pinpoint-sized

166

accretion disk might be visible in a high power telescope. They had one on a special gimbal mount designed by a famous Hollywood action cinematographer, who claimed that it would be able to track the fast-moving black hole. This would be the only orbit passing close to any kind of an operational solar observatory, and they were going to try.

The singularity flashed over the south shore of Big Bear Lake at an altitude of less than 20,000 feet. Nikki pulled up and slowed to subsonic cruising speed, fearful of going too fast this close to the ground. Major Runner followed. Dud was able to track the singularity down to where it penetrated the Earth in the San Bernardino Mountains between Big Bear Lake and Lake Arrowhead. It disappeared into the ground without so much as a puff of dust.

All the crazies down below did their dances, prayers, sexual acts or whatever as the singularity passed overhead. The scene on the ground was more bizarre than anticipated, and they had been anticipating quite a bit. None of it had the slightest effect on the black hole. The idiot with the sniper rifle missed the tiny accretion disk with his shot, but did manage to accidentally take out a convenience store window downrange in Big Bear.

There was some concern that the passage of the singularity this close to the San Andreas Fault, which separates the San Bernardino Mountains from the San Gabriel Mountains, might cause an earthquake. Nikki and the scientists on her team thought it was still far too small to have any such effect. Citizens in Los Angeles were not so sure, and many people went outside during the singularity passage just in case it did trigger "the big one." There was a lot of hype and hysteria, and Nikki was relieved when the singularity passed close to the fault and nothing happened.

After checking that the F/A-18 had sufficient reserves of fuel to return to base, "Ridge" Runner peeled off and headed back to Nellis in his F-22. Nikki flew the short distance northward to Edwards and landed without incident. Her landing was smooth, gentle and far less dramatic than she had led Dud to believe. A terrestrial runway was one thing, but it was the landings on carriers that were much faster, more violent, and very abrupt. Coming onto a pitching deck at the steep angle of descent required the pilot to properly line up with the red approach beacon, universally called "the meatball," and then attempt to catch the second wire on the tailhook. This was no mean feat. The arrest wire stopped the plane almost instantly, pitching the pilot forward into the restraining straps. Nikki had received an embarrassing and rather painful bruise across a female body part during one of her early landings, because a buckle on the chest straps had not been aligned properly. Although she was now a veteran of dozens of carrier landings, including several at night, they still terrified her just as much as her first one. She had no intention of ever taking Dud through one of those controlled crashes.

Once on the ground, she and Dud labored to retrieve their instruments and download the massive files of data collected during their flight. They transferred everything into the Gulfstream jet still sitting where they left it on the tarmac. The crew from Nellis would soon return to claim the F/A-18. All in all, Nikki thought it had been a successful mission. The next one, over the South Pacific, would be the real deal; the real attempt to tame the singularity and save Earth. It would test the limits of the aircraft and pilot. Me, she reminded herself. It will be testing the limits of me.

Chapter Eight: The Second Singularity

Leon Hammermesh and Karl Barski were personally escorting Dr. Geoffrey Finch to Geneva. They were on their way to CERN, where the LHC would be used to create a second black hole to nudge Finch's original black hole into a safe orbit high above the Earth. Finch was cooperating, at least on paper. Barski had given him a little "come to Jesus" talk before they left Maryland, and clearly explained his situation and the cost of non-cooperation. Finch reluctantly agreed to play ball. Given the fact that his choice had been to either help or remain incommunicado in prison indefinitely, he was even behaving tolerably well.

Then Nikki sat him down for a chat. She explained bluntly that she had protective custody of him from the U.K. authorities as a special agent of the United Nations. She explained further that many members of the public had threatened him with fates worse than death, and he was not safe out of her custody. Finally, she told him that if he failed to cooperate, work hard and do his level best to help, she would simply turn him loose in a crowd and announce to everyone just exactly who he was. Nikki had become totally exasperated with Finch, who argued every point, debated every decision, and dripped arrogance covered in sarcasm. She had refused to accompany him and Barski to CERN, under the theory that being cooped up with Finch in an airplane for eight hours was a recipe for murder. His. She pressed Leon Hammermesh to go in her place.

They were using a C-17 military cargo jet to get there. This effort was too important for commercial jets and public airports. The new mini-black hole would be transported aboard this aircraft in a magnetic

169

containment vessel. They were to deliver it to New Zealand, where Nikki would take it out to the Roosevelt in a Hornet.

They stopped at Tenerife in the Azores to refuel. Although the big jet had more than enough range to "cross the pond," they couldn't get all the way to New Zealand without refueling. Barski thought it would be more discreet if they landed in the remote Azores and gassed up there before heading into Europe. They couldn't risk being noticed in a larger airport like London, Paris, Madrid, or even Geneva. The President had wanted this mission to be kept very, very quiet.

They landed in Geneva after dark. The plane taxied into a hangar, and the doors were slid shut as soon as the pilot killed the engines. They were met inside by a United Nations car and driver. Janos Tomczik, the director of CERN, was in the front seat. He had been called in by Dr. Nicole Shelton to help hold Finch's leash, and get him to produce a second black hole of the proper size and mass as quickly as possible.

The limousine took the four scientists out a back gate of the airfield, and through the small Geneva suburb of Meyrin. They passed the large sphere marking the entrance to the CERN visitor's center, and entered the scientific complex before reaching the Swiss-French border crossing on Route de Meyrin. The limo made its way down Route Arago past the labs, shops, dorms, cafeterias and other support buildings for the large particle physics facility. They turned off onto Route Enrico Fermi, and continued to Route Max Planck. The driver stopped the vehicle and deposited the four scientists at the entrance to the Super Proton Synchrotron. This device created the heavy particles that were then injected into the adjacent Large Hadron Collider (LHC) for super-high acceleration and collision.

170

"What is the meaning of this?" Finch asked indignantly. "You surely don't expect me to begin work immediately? Why, we haven't even had dinner and I'd like to spend a little while in my hotel room to freshen up. It was a rather long trip."

"Dr. Finch, you are not here on holiday," said Tomczik, irritably. "Time is of the essence. You had nine hours on the plane to relax, and they fed you twice. We need you to set up the synchrotron parameters for the LHC immediately so we can begin creating and coalescing the singularities. It is going to take us a minimum of eight days working around the clock to manufacture a black hole of the size requested by Dr. Shelton and her committee. In ten days she needs it to intercept the other singularity that you recklessly created and let loose. If she misses this opportunity, the orbits of your black hole will emerge from the Earth above populated areas for another two weeks. If we are forced to collide the two singularities over population centers, it could kill millions. Unless you want those deaths on your head, I suggest you get cracking and start to solve this problem that you created. We must have the second singularity in time for the New Zealand orbit."

Finch looked at Tomczik with smoldering anger in his eyes. "Well, at least get me some coffee and pastries or something. I probably should not be calibrating the LHC with low blood sugar."

****

They gave Finch everything he needed. Computers, equipment, tools, and personnel were at his disposal. The machine shop was busy turning out an electromagnetic cage to contain the new singularity once it was made. They assigned him a bunk in the CERN dormitory instead of a 5-star hotel room on the shores of Lake Geneva. They worked him 18 hours a

171

day, and he was never alone. Hammermesh, Tomczik, or Barski were at his side constantly, keeping an eye on him virtually every waking moment. Finch objected, complained, threatened to quit, threatened a work slowdown, and every time, Barski told him soberly that if he didn't want to face certain death with most of the rest of humanity in less than a year, he would cooperate. This cold dose of reality usually calmed him down, and the work resumed. Occasionally, Dr. Hammermesh assured Finch that if they didn't find a way to fix this, he would personally see to it that Finch made history by being the first human ever to cross the event horizon of a black hole. Although if it came down to it, he would not be the last.

They were using americium nuclei to create the mini black holes instead of the lead they had used the first time. Americium was denser and therefore more efficient. As a man-made element, it was also considerably more expensive, but at this point, cost was irrelevant. The atoms were stripped of their electron shells, and the heavy atomic nuclei were then injected into the Large Hadron Collider. A series of superconducting electromagnets pulled and pushed the nuclei around the large circular track, continuously accelerating them like a maglev train or a rail gun. Two beams of nuclei were run in opposite directions around the track. When the velocity of the atomic nuclei reached 99% of the speed of light, the beams were crossed and allowed to smash into each other. The nuclei collided at incredibly huge energies measured in billions of electron volts, overcoming repulsive electrical fields, the weak nuclear force, and the strong nuclear force to ram together and create tiny spheres of hyperdense neutronium. This was identical to the process that went on inside a supernova, except on a microscopically smaller scale. Some of the neutronium spheres were dense enough to form rotating singularities. These singularities were given an

172

electrical charge and steered into each other before they could evaporate from Hawking radiation. In this manner, the combined singularities created a mini black hole that was large enough to be stable. It steadily gained mass as more singularities and neutronium were added.

Finch tried adding more mass by creating more neutronium. The work was painstaking, tedious and slow to produce results. An incredibly small black hole, with the mass of a grain of rice, had taken nearly two days to create. They needed something with the mass of a car if they wanted to give the first singularity enough velocity to achieve high orbit.

Finch tried adding more mass by creating more neutronium. The size of the black hole grew slowly. One of the assistants suggested that they start feeding it normal matter, just because it was more available than neutronium. Finch spent a few hours away from the LHC to design a device that would deliver a fine wire made of copper into the event horizon of the tiny black hole, atom by atom. By running it full out, they got several kilograms of mass into the singularity within a day. It now weighed the equivalent of a bag of cat food.

The next day, Finch decided to continue adding normal matter along with neutronium to increase the mass. Some additional safety precautions were needed, however. Adding mass too fast would create dreadful amounts of radiation, poisoning nearby workers, including Finch, and could even destroy the facility. Feeding matter into the black hole required patience, extremely high-precision, and tight control of the magnetic fields if there was to be any hope of hitting the tiny event horizon. It was like trying to shove cotton candy into the opening of a hypodermic needle.

173

Finch had the machine shop draw out the remaining americium into a thin wire. With the singularity clamped into an electromagnetic cage in the deepest tunnel at CERN, a remotely controlled stepping motor fed the wire slowly into the event horizon. The singularity gained mass more quickly than when they were feeding it copper atoms. Radiation levels were high underground, but remained safe on the surface. Finch fed the wire into the singularity at the highest radiation level they could tolerate. They also gave it neutronium spheres and mini black holes as they were created in the LHC. By the end of day five, the singularity had the mass equivalent of a piece of heavy furniture. It wasn't a car yet, but they were getting there.

Nikki Shelton arrived via commercial flight on day six. She had been hoping the singularity would be nearly completed and ready to transport. Nikki didn't like tight deadlines, and the sooner she got this thing settled aboard the Teddy Roosevelt, the better. She was disappointed to learn from Tomczik that while Finch had been making progress, he wasn't exactly blowing the schedule out of the water. They needed to get some heavier mass into the new singularity, and quickly. The orbital mechanics of the first singularity gave her no leeway. It would be in the appointed place at the appointed time, and if she was not there because Finch was behind schedule, they wouldn't have another chance.

Nikki asked Barski and Hammermesh to meet her in a conference room, and got the other members of her team connected via phone and internet.

"We need some ideas, folks. Finch is behind schedule building up the mass of the second black hole. I need to know the minimum mass we can get away with, and how we can achieve that by the end of tomorrow."

"What size is it at the moment?" asked Dr. Maneesh Kelkar on the phone from Mumbai.

"A little more than forty kilograms," Hammermesh answered him. "Finch is adding mass as fast as he can, but the radiation levels are very high."

"We can trade mass for velocity," said Dr. Heidi Schwimmer via Internet from Berlin. "If we can increase the speed at which the two objects merge, mass is not as critical a factor."

"I agree," Dr. Boris Pavlov chimed in from the Russian Academy of Sciences in St. Petersburg. "Especially if the collision is timed to happen exactly at apogee when the object is at its slowest speed. Any increase in velocity there will be magnified greatly along the remainder of the orbit."

"Some U.S. antiaircraft missiles can move as fast as Mach 5," Barski offered. "If we can fit this singularity into one of those, it might work."

"That would be an improvement over just flying a drone aircraft into it with the new black hole strapped on," said Nikki. "I wasn't sure how we'd hit it with a drone, anyway. A missile can use infrared tracking and zero right in. What did you have in mind?"

"A Phoenix," Barski replied. "They have some onboard the Roosevelt, even though the model is officially retired. The standard missile is radar guided, but it can be modified for infrared targeting fairly easily. It is heavy and designed to launch off a Tomcat."

"What is the payload?" asked Pavlov in St. Petersburg. He was a weapons designer as well as a theoretical physicist.

"About 50 kilograms of high explosive," Barski replied.

175

"Well then, that is the target mass of your new singularity," said Pavlov. "Whatever the missile is designed to carry. It will have to be enough."

"Will it?" asked Nikki. "Let's walk through the calculations, people. I need to know if 135 pounds of super condensed matter moving at Mach 5 will be enough to kick that other singularity off the planet. If it's not enough, we need other options."

"The Russian Vympel R-37 air-to-air missile can carry the same mass at Mach 6, if you are interested," Pavlov offered. "One extra Mach number might make the difference."

"Can it be modified for infrared?" Barski asked quickly.

"Yes, probably with no more difficulty than modifying the Phoenix," Pavlov replied. "Also, the launch rails have been replaced with new ones that fit onto European Union standard ordinance racks. We had hoped to export this model."

"All United States Navy aircraft use NATO standard racks, which I believe are the same specs as the EU design," Nikki said. "We could mount one of these racks on the drone and attach the missile."

"Boris, how fast could we get a couple of these missiles?" asked Barski.

"For you, my good friend, we can deliver them immediately. The impending doom of the planet has nothing to do with it. You will, however, owe me a bottle of vodka."

"Of course. If this works, I'll buy you an entire case of Stoli. Thank you."

"Like every other military organization on the planet, the Russian Navy has been busy with the lifeboat project. However, I shall contact the right people, and see if we can arrange for you to pick up the missiles on your way to the Roosevelt. The logistics might be a bit difficult, but I will do my best. If your route will take you within flying range of the Black Sea, I may be able to arrange for an SU-33 to transport the missiles from the Russian Navy base at Sevastopol to a rendezvous."

"Tell me the range of an SU-33," Nikki said, "And I will make sure our route is close enough."

****

The new black hole reached a mass of 50 kilograms the next morning. Three days remained before Nikki would be making the interception. She told Finch they had reached the goal, and that his work was finished. She thanked him, but instead of being gracious about it, he went off on a rant about how poorly he had been treated, housed and fed. They had worked him like a field slave, with no compensation, and allowed him virtually no free time. It was completely unacceptable and he was going to lodge complaints with all of the appropriate authorities.

Nikki looked at him like he was a bug in a jar. What universe was this guy from, anyway? He had created and lost a singularity by performing irresponsible and illegal physics experiments. His careless mistake was about to destroy the entire planet and all life on it unless they found a way to fix it. By creating a second singularity that they could use to accelerate the first one off the planet, Finch had contributed significantly to saving the world. Instead of feeling redeemed, however, he whined and complained. She just didn't understand people like that.

Finch with his big mouth and thoughtless remarks needed to be protected from the public. As long as the singularity was loose inside the Earth, they needed to keep the arrogant bastard alive. His expertise in creating the second singularity was a case in point. Once they had extracted the damned thing out of the planet and put it in a safe, distant orbit, the world justice system could settle up accounts with Finch. As far as Nikki was concerned, a little frontier justice might be even more suitable.

Nikki turned him over to the care of Janos Tomczik, and asked Janos to keep him under wraps. After Finch complained again about being forced to sleep in the CERN dormitory, Tomczik told Nikki that he was unable to deal with him, and requested that the obnoxious British scientist be relocated to the Geneva city jail. For his own protection, of course. Nikki concurred with the request, and spoke to the city authorities. As Finch was led away by the Geneva police, who completely ignored his loud protests, Tomczik told him that he hoped the new accommodations were an improvement over the humble CERN dorms. The jail had plenty of empty cells, so at least he wouldn't have to share a room.

With Finch on ice, Nikki, Barski and Hammermesh got the new 50 kilogram black hole loaded aboard the C-17 cargo aircraft. Nikki would accompany it to the South Pacific, while Barski and Hammermesh planned to return to the U.S. on a commercial flight. They would monitor progress with Barney's team in College Park. The singularity transport container was a square aluminum equipment case the size of a small steamer trunk. The black hole was contained in a strong electromagnetic field shaped by a superconducting grid. The field generator and superconductor cryogenic temperature control were powered by a set of a dozen lithium batteries guaranteed to last 48 hours. Nikki figured it would take her 12 hours to fly

178

from Geneva to Christchurch in New Zealand, including a stop in Istanbul where she would meet up with the Russian aircraft bringing the two Vympel missiles across the Black Sea. At Christchurch, she would transfer the singularity case to the back seat of an F/A-18, attach the missiles to the ordinance racks, and spend two more hours flying out to the Roosevelt. There should be plenty of leeway on the battery life to sustain the singularity electromagnetic field, but she had two extra battery sets along just in case.

As soon as the C-17 took off, Nikki made contact with Ted Lewis on the Roosevelt. Boris Pavlov had been as good as his word, and two Russian long-range Vympel R-37 air-to-air missiles would be waiting for her in Istanbul. They were currently traversing 300 miles of Black Sea waters slung beneath the wings of a Sukhoi-33 advanced fighter jet. Lewis and the Roosevelt's ordinance technicians were poring over engineering drawings sent by Pavlov to figure out ways to modify the big Russian missiles to carry the second singularity as the payload. He told her they would have it solved by the time she arrived. Nikki was pleased by the news.

She was not so pleased by her attempts to contact Dud. She had not spoken to him since they parted ways after chasing the singularity in California. Once they had uploaded all the data to the team in College Park, she was ready to return to Washington, but he had other plans.

"I am going to Hawaii for awhile, Nikki. You will be extremely busy in the next few weeks, and I don't want to be a distraction. There isn't anything I can do to help at this point, and I'd just be underfoot. I have a friend at Hawaiian Volcanoes Observatory who promised to show me the active lava flows if I ever made it out there. Since we are in California, I decided to continue on to Hawaii."

179

"But Dudley, I was hoping you would be there when we finished this thing. I need your support," Nikki protested.

"No you don't," he replied. "Nicole Shelton, I've watched you develop over the past few months into a strong, assertive leader. You may want to have me around, but you don't 'need' me. Ever since the rig explosion and Barney's injuries, you have taken on huge responsibilities and done what needed to be done. I am incredibly proud of you. I am also absolutely confident that you can tame the singularity on your own, and save the world in the process.

"Everything from here on out has to do with high energy physics, military flying, and firing missiles. I don't know anything about any of that stuff, and I'd be a fish so far out of water that I would feel like smoked salmon. I really want to go to Hawaii, dear heart. It may be my last opportunity to see flowing lava, after a lifetime spent studying the solidified versions."

"Well, if you feel that strongly about it..." Nikki started to say.

"Nikki, love, I can't be there when you take this thing on," he said quietly. "I know you are a good pilot, and I know the United States Navy will give you the best equipment they have. I'm sure you've worked out all the details about how to approach the singularity, and slam a second one into it hard enough to knock both of them completely off the planet. I am confident in my heart of hearts that you will be successful and return safely. But I just can't watch." He looked at her pleadingly.

Nikki finally began to realize just how much of a toll this little adventure had been taking on Dud. He wasn't military, and some parts of her world must seem incredibly alien to him. He had helped out on the deep drilling in St. Croix under orders from the British government, and falling in love with Nikki hadn't been part of the plan. But it had happened, and Dud had been a great source of strength to Nikki in the dark days after the drill rig was destroyed. He had even gone to Washington with her and testified before Congress. As a citizen of the U.K., he could have ignored the U.S. Congress request to testify, but he went partly to support Nikki, and partly to make sure that she didn't get blamed for any of the mess that followed the terrorist attack. Now that so much of the singularity work was taking place at levels that were way beyond Dud's skill sets, he was feeling helpless and scared. He wanted to get out, and frankly, Nikki couldn't blame him.

"All right, Dud," she had told him. "Go to Hawaii and look at your volcanoes. I know this stuff with the black hole must be overwhelming. It is getting that way for me, and I can only imagine how difficult this must be for you. You'll be happier away from all this in Hawaii, and I'll be happier knowing that you are safe and out of the way. Once we take care of this, I will fly into Pearl and meet up with you on Oahu. Just keep your cell phone charged up and turned on."

He promised he would, but he hadn't. Nikki had tried calling him again and again, from Washington and from Geneva, but got only his voicemail. Now, as the C-17 sat on the ground being refueled on the island of Diego Garcia in the Indian Ocean, she tried once more, still getting connected straight to Dud's voicemail.

"Hello, this is Dudley Gardner. Sorry I missed your call–please leave a message," the recording said in Dud's mild British accent that she loved so much.

"Dud, it's Nikki. This is like the fifth message I've left on your phone. I don't know why you are not calling back, but we have Finch's new

181

singularity in a cage and I'm on my way to New Zealand. I'll be out of touch from now until I get to Hawaii. We are going to be in a remote part of the South Pacific, and I won't have any cell phone access out there. I love you and miss you, and I hope everything is okay. I am looking forward to seeing you in Hawaii at the end of next week. However this works out, positive or negative, I will do my damnedest to be in Hawaii afterward. See you then, sweetheart."

She wanted to say more, but the annoying female computer voice came on and told her the voicemail only have 5 seconds left. Quickly, she finished up.

"I love you, Dudley. No matter what else happens, please remember that."

****

Sir Geoffrey Holmes Finch, dipl. H. Sci. (cum laude), M.Sc. (honours), Ph.D., languished in a Geneva jail cell like a common criminal. Well, maybe not quite so common, he thought. After all, he did have the cell to himself, and wasn't forced to share the facilities with some barbarian off the street. His iron-barred window showed a pleasant if narrow view of the town below, including a piece of lakeshore, and a few peaks of the Jura Mountains in the distance. The food was palatable, if not exactly five star cuisine, and they even brought him a decent cigar and some wine every once in awhile. He had a laptop computer, but no Internet access. He had started writing his memoirs.

Finch still couldn't understand why that horrible Shelton woman had put him in jail. He hadn't actually done anything criminal. She had claimed that it was merely protective custody to save him from an enraged populace, who were ready to blame him for the potential destruction of the

182

world. Finch sniffed. If they were going to blame anyone, they should blame the unreliable French power grid, he thought. If it had not hiccupped when it did, they could have held on to the singularity in the first place, and none of this would have happened. In that case, Finch would have been able to gift the world with a nearly endless supply of electrical power derived from a large, stable black hole, and been treated as a hero. They would have put him in a gold palace, he thought glumly, not an iron jail cell.

Nikki Shelton. What a piece of work! She was definitely a looker, but didn't seem to know it. Her brunette hair was cropped short in a military cut, and her only wardrobe seemed to consist of a formal Navy uniform, camouflage fatigues or a flight suit. She never wore makeup, and none of this military crap did anything to flatter her as a woman. Finch had initially pegged her as a lesbian, until he found out that she did indeed have a boyfriend. That geezer from the British Geological Survey, who was at least twice her age! Well, at least she had the good taste to take up with a Brit.

Finch sensed strength in Nikki, but there was an underlying weakness, too. Almost as if the strength had been a recent development, and was little more than a veneer. He could feel the presence of a timid, frightened mouse underneath the bravado. He wondered if he could find a way to exploit that against her. If this whole ridiculous farce ever came to a trial, he might be able to call Nikki as a witness. He suspected that with the right approach, he could intimidate her and make her look weak and indecisive. It might give his plea for innocence a slight edge. But how could he turn that to his favor?

With little else to do as the days slowly dragged by in Geneva, Dr. Geoffrey Finch sat in his jail cell and schemed.

****

"Mr. President, we need to make some plans." Charles Godell, the U.S. Secretary of Commerce, was clearly concerned. "Our government and many others have been building spacecraft like crazy to serve as escape lifeboats. Our economy is in a shambles because of this effort, our military has been gutted, and our industry is strained to the breaking point. Nobody has been complaining because the end of the world as we know it is imminent. But what if it is not?"

"What on Earth are you talking about, Charlie?" President Jackson was physically tired, and mentally exhausted. He had a throbbing headache that never seemed to clear up, although the Army physicians at Walter Reed could find nothing wrong with him. The painkillers held it at bay for awhile, but it always returned. It was just one more piece of the nightmare that had been steadily unfolding since he first heard mention of Doctor Geoffrey-be-damned-Finch and his missing black hole.

After the destruction of the drill rig in the Virgin Islands, Jackson had taken a personal role in the evacuation of Earth. He was putting in 20 hour days, working on logistics that were frightfully complex, and making decision after decision where the need was constant. He had already decided that he would remain behind on Earth. It was important to set an example, and it would be better for humanity if his spacecraft seat was occupied by someone who was more useful to the survival of the species than a middle-aged attorney turned politician. Even if his JD was from Harvard. His only legacy to his family would be to make sure that his daughters were onboard one of the ships. Amid all this distraction, he now had to figure out what was bugging Charles Godell. He tried to clear the cobwebs from his head.

184

"All right, Charlie," said the President, looking up at the Commerce Secretary. "Start over and take it slowly. I've got a brain overloaded with information right now, so you will have to spoon feed it to me."

"Yes, Mister President." Privately, Charlie Godell was appalled at the toll the singularity incident was taking on his friend Barry Jackson. The Chief Executive was gaunt, his dark hair had turned iron grey, his left hand shook constantly, and he was chain-smoking cigarettes, which he had started again after famously quitting in his first term. He didn't work out anymore, jog, play basketball, or even go for walks. About the only thing he consumed for sustenance these days was coffee. Godell vowed at the end of this to personally shoot Finch for the destruction heaped upon such a great man as Jackson, but he figured he might have to wait in a long line.

"Sir, all of our thinking and planning for the past year has been based on the premise that Barney Freeman's team would fail at taming the singularity. But what if they succeed? I know it's a long shot, but if the threat goes away, Mr. President, what do we do next? Our world is going to be stuck with a huge number of brand new, fully operational spacecraft. The construction of these craft has strained the resources and ruined the economy of every industrialized nation on the planet, along with most of the non-industrialized ones. How can we end this massive construction program without crashing the entire financial system? In our country alone, there are 300,000 nearly complete spacecraft at the Nevada Test Site, with another 50,000 at Dugway Proving Ground in Utah. What are we going to do with them?"

Jackson chose his words carefully before speaking.

"Charlie, your questions answer themselves. It would be economic suicide to halt the construction of the remaining spacecraft, tear them all

185

apart and return things to the way they were before the accursed Dr. Finch and his escaped singularity caused all this ruckus. I don't believe we ought to go back to that anyway. The singularity itself is a wakeup call, and a warning. Even if Lieutenant Shelton somehow manages to save the day, any number of things, both natural and man-made, could destroy this fragile planet in the future. If we survive this current disaster, then for the sake of the safety of the human race, we must not be confined to one world.

"Since we now have a massively overbuilt capacity to go into space in a big way, we should go there, whether or not the singularity consumes the Earth. Humanity needs viable settlements on the moon, people on Mars, and O'Neill colonies at the Lagrange points of the Earth's orbit. Developing a new space economy will open up supplies of raw materials, energy and labor. It is the future, Charlie, and we need it. I want you to pull together a blue ribbon panel to look into this, and be ready to give us some directions on how to proceed if and when Nikki Shelton does indeed tame the singularity. Make the group international and center it at the United Nations, but keep it small and discreet. I don't want the media to get wind of it, because it will distract attention away from the lifeboat effort. That is still our number one, top priority, and we have to keep it moving forward under full steam. The odds are still high that we are going to need those vessels very soon for the survival of humanity. We're not out of this yet."

Chapter Nine: The Taming

They were planning to get the second black hole into the proximity of the first one aboard a modified MQ-9 Reaper drone. The Reaper was an upgraded and much faster version of the older MQ-1 unmanned aerial vehicle or UAV known as the Predator. The Navy flew a turboprop version of the MQ-9 UAV called the Mariner, but the U.S. Air Force Reaper was powered by a high compression turbofan jet engine, which allowed the craft to fly at speeds of up to Mach 0.8. They needed something at least this fast to catch Finch's singularity, even at apogee.

Nikki delivered the newly manufactured singularity from CERN, along with the heavy, Russian-made Vympel R-37 air-to-air missiles onto the hangar deck of the USS Theodore Roosevelt. Doc-Doc Ted Lewis and a small army of technicians got busy with one of the missiles mounting an electrostatic cage into the nose cone. The missile with the cage inside would then be mounted onto the drone by attaching to the NATO-standard launch rails on the unmanned vehicle. The plan was to vector the Reaper to within a dozen kilometers of the orbiting singularity, and fire the missile when the black hole reached the slowest part of its orbit. This required careful planning and perfect timing, because the Reaper was not capable of supersonic speeds. If the singularity got too far ahead, the drone would never catch it.

Once launched, the high speed missile would intercept the singularity from behind at more than 4,200 miles per hour. Hitting the target shouldn't be a problem; because the two black holes had opposite electrical charges, as long as the missile was reasonably close, they would mutually attract and collide. In the process, the smaller but faster moving singularity on the missile would fuse into its cousin, transferring a huge amount of momentum to the pair, and boosting the now combined black hole into high orbit. It was going to be like hitting an eight ball with a precisely aimed cue ball, and transferring momentum with nearly 100% efficiency.

The catch was that transfer was "nearly" 100% efficient. Remnant energy left over from the collision of the two singularities would release a large amount of heat, light and radiation from the accretion disk. It was expected to be equivalent to a 20 megaton hydrogen bomb. That was why they were launching the Vympel from a drone, and not a manned fighter jet. Any fighters in the vicinity needed to be hundreds of miles away and moving ever farther on full afterburners.

Lewis had brought a group of NASA orbital engineers aboard the Roosevelt to track the singularity on radar and calculate orbital elements in near real-time. The intent was to get the information about any orbital changes out to the authorities as quickly as possible. The team was prepared to report on one of four possible outcomes: 1) they'd fixed it, 2) they had almost fixed it and doomsday would arrive later, but still arrive, 3) they did not fix it and doomsday would arrive as previously scheduled, or 4) they had somehow made everything worse and now the end was very near. Ted Lewis wasn't normally a pessimist, but he wanted to be prepared.

Nikki would be up in a chase plane, with an Air Force sergeant from Indian Springs in the back seat guiding the drone. Even at apogee, the orbital speed of the black hole would still be quite fast. They ran the risk of having the UAV fly out of range of the radio controls if they tried flying it from the deck of the Roosevelt. They could have used a satellite relay, but

188

everyone was nervous about this mission, and felt that having direct control of the drone from a nearby chase plane was a better option.

So when the singularity was tamed, Nikki would have a front row seat. The plan was for her to hit the launch button for the missile and light the afterburners on the F/A-18 simultaneously, turn hard to starboard and boogie on out of there while the missile flew downrange to the target. At the calculated closing speed and from an optimal launch distance, the flight time for the Vympel to reach the target would be about five minutes. In five minutes under full afterburners, the F/A-18 carrying Nikki and the Air Force sergeant would be approximately 120 miles away. It was still a little close for comfort, but it should be survivable. She was both excited and scared, and her stomach was twisted in knots. It was like the first day of flight school. Nikki had never flown in actual combat, only on training missions, but she thought that this is what it must be like. She wished she could have spoken live with Dudley before all this. It would have calmed her immensely to hear his voice. The only way to reach him now was by satellite phone, but the use of such communications gear for personal reasons was frowned upon unless it was a genuine family emergency. A case of the butterflies probably did not qualify as such.

She hadn't been on the carrier for an hour when she was paged over the ship's public address system and ordered to report to the bridge. The captain and first officer were waiting for her in the wardroom.

"Lieutenant Shelton, please allow me to welcome you aboard," Captain Goodfriend said warmly. "I trust your trip halfway around the world was not too unpleasant?"

Nikki saluted them both smartly. "Thank you, sir. The trip was not bad, considering the circumstances. The detour into Turkey to pick up the Russian missiles took a bit longer than I wished for, but it was important to acquire them, and we still made it here on time." Commander Helen Marino, the first officer, smiled at her.

"Excellent," said Goodfriend. "Well, we don't want to keep you too long, Lieutenant. We know how much you have to do, but there are a couple of articles of business we need to handle." He nodded at Marino, who dialed a satellite phone and placed it into a cradle that connected it to a speaker.

A familiar voice came out of the speaker. "Jackson here. I trust you have Lieutenant Shelton with you, Captain Goodfriend?"

"Yes, Mr. President," Goodfriend replied. "She is here."

"Hello, Mr. President," Nikki piped up. "Nice to hear from you again."

"Indeed, Lieutenant," Jackson replied. "I wanted to touch base with you before you go chasing off after that infernal singularity thing in a few hours. First of all, I am going to remove you from under my direct command, and attach you to the Roosevelt. You will report to Captain Goodfriend for the duration of this mission. I want him to have on-the-spot command authority from here on out, because there is not much I can do from back here in Washington. Please know, however, that we will all be watching you, and my prayers go with you for success. Secondly, you are promoted as of now to lieutenant commander."

Nikki's eyes grew wide. She hadn't expected that, and was surprised and stunned. "Why, thank you, Mr. President!" she finally managed to stammer.

"Congratulations, Nikki, you have definitely earned it. This would have happened sooner, but we needed to wait for your service anniversary to ensure that you would have enough time-in-grade. Even a president can't overrule that requirement.

"So, Lieutenant Commander Shelton, I want to know if you need any additional assets to carry out this mission. Even though most of the military is tied up with the lifeboat project, we will break free whatever personnel and equipment might be needed to assist you. Anything at all...just name it."

"Uh, Mr. President, I was thinking that we should try to keep this mission as small as possible. I think one aircraft, piloted by me, with a backseat drone operator to guide the Reaper should be the only personnel we risk sending in so close to the singularity."

"Why is that, Nikki? Surely you could use a wingman or some other help up there."

"Negative, sir. The problem is that we don't really know how much energy will be released when the two black holes collide. The models suggest the equivalent of a 20 megaton blast as a lower limit, but it could go much higher. Possibly 100 or maybe even 200 megatons. In any case, the radiation will be severe. One of the main reasons for selecting this particular orbit for taming the singularity was because we will be over an unpopulated ocean area, far from land. I intend to stand off a good distance from the drone, have it fire the missile, and then get the hell out of there on full afterburners. I plan to be several hundred miles away before the two event horizons collide and merge. There is no reason to endanger additional personnel."

191

"I see your point. Okay, Lieutenant Commander Shelton. It will just be you and an unlucky Air Force technical sergeant from Nevada who's only offense was to be the best drone operator in the world."

"Thank you, Mister President."

"Godspeed, Nikki."

Within 24 hours of Nikki's arrival onboard the USS Theodore Roosevelt, all preparations for the mission had been made. The Air Force drone operator was onboard the carrier, looking a little befuddled at the vast expanse of ocean that had replaced his previous view of a vast expanse of desert. The new singularity had been loaded into the Vympel, the missile had been attached to the ordinance rail on the Reaper drone, and both the drone and the F/A-18 Super Hornet were fully fueled, checked out and cleared for launch. All they could do now was wait on edge for the black hole to show up.

****

Hermann Gantz was a survivor, and he was used to getting his own way. He had made his fortune running drugs into East Germany under the old Communist regime. Despite the miserable working conditions and low wages in the socialist worker's paradise, or perhaps because of them, Gantz couldn't even begin to meet demand for drugs in the east. He was caught a few times by East German border guards, but a hefty payoff in high street value cocaine was enough to get him released. The reunification of Germany caught him flat-footed, but he soon recovered, discovering that a lot of high ranking members of the former regime wished to be quickly and quietly relocated with their private fortunes to obscure countries in South America. So he added human smuggling to his resume, along with prostitution rings, arms trafficking, and many other criminal diversions.

Profits from these enterprises were an added bonus on top of the nice, steady income from the high demand for drugs. By the time he was 40, Hermann Gantz was worth two billion Euros, and wanted by police in dozens of countries. Every time they picked him up, however, evidence disappeared, witnesses refused to testify, and key informants vanished. All the cops had on Gantz was a big fat zero, and he remained a free man.

Gantz was living the high life, with top shelf liquor, premium Cuban and Dominican cigars, several Italian sports cars, a beach house on the Riviera, another in Tahiti, and a mansion in Berlin. He had a yacht docked down in Monaco. His women friends were so hot that any one of them could easily grace the centerfold of a men's magazine. He often had marathon bouts of sex with two or three at a time. Life was just grand, until this.. this THING had happened. The end of the world as we know it, like that stupid popular song. No one ever suspected that it might be real. The first thing he thought of was to set up a contract killing of that *Gott verdammt* Dr. Geoffrey Finch, but Finch might still have uses and the personal survival of Hermann Gantz took precedence. Once that was assured, he would take care of Finch.

Like everyone else on Earth, Gantz hoped that Nikki Shelton would succeed in taming the singularity. But if she failed, he wanted a way off the planet. Several of his wealthy associates were scheming for ways to build their own spacecraft, but the necessary materials were extremely difficult to obtain. Nearly everything of use to a spacecraft had already been committed to the lifeboat program, under force of arms if necessary. Large sums of money could buy many things, but not something that simply wasn't there. Even worse, the skilled labor force needed to construct an escape vessel was impossible to get at any price. Governments around the world had recruited these people into the lifeboat construction brigades by promising them better odds for family members, and they could not be bought at any price.

A group of drug lords in Columbia had brazenly kidnapped a dozen NASA engineers and their families in Houston, and spirited them away to a remote jungle location. The plan was to hold the families hostage while the engineers were forced to construct an escape spacecraft for the drug cartel using aircraft parts that had been procured from all over the world. It might have actually worked if the entire U.S. Army 101st Airborne Division hadn't dropped in on them unexpectedly, rescued the hostages, and freed the engineers. Notably lacking any sense of fair play, the soldiers killed every last member of the drug cartel, while suffering only three casualties of their own.

A British airline magnate, who was much more of a businessman than an engineer, had begun development of a commercial space plane years before the singularity got loose. His employees had all been recruited to work on the lifeboat project, so he spent long hours alone in his hangar, trying to teach himself enough engineering to complete the assembly of the prototype space plane so it might fly. He was simultaneously learning to become a pilot.

Hermann Gantz could not hold a group of engineers hostage, and it would take him a thousand years to learn enough engineering to construct his own escape spacecraft. No, the only way for Gantz to survive was by guaranteeing himself a place one of those escape lifeboats. He would spend his entire fortune to that end if necessary, holding back only enough money to make sure that Finch was one of the first to get sucked down the rabbit hole.

They were assigning berths on the lifeboats by a lottery. There were to be two drawings; the first would fill the billion berths available on the lifeboat fleet. The second would fill available berths on lifeboats that were making second or third trips. First of all, Hermann Gantz was too old to qualify. He was 53, a full 180 degrees from the lottery cutoff age of 35. Secondly, even if he could get in the lottery somehow, there were four billion qualified people for the guaranteed one billion berths. So the chances were only one in four that he would get selected anyway. There were billions more qualified for the second drawing, but with no guarantee of a ride. Gantz didn't like the odds of either drawing. So he set about changing them.

Identities could be bought, created or stolen with enough money. Everyone eligible for the lottery had been assigned a number from 1 to 12. Three of those numbers would be selected to fill the lifeboats. In order to guarantee success, Gantz needed to cover them all.

It cost him a huge amount of money to bribe lottery officials for the names of twelve men with blond hair and blue eyes, age 35 at the time of the lottery, and assigned to each of the groups. He could have offered each individual a small fortune to buy their identities, but since the lottery was a life or death situation, he figured they weren't for sale. So the men had to be killed, but in a manner that couldn't be connected or traced to Gantz. For that, he needed very good, highly trained, professional hit men, which cost him even more money. Finally, Gantz spent an enormous amount of money on an extremely talented computer hacker to substitute his biometrics for each of the twelve dead men in the lottery database.

In the end, he was down to his last few million, but he had a guaranteed spot on the lifeboats. Three of those twelve identities would win

195

the lottery, and as soon the winning numbers were announced, Gantz would become one of those men, and board a ship. His biometrics would match the data in the ship's computer and no one would suspect. The other two winners would of course not show up, but who was going to miss two people out of a billion? The scheme was virtually foolproof.

Amid the general preparations of an evacuation from Earth, hardly anyone noticed the unexplained disappearance of a dozen men with nothing in common except a similar age, hair color and body shape. Except for those whose job it is to notice. In Leipzig, Germany, a Special Forces detective attached to Interpol by way of the United Nations Security Directorate began to take an interest. He was a Sikh from the Indian federal police, known only as Mohan.

****

Nikki could tell from her instruments that something was wrong. The drone was moving too slowly and its course was erratic. The U.S. Air Force sergeant in the back seat was having a difficult time controlling it.

"Sergeant MacDonald, what the hell is going on?"

"I don't know, lieutenant commander, ma'am. The drone is having communication errors. Most of my commands seem to be getting through, but some are not. It is causing control problems. The last time I saw something like this, the radio transmissions had been hacked."

"Hacked? By whom? And why?"

"Back then, it was jihadists in Afghanistan. This time, I don't know, ma'am."

"All right. Keep working on it. I'll try to get us in closer." She slid the F/A-18 alongside the Reaper, hoping the proximity would aid

MacDonald's communications. He might even be able to over-ride the hackers and regain control of the craft.

Seconds later, the UAV banked steeply toward them and Nikki instantly dodged. She did not want a midair collision with any aircraft, and most especially not with one carrying a missile containing a mini black hole. If the electrical fields were cut off by a crash, they could lose the second singularity and have it fall into the Earth, creating another problem as bad as or even worse than the first. Fortunately, the big Vympel missile mounted on top of the Reaper made it somewhat sluggish to maneuver, and Nikki was able to nimbly move her much larger aircraft out of the way.

"Okay, Sarge. We now know something."

"What's that, lieutenant commander?"

"They are watching us very closely."

"Yes, ma'am. I assume you mean whoever is controlling that drone."

"They reacted too quickly to our presence for any other explanation."

"I agree, ma'am. If they have access to the controls, then they would have access to the cameras as well. The two systems are linked."

Nikki called Ted Lewis on board the Roosevelt and informed him of their plight. If they didn't regain control of the Reaper very soon, she was going to miss the optimal orbital insertion window, and there would be no second chance. The models showed that the singularity was getting very near to the inflection point where it would begin to gain mass rapidly. As the singularity collided with more matter, it would lose momentum, and the apogee of each successive orbit would be significantly lower than the

197

previous one, until it stopped emerging from the Earth altogether. The remaining two dozen above-ground orbit tracks were unfortunately going to be located over densely populated areas of South America and Asia, where they didn't dare stage a collision, except perhaps as a last resort. Nikki sincerely hoped it wouldn't come to that. While it might make sense from a planetary survival perspective to kill a hundred million people in order to save billions, Nikki wasn't sure she could do it. This collision just HAD to work, and on this orbit.

Lewis and the Navy technicians aboard the Roosevelt were working on the drone control problem. Using the ship's powerful communication gear, they had determined that the hackers were transmitting through a commercial satellite over Samoa. They were trying to get it shut down, but it would take time.

Time was something Nikki did not have. Even though it was slowing down as it approached apogee, the drone control problems were causing the bright star of the singularity to pull away in front of them. The infrared sensors on the modified missile had a range of only about 25 kilometers. If they didn't get close enough to hit the black hole just right at the slowest point in its orbit, it wouldn't have enough speed to get into a higher, safer orbit. The UAV was moving too slowly and in an erratic pattern. Nikki needed to act within seconds.

"Sergeant MacDonald, can you swim?" she asked abruptly.

"Why, yes lieutenant commander. I'm actually a fairly good swimmer, ma'am."

"Good. I'm going to eject you, and you will float down into the ocean on a parachute. It's all automatic – you don't have to do a thing. Your emergency locator beacon will come on as soon as your chute opens, and a helicopter from the Roosevelt will pick you up in ten minutes. The water will protect you from neutron radiation. Keep your eyes averted from the sky, because when these two black holes collide, it is going to be the world's biggest flash. All right, now pull down your helmet visor unless you want a shot of 500 mile per hour air in the face. You are out of here in four seconds. Thank you, MacDonald, and good luck."

"But..." Before he could say anything else, there was a blast as the rear canopy section came off. MacDonald yanked down his visor as the seat accelerated upward and left the aircraft on rocket engines. He found himself transcribing a lazy parabolic arc above and behind the F/A-18 until the chute opened seconds later, the seat dropped away, and he began his long descent to the ocean below.

Inside the Combat Air Command situation room on the USS Theodore Roosevelt, Commander Helen Marino saw the locator beacon light up on Nikki's mission profile screen when MacDonald ejected. She grabbed a mike.

"Athena, this is Roosevelt, over. Lieutenant Commander Shelton, what the hell do you think you are doing?"

"Carrying out my mission, ma'am," Nikki answered back. "I am here to ensure that the black hole on the Reaper collides with Finch's singularity at the proper speed and at the proper instant. Don't see any way to do that now except manually, and the good sergeant didn't need to be a part of it."

"Nikki, don't do this. Back off and we'll find another way."

"No, Commander. With all due respect, there is no other way. If we don't get it on this orbit, the singularity goes over populated areas and we kill millions or lose the planet. Someone who knows this is hacking the drone's electronic commands to try and stop us. I intend to snag the UAV and make sure it gets to where it needs to be." She maneuvered the Hornet behind the unmanned aircraft so the nose spike was lined up on the Reaper's jet exhaust port.

Commander Marino called Captain Goodfriend on the bridge. "Captain, this is Marino in the CAC. You'd better get down here, sir." She re-keyed the mike to talk to Nikki.

"Athena, this is Roosevelt. I am giving you a direct order to break off and land. We will recover the UAV and try again. You are not, repeat, not to take action up there on your own."

"I am sorry to disobey, Commander," Nikki replied. "But I know the physics far better than you, and I know the orbit. It has to be done on this orbit, and it has to be done now." Captain Goodfriend entered the CAC during this exchange.

"Nikki, please..." Marino pleaded.

"Commander, I am sorry, but I'm going to be very busy up here for the next few minutes. I don't really have time for this argument."

Goodfriend took the mike from Marino's hand. "Stand down, Helen," he said.

"Lieutenant Commander Shelton, this is Captain Goodfriend. I cannot authorize you to proceed, but I can't stop you, either. We all know what is at stake, and I admire your heroic actions. If you perish, I will make sure that the world knows what happened. Do you have any messages?"

"Messages?" Nikki was taken aback. Yes, messages. She was almost certain to die up here. She felt her insides go watery. They had originally planned to be 120 miles away from the blast moving at top supersonic speed on full burners when the two objects collided. Now she would have to be up close and personal. And likely vaporized.

"Just one message, Captain. Please tell Dudley Gardner that I love him and I will miss him. He once told me that nothing in nature is ever destroyed, just transformed. Remind him of that. Thank you, sir. And now I have work to do. Athena over and out." She turned off the cockpit radio so there would be no more interruptions from the Roosevelt.

Commander Marino called Nikki a few more times from the CAC before realizing that the radio in the F/A-18 was turned off. Dammit! Well, if the lieutenant commander did somehow make it back, she would be brought up on charges and dragged into a full court martial to be busted back to ensign. Right after they pinned a slew of medals on her. In the meantime, Marino called the Roosevelt sea rescue detail and told them to get a chopper out to retrieve that poor Air Force sergeant from the drink.

Nikki increased the thrust from her engines to move the nose of her aircraft into the jet exhaust port of the Reaper. This was certainly not going to be pretty. When she was a few feet back, the front of the Hornet began glowing a dull red from the engine heat of the drone. It was moving on a steady course now that the comsat had been shut down. The hackers had succeeded in getting it to fall far enough behind the singularity that it couldn't catch up with its small jet engine. Additional thrust was going to be needed. Nikki hit the emergency kill switch for the drone's engine on the auxiliary control panel, and activated the F/A-18 afterburners at the same time. The engine on the Reaper abruptly cut off, and the tapered nose of the Hornet rammed into the jet exhaust port, effectively spearing the drone. It sat on the front of her aircraft like a bizarre hood ornament.

Nikki adjusted her angle of attack and increased thrust to make up for the extra weight. She aimed the impaled UAV on the front of the F/A-18 at the small, brilliant star of the singularity, which was just reaching apogee. At full burner, the Hornet and drone rapidly closed the distance.

Nikki hoped all the other systems in the UAV and missile were operational, and that the black hole aboard the missile was securely pinned in an electromagnetic field. She did not want to lose it under the wild acceleration. Her indicators told her the electric fields were holding and the black hole was still inside the Russian missile.

She cut off the afterburners and slowed back down to cruising speed. The joined aircraft were about 10 kilometers behind the singularity now. Nikki wanted to make sure the Vympel missile was tracking the singularity in front of her with infrared sensors. Her display showed that it had detected a source of infrared ahead of them.

The original plan had been to fly the second black hole into the first one from a safe distance at high speed using the Vympel missile. Because the hackers had caused them to lose control of the Reaper, Nikki had to bring the missile within range using her fighter. Now she would have to launch the missile from here, and there would be no getting away from the radiation. The dose would likely be fatal. She decided philosophically that it didn't really matter – she would die a hero if this worked, and if it didn't, well they were all doomed in a few months anyway.

She armed the Vympel and got the booster rocket "hot" for launch. The missile was actively tracking the glowing accretion disk now. Her headset changed from beeping to a steady tone as the missile found the target and held it. They were locked and loaded, and this was it.

Nikki took a deep breath, and cleared her mind. She was going to just do this, and not think about the consequences. There wasn't a whole lot of time for philosophy. She briefly wondered about Dud's concept of free will. As she saw it, there was no choice except to save the world, and no one could save it but her. Nothing very free about that. She felt a brief pang of regret for the loss of what could have been a bright future with Dud, but if she didn't do this, there would be no future for anyone. The old timid Nikki was gone. She set her jaw in determination and hit the firing button. The big Russian missile shot off the rail and accelerated toward the orbiting singularity. The F/A-18, with the UAV still impaled on its nose, angled up and twisted to port as the heavy missile shot away. Part of Nikki's forward canopy was blackened by the missile exhaust.

Nikki brought the aircraft under control, and followed the contrail of the missile as it streaked upward toward the singularity. She could have peeled off and dove away, but with the heavy drone on the nose and possible damage to the airframe of her Hornet, a steep dive would probably end in a crash. It was better to stay up here and make damn sure this worked.

From 20 kilometers away, Nikki watched as the missile arched up into the singularity. The negatively charged electrical field surrounding Finch's orbiting singularity latched onto the positively charged black hole in the missile like a tractor beam. It drew the other singularity toward it as the missile approached at six times the speed of sound.

A huge amount of kinetic energy was transferred from the second singularity as it collided with the accretion disk of the first. There was a brilliant flash of light, and the thrust from the missile rocket motor continued for a few additional precious seconds to accelerate both objects forward. Nikki had tilted her head down below the cockpit control panel to shield her eyes from the intense flash of light as the two event horizons collided. Although protected from the light, the titanium airframe could not protect her from the radiation. Nikki's body was sleeted with an intense dose of gamma rays, x-rays, and neutrons, but she felt nothing except for a faint tingling on her skin.

The blast wave hit seconds later, causing Nikki's airplane to shudder violently, and knocking the drone off of the nose. The Reaper spiraled downward as it fell into the sea. Nikki checked immediately to see if her aircraft had sustained damage from the impaled drone. The front part of the Hornet's fuselage was dented and scraped, but apparently intact. Tough old bird.

A lot tougher than the pilot, apparently. The data on the radiation monitor in the cockpit showed that Nikki had received a massive dose of more than 20,000 rem. The chart on the front of the meter indicated that such an exposure would certainly kill her from acute radiation poisoning within 24 hours. There was no way to stop it. Nikki realized that she was already dead, but just hadn't quite died yet.

She thought about her options for a few moments, before turning the radio back on to call the Roosevelt.

"USS Roosevelt, this is Athena, over."

"Athena, this is Marino on the Roosevelt, over. Please state your status."

"I am fine at the moment, Commander. Missile launch was successful. Target was acquired and struck. Cockpit meter says I caught a lethal radiation dose, but I am okay for now."

"Affirmative, lieutenant commander. Return to the ship and we will get you into sick bay."

"Negative, Roosevelt. I need to stay up here until we are sure the orbital correction has been sufficient. Please let me talk to Ted Lewis so I can get the orbital elements."

"Lieutenant Commander..."

"Please, Commander Marino. I need to know if this worked."

Captain Goodfriend was watching a radar screen on the other side of the CAC. He looked up at Marino and nodded.

"All right, Athena. Stand by. We will fetch Dr. Lewis."

A few minutes later, Ted Lewis called her on the radio. He and his team were updating the orbital models from the Roosevelt's radar position data.

"Nikki, this is Ted, do you read?"

"Roger, Ted. What is happening to the orbit?"

"I'm sending the latest data and model projections up to you now," he replied. "You moved it enough to keep it out of the crust of the Earth, but the orbit is still very low. It is going to re-enter the atmosphere on every perigee. The stronger gravitational gradient of the larger black hole will draw in more air, which will eventually slow it down enough to crash back into the planet. You don't happen to have another missile up there you can shoot at it, do you?"

"Sorry, Ted. We only brought the one. It was all the drone could carry." Dammit, she thought. Even hitting it at Mach 6 with a second 50 kilogram singularity wasn't enough to knock it into high orbit. Their calculations assumed that the impact would take place at the optimum

205

timing for momentum transfer, which they must have missed by a few minutes due to the hacker's interference with the drone. Somebody ought to pay for that. In the meantime, they would have to think of something else, and fast.

She looked at the new orbit on her cockpit computer screen. Apogee was now a third of the way to the moon, deep in cis-lunar space. It was high and out of reach, unless one of the new spacecraft could get to it. Even then, it would be damned hard to find the thing in the vacuum of space, where there was almost nothing to pull into the accretion disk for illumination. Perigee would skim through the Earth's atmosphere as low as 20,000 feet above sea level. The black hole wouldn't be immediately dangerous to anyone on the ground, but because it would be colliding with air along this part of the orbit, it would drop lower with each successive pass. Eventually it would make contact with the surface of the Earth, slow down considerably and drop underground again. Because of the increased mass of the singularity, the problem would be worse than ever. Orbiting objects moved fastest at perigee, so they would have a hard time catching it in the atmosphere with anything slower than an intercontinental ballistic missile. It had to be now or never.

"Well, we've got a breather for a little while, anyway," Ted replied. "The new orbit should be good for a few weeks, maybe even a month or two. Why don't you come down? We'll keep track of it in the atmosphere, and figure out another way to hit it."

"How fast is the singularity moving now, Ted?" she asked.

Lewis replied after a moment. She assumed he was checking the radar. "The missile collision increased the speed from 900 to 1500 miles per hour. It is just past apogee, so it will continue to accelerate and move into a

206

higher orbit. The second black hole transferred enough momentum to get it well out of the atmosphere on part of each orbit, at least for awhile."

"And if I could add more momentum?" she asked.

"Well, that was why I was hoping you might have a second missile up there to fire at it. Most of the major orbital element changes have been made. Adding more momentum right now while it is still near apogee could loft the orbit completely out of the atmosphere and into space. Any mass that can hit it from behind within the next ten minutes would be helpful. You could even fly that drone into it, since we don't need it anymore."

"Sorry, the drone is gone. I do have other options, though. Thank you, Ted."

He must have sensed what she was considering. "Good luck, Nikki. We all love you."

She flew the F/A-18 behind the brightly glowing star as it accelerated downward after passing the top of its orbit at 60,000 feet. The singularity was moving at 1500 miles per hour, but the top speed of the Super Hornet carrying no under-wing ordinance was at least 1800 miles per hour. She ought to be able to catch it, and give it some more of that precious momentum. It took Nikki a few minutes to work out the math. The available mass, plus acceleration, should be enough. The trick was going to be getting a lock on the still tiny accretion disk. The collision with the Vympel and the other black hole had expanded it out to the diameter of a wedding ring, but it would soon shrink back down to pinhead size.

She approached the singularity deftly, with her radar gun sight set for maximum resolution. When she was a mere 100 yards behind the object, the gun sight indicated a target lock. Nikki squeezed the firing button on the throttle, and the M-61 Vulcan Gatling gun mounted in the nose of the F/A-18 opened up. The accretion disk of the black hole was hit with more than 500 rounds of high-velocity 20 millimeter shells. Nikki watched the bullets and tracers angle eerily into the tiny disk as the gravity of the black hole caught them in a spiral and pulled them in. She couldn't miss. The heavy slugs transferred momentum to the singularity while radiation from the impacts poured over Nikki. Not that it mattered. It couldn't make her any more dead.

She no longer had anything left to hit it with, except for the Hornet itself. She edged the jet forward, until the nose barely contacted the brightly glowing accretion disk. The singularity event horizon in the center was a tiny black speck that Nikki thought she could almost see. She felt the flight controls stiffen in her hands as the F/A-18 became locked to the singularity by gravity. The aircraft was stuck in the accretion disk.

U.S. Navy Lieutenant Commander Nicole Marie Shelton smiled grimly to herself, secure in the knowledge that she wasn't going to die of radiation poisoning after all. She shoved the throttles all the way forward to the stop, and the Hornet began accelerating into the black hole on full afterburners.

Although the accretion disk was less than an inch across, the gravitational gradient of the singularity was enormous at close range. The nose section of the aircraft began collapsing inward. Pieces of the Hornet broke off and fell into the spinning disk, each creating a flash brighter than a lightning stroke as it crossed the event horizon, and dosing Nikki with even more lethal radiation. Her skin began to blister, and her vision got cloudy.

She maintained acceleration. The gravity from the singularity pulled the massive Gatling gun out of the nose cone of the FA/-18, and it

208

disappeared into the black hole with a brilliant flash. The searing light blinded Nikki. The front of her aircraft was starting to wrap itself around the event horizon, but she kept the engines on full afterburner by feel alone. Any little bit would help. Each extra mile per hour would put the black hole that much farther from Earth. The Hornet shuddered as it was being swallowed by a monster.

A few moments later, Nikki's engines cut off. She was out of fuel, and whatever speed she had given to the singularity would have to be enough. The front part of her aircraft twisted around the accretion disk and began falling in. It was disappearing quickly. Tidal forces were pulling on the tail section and the aircraft groaned as metal fought gravity. Burned, in pain and unable to see, Nikki wanted out. Working by feel and training, she blew off the canopy above her head, and grabbed the ejection lever. Just as she pulled it, the F/A-18 collapsed in the center and wrapped both ends of itself around the accretion disk.

Nikki Shelton ejected directly into the event horizon of the black hole. For a brief second she registered the heat of the accretion disk, and felt tidal forces pulling on her head and feet like two implacable giants. Her body was ripped in two at the waist by the gravity while simultaneously being vaporized in the intense radiation, and Nikki's universe ended quickly and painlessly in a brilliant flash of white light. The momentum of her 55 kilogram body from the ejection seat added slightly to the orbital speed of the singularity. Then the aircraft fell into the black hole behind her, its bulk setting off an explosion equivalent to one of the larger hydrogen bomb tests done in this area of the Pacific decades earlier. Because the jet had been pushing into the singularity from behind, the force of the blast was directed backward like a rocket, and gave the singularity the final forward velocity it needed to escape the atmosphere and achieve a high, stable orbit.

From the bridge of the USS Theodore Roosevelt, Captain Goodfriend and First Officer Marino watched a distant chain of small and large mushroom clouds form in the atmosphere.

"Do you think she succeeded, Captain?" Marino asked.

"Only time will tell, Helen. It looks like she gave it everything she had, and then some. I'm sure they are carefully plotting the orbit. We can only hope that her sacrifice was not in vain."

Ted Lewis entered the bridge moments later from where he had been monitoring the radar unit in the CAC. "We have preliminary orbit data. It will make one more pass close to the Earth's surface, and then stay in outer space for good. Nikki did it."

****

In College Park, they were running the orbital models as Lewis's radar data feed came in. Leon Hammermesh fed it into the orbital computer model, which immediately began cranking out a corrected orbit. The team looked at the results in astonishment.

"She did it," said Barney Freeman from his wheelchair. "Good God, the orbit has changed. The velocity is so great that it is describing a final hyperbolic pass a few hundred meters above the surface of the South Atlantic, and then heading out into space on a high, elliptical orbit."

"How elliptical?" asked Karl Barski. "And how high?"

"Too soon to be sure, but the model predicts that it will probably be almost circular, and a third of the way between the Earth and Moon. It is definitely gone!"

210

The cheers were deafening.

"I can't wait to see Nikki so I can congratulate her," Barney Freeman was telling Barski. "Her plans for this operation worked perfectly. In fact, better than perfect. That singularity is precisely where we wanted it. She couldn't have done any better."

Barski's cell phone rang with a special tone, and he excused himself to take it.

"Yes, Mr. President. It worked and the singularity will soon be in high Earth orbit. Yes, sir. We are all celebrating here, sir. Sorry for the noise. What was that? She did what? Oh my God."

"I just got the word from the captain of the Roosevelt," said President Jackson. "Their radar data confirms that the orbit has been altered enough to take the black hole out of the atmosphere and into cis-lunar space. Dr. Lewis said that the accretion disk was heated up quite a bit by absorbing Nikki's aircraft, and it can easily be seen using infrared detectors. Lewis thinks it will be visible for several months, even in space. We are getting a spacecraft ready out of Nellis to go chase it down and cage it. Once we put a leash on that thing, it should be safe. U.S. Navy Lieutenant Commander Nicole Marie Shelton made a great sacrifice. She did what was necessary and she is a national hero. Actually an international hero. We will honor her memory around the world that she just saved. In the meantime, I will talk directly to her family, before this gets out in the media. I'm going to have to give a press briefing in moments. Karl, the people there ought to know about this."

"Yes, Mr. President. I'll make sure they are informed."

The celebration was considerably more subdued after he gave them the news.

211

****

President Jackson was sitting alone in the Oval Office, rocking slowly back and forth in the wicker chair that had once belonged to President Kennedy. He could sit here for hours, thinking, reading briefing papers and coming to decisions about important matters of the day. He found it comforting to know that John Fitzgerald Kennedy had often sat in this very same rocking chair and made similar hard decisions, and that they had generally been the right ones.

Jackson was thinking now about the death of Lieutenant Commander Nicole Shelton, and how he had broken the news to her parents. Her father was a humorless, dour man who made it plain that he did not vote for this President, did not support the policies of this President, and in fact, was of the opinion that if the current administration had not wasted people's hard-earned tax dollars on stupid science experiments that were dangerous and proved nothing, none of this would have happened. According to Mr. Shelton, his daughter had died because of the misguided policies of tax-and-spend liberals, the internationalists at the U.N., the ungrateful French, reckless Swiss, snobby British, and multinational corporations that had supported the construction of the Large Hadron Collider at CERN, and allowed Finch to build the singularity. If all that tax money had been spent on more useful pursuits, like fixing roads, rebuilding the military, or most of all, giving hard-working, ordinary Americans a huge tax cut, none of this would have happened. The President was far too good of a politician to try arguing with or correcting the man. He had thanked Nikki's father for his input, and expressed condolences for the loss of his daughter. They seemed like a rather strange, straitlaced religious family. He wondered how they had produced a remarkable young woman like

212

Nikki. Perhaps her efforts in overcoming her family roots had led to the strength of character she had exhibited later in life. His headache was worse than ever when he got off the phone.

His reverie was interrupted by a knock at the door, and the Secretary of Commerce entered.

"Come in, Charlie," the President said, with a wave of his hand. "I've got a press conference in five minutes, but I wanted to be the first to tell you that you were right. The singularity is tamed, and safely in high orbit between the Earth and moon. So what the hell do we do next?"

"Thank you, Mr. President. That's the best news we've had since this whole mess started. The success of Barney Freeman's team was always a long shot, but I still wanted us to do some contingency planning. They used to say that nothing settles a man's mind like knowing he will be hanged in the morning. We've had quite a bit of that mindset around here lately, but now that the hanging has been called off, we need to live again. The committee you had me assemble has been working hard to come up with some plans for reviving the world economy and moving us forward."

"Great, Charlie. What did they recommend?"

"First and foremost, Mr. President, they recommended that we get off this planet."

President Barry Jackson smiled, for the first time in months. His headache had gone away.

Chapter 10: Aftermath

Dud Gardner hadn't heard from Nikki since leaving California. He had left his cell phone on, but it never rang for calls or beeped for waiting voicemails. Then he forgot to check it for a couple of days because he was busy with the volcanoes. When he finally did check it, he realized the battery was dead. Apparently it had been dead for quite some time, and despite several attempts, it wouldn't hold a charge. He needed to go into town and buy a new battery before this mobile phone would work again.

Dud's pal Dale Richmond was a USGS research volcanologist at Hawaiian Volcanoes Observatory (HVO) with full access to Kilauea crater. Dud had arrived on the Big Island from California in the afternoon. He drove his rental car from Kona through the saddle between Mauna Kea and Mauna Loa, and arrived at the modest home of Dale and his wife Evelyn in the evening. They lived in the town of Volcano, just outside the gate of Hawaii Volcanoes National Park. Evelyn had made a traditional Hawaiian dinner of roast pork, raw fish, pineapple-banana gelatin, sweet potatoes, rice and poi. After dinner, Dale asked if he'd like to see the lava flows.

"At night?" Dud had rarely done any geology at night, except for one poorly organized and memorable field trip in the Sahara, where the sun had set while they were still on the outcrop debating the crystallization history of an igneous rock, and they were an hour away from the vehicles. That wasn't exactly geology at night, just a dangerous return hike to the trucks in moonless, full darkness through rocky desert terrain.

"Sure," Dale replied. "The lava flows are easiest to see at night, and the fountains are spectacular. Madame Pele has been quite active over the past few weeks."

"Then I picked a good time to come." Like nearly all volcanologists, Dud Gardner was well aware of the legendary Hawaiian volcano goddess Pele. People who trespassed on her volcanoes without showing the proper respect, and took samples or souvenirs of lava home without her permission were said to suffer incredible streaks of misfortune. The HVO reception area had a large collection of lava rocks returned by tourists with notes describing the dreadful runs of bad luck experienced by these people after returning home from Hawaii with their illicit treasures. Financial disasters, collapsed marriages, job losses, auto accidents, house fires, personal injuries...even the most rational and cynical scientists in the observatory respected the legend of Pele, leaving small gifts or coins for her on the outcrops, and asking for permission with a brief prayer before collecting samples. One did not want to get crosswise with this goddess. Dale said that there were two things about Madame Pele on which everyone could agree: she was literally the hottest woman on the island, and her temper was volcanic.

They drove around the Pahoa road to Kalapana on the southeast coast below Kilauea. Lava flows here in recent years had blocked off Chain of Craters Road, which led down from the national park, and surrounded a nearby housing development called Royal Gardens. Some of the homes in Royal Gardens had been destroyed by the slow-moving lava. The remainder had been hurriedly dismantled and relocated elsewhere. The government evacuated everyone, and former development was now little more than a grid of abandoned streets in the middle of a lava field.

215

They drove to the end of Kaimu Road at a place called Kapaahu. Dale got out flashlights, and told Dud it was about a half-mile hike to the active flows. They walked over glassy and cindery solidified lava. The broken and blocky stuff was known to geologists by its Hawaiian term, aa, and the looping, ropy flows were also called by their Hawaiian name, pahoehoe.

Dale pointed out a reddish orange glow to Dud that was visible just ahead. It was the outside of a lava tube, glowing from the heat of the molten rock moving through the hollow inside. They turned to follow the lava tube toward the sea.

At the sea cliffs, they could see the glowing orange lava pour slowly out of the tube and drop into the ocean. The water sizzled when it hit, and billowing clouds of steam rose up. The whole place stank from sulfur, seawater and hot rocks.

"Here it is," Dale told him. "The very newest land in the United States."

Dud hoped this land would have a lifespan of more than a few months. To be created in such fiery drama by a process eons old, only to be sucked into the maw of a black hole was a fate that this land, and in fact this entire planet didn't deserve. He prayed to the God of the universe and the goddess of the volcano to help Nikki succeed in her quest. Sometime in the next few days, she would try it.

Dale's wife Evelyn was glued to the television news channels hoping for any information at all about the outcome of the attempt to remove the singularity from Earth. Dud was avoiding the news, because he didn't want to know the exact date and time his lover would be in the greatest danger. He felt that he owed it to Dale and Evelyn to inform them about his relationship with Nikki, and to express how worried he was about her upcoming attempt to tame the singularity. They were sympathetic and seemed to understand his decision to isolate himself from the minute by minute news coverage of the attempt.

He and Dale were out viewing some of the hydrothermal vents around Kilauea the day Nikki tamed the singularity. They were down in the crater and away from the vehicle for most of the day. As they returned to the truck and came within range of a cell phone tower, the message light on Dale's phone lit up like a strobe.

It was Evelyn. She had left him two text messages, the first to tell him that the singularity was on its way to cis-lunar space, thanks to Nikki. The second message was that Nikki Shelton herself had not survived the encounter, and both she and her aircraft had disappeared, apparently into the black hole. Dale was left to break the news to Dud.

Dud took it rather well. He felt a sharp pang of loss to be sure, but he had also been half expecting this, knowing Nikki. It wasn't really a surprise, for a woman who flew supersonic fighters and jumped out of airplanes. He went into Hilo and replaced his cell phone batteries once he realized they weren't working. The five voice mails from Nikki were the last words he ever heard from her, and he saved them forever.

Dud also had a message from a Captain Joseph Goodfriend of the United States Navy requesting a callback. He punched in the number, and was surprised to find himself connected via satellite phone to the commander of the aircraft carrier USS Theodore Roosevelt, on its way back to San Diego from the South Pacific. Captain Goodfriend passed Nikki's last message on to him, and Dud found it comforting. The captain also told him the circumstances of Lieutenant Commander Shelton's death, including the

217

problems with the uncontrollable drone, and her decisive actions to deliver the second black hole and the momentum from her aircraft into the singularity, lofting it into a higher orbit. Nikki had done nothing less than save the Earth with her quick thinking and selfless sacrifice. Dud realized that Nikki would have refused any other course of action, and felt an immense surge of pride to have known her.

Several days later, Dudley Gardner left Hawaii for Nottingham, England, determined to move his life forward. It was time to stop hiding out on Tortola. Dale had told him about a new American initiative to explore the moon and find suitable locations for additional living space. President Jackson had announced that the thousands of new spacecraft built as lifeboats would be used instead to establish a large lunar colony and other habitats in space. No longer would humanity be restricted to living on one fragile world. Since most of the moon was volcanic rock with no atmosphere, and the living quarters were to be excavated below ground to provide protection, people with Dud's talents were needed. Dale told him that Karl Barski himself had passed the word that Dudley Gardner was welcome to join the expedition. The European Space Agency was partnering with the Americans to establish the new lunar colony, and they were hoping Dud would lead the British Geological Survey contingent. After the singularity disaster and the near loss of the entire planet, many governments realized that it was simply not wise to keep all of one's habitat eggs in a single basket. The Russians and the Chinese were looking at Mars.

Although the media played the story continuously, at first no one knew for sure why Nikki had flown her jet into the black hole. Days later, word slowly trickled out from an Air Force sergeant who had been in Nikki's back seat operating the drone. Sergeant Elwood MacDonald told the media that Lieutenant Commander Shelton had ejected him because she needed to use her aircraft to pursue the singularity. They couldn't catch it with the drone as planned, because of interference with the controls from a remote source. MacDonald expressed his opinion that the behavior of the unmanned aircraft over the Pacific strongly resembled similar control problems he had experienced when jihadists hacked into drone flight programs in Afghanistan. In particular, he noted that the drone attempted to attack them personally once the hackers became aware of the nearby U.S. Navy jet. It was only quick thinking on the part of Lieutenant Commander Shelton that avoided a potentially fatal collision.

Commander Helen Marino of the USS Theodore Roosevelt then confirmed in a separate interview that Nikki had impaled the drone onto the nose of her aircraft, carrying it and the attached missile to within firing range of the black hole. She was too close when the Russian missile impacted the singularity, and received a lethal dose of radiation. Marino confided that the cockpit radiation sensor had informed Nikki that the radiation dose she received was enough to kill her within 24 hours, and it was going to be a miserable death. Radio traffic between Nikki and Dr. Ted Lewis on the Roosevelt soon after the missile strike indicated that the singularity would still need additional momentum to get safely into space. Commander Marino could only speculate that in light of the untreatable and certainly fatal radiation poisoning, Nikki chose to use whatever options she had left, including the F/A-18 itself, to impart as much additional velocity to the singularity as she could. It worked and Nikki was an international hero, but her death could have been avoided if the drone had taken orders as planned.

The public outrage at the interference by the jihadists in Lieutenant Commander Shelton's mission was intense. Renewed military action was taken against the strongholds of Tora Bora in the mountains of Afghanistan. The attacks were relentless, and the jihadists were dispersed and driven underground. Still, they hung together, and with village sympathizers, message drops, and word of mouth, they kept in touch, made plans, and waited patiently for the melee to die down.

The public outrage was nothing compared to the anger felt in the engine room of the USS Theodore Roosevelt by Chief Warrant Officer Ibrahim Mohammed when he heard the news about Nikki. His eyes narrowed as he realized that a Navy pilot, who was an honorable officer and an incredibly brave lady, had become a casualty because of information he had provided. They had promised him the interference would be distant and harmless. The imam told him it was the will of Allah that the world should be destroyed.

Well, the world was still here, and apparently the imam did not know the will of Allah quite as well as he claimed. He had lied to Mohammed to get the information he needed for the militants. The jihadists had not only hacked into the controls of the drone to try preventing the rendezvous with the black hole, but they had actually attacked the nearby U.S. Navy F/A-18 with the intent of bringing it down. They had promised him there would be no killing. Chief Mohammed felt betrayed and angry. He vowed that no matter what it took, this could not be allowed to stand.

****

Hermann Gantz was trying to rebuild an empire. Now that the singularity had been tamed and the Earth was likely to remain intact, he needed to recoup the fortune he had spent assuring himself a place in the

220

lifeboats. The economy had changed, and the old drug and smuggling businesses just weren't as lucrative as they had been in the past. But Gantz was nothing if not creative, and he figured he would soon find an opportunity to make some serious cash.

He found it when a conversation with an old pal who was into real estate schemes mentioned that the U.N. was inquiring about land availability on the island of Maui, in Hawaii. No one knew why they would want land on a tropical volcanic island, but the queries were rumored to have come from the U.N. Space Directorate, the organization that ran the lifeboat program.

Gantz made a quick trip to Hawaii. With what was left of his fortune, he bought 10,000 acres of sugar cane and vegetable farms on Maui just west of the town of Pukalani, in the flat saddle of the island. His well-paid and highly cultivated contacts from the lifeboat program had told him that the U.N. Space Directorate wanted the land between the slopes of Haleakala volcano and the rugged mountains of West Maui for a spaceport. His contacts told him the U.N. would pay top dollar.

Within a few months, working from his Berlin mansion, he had remade a sizeable fortune by selling small parcels to land speculators, buying it back at a profit, and reselling it. Gantz was able to spread rumors and misinformation about the land's worth and the degree of U.N interest in the spaceport project, causing the prices to fluctuate wildly. Since he was controlling the rumors, he was able to buy low and sell high, over and over again. His offshore bank balance began to creep back toward a billion euros. Eventually, the U.N. Space Directorate did buy the land for the Maui breech-lock of a maglev-railgun spacecraft launching system. They paid Gantz ten

221

times his original cost, which when combined with the land speculator profits, netted a very tidy sum indeed.

He had almost completely forgotten about his arrangements for a spot on the lifeboats, and the desperate days when everyone thought the world would end. Inspector Mohan and the U.N. Security Directorate didn't forget, however. Painstaking research of computer records and biometric identifications were turning up discrepancies and fraud. Corrupt officials were beginning to talk. Patiently, thoroughly, and carefully, Mohan and Interpol began to pull together enough information to make a case.

Gantz was utterly surprised when they came for him. He was in the hot tub with Britta, one of his favorite girls. They had just finished making love and were sipping properly chilled white wine, when the patio was suddenly surrounded by five government agents in urban camouflage. They were heavily armed and very professional. The mansion's security system had been expertly breached and the bodyguards immobilized. The leader of the group was a dark man in a turban. He was the only one who spoke, in perfect, colloquial German.

"*Guten abend, Herr Gantz*. My name is Mohan, and I am with the United Nations Security Directorate. Also Interpol. Let me get straight to the point. Although the lifeboat program was shut down with the taming of the singularity, we have continued to check all of the lifeboat data files for mismatches. Our supercomputer search engine found twelve duplicate records of your biometrics in the lottery files. Each record was linked to a different name that belonged to a recently deceased young man. All these young men were of similar appearance, and in fact, they all happened to resemble you. In each instance, a different number of the lottery was assigned. We believe this was an attempt by you to guarantee a seat on a lifeboat, by murdering or causing to be murdered a dozen innocent people to create spaces for yourself. Of course, it could just be an incredible coincidence, but until we hear a satisfactory explanation, you are under arrest."

"What is the charge?" asked Gantz, feeling his world crumbling around him.

"Twelve counts of premeditated, first degree homicide will do for a start, plus bribery of government officials and tampering with data in government data banks," Mohan replied. Although he smiled, there was no merriment in his eyes, which remained hard and piercing. "I am sure more will come to light as we investigate."

The girl, Britta, cowered at one end of the hot tub, desperately trying to cover herself. She looked at Gantz with horror in her eyes. Mohan handed her a towel, and told her she was free to go.

Her only words were, "Hermann, how could you?"

"Come, my dear," Mohan answered. "How do you think he acquired this fortune?" He waved a hand airily around at the estate. "By selling apples on the street?"

"I didn't think it included cold-blooded murder," she replied, with a shudder.

In handcuffs and wearing only a bathrobe, Hermann Gantz was frog marched out of his fabulous Berlin mansion under the watchful eye of two Interpol inspectors with guns drawn. It was the last time he would ever see it.

****

With nearly a million spaceships available, humanity was spreading rapidly into space. A second human habitat called Luna City was being constructed on the moon, on the nearside and deep underground near the first moon landing site in Mare Tranquillatis. Moon Base Alpha was still being dug deeply into the lunar farside, and in all, the moon was expected to house upwards of two billion inhabitants. Several nascent, O'Neill-type space habitats had been started at the Lagrange points of the lunar orbit, with the intention of being supplied with construction materials from the moon once the colony there was a going concern. There was already a fair-sized settlement on Mars, which didn't need to be dug in like the lunar bases thanks to the planet's thin atmosphere. The prefab living structures scattered across the desert landscape somewhat resembled a sprawling mobile home park. Some of the more adventurous humans had gone to live in the asteroid belt, prospecting for metals and materials like ice and hydrocarbons in an atmosphere reminiscent of the 1849 California gold rush, complete with saloons, dance halls, and whorehouses. The moons of Jupiter and Saturn were also being explored.

Dud Gardner, along with Dale and Evelyn Richmond, had joined the lunar colony program. Deposits of titanium and iron had been found in the ancient, hardened lava flows of Mare Imbrium. Most geologists thought the metals came from the parent asteroid that had collided with the moon eons ago to create the Imbrium Basin. Other resources had been found in the ancient rocks of the lunar highlands, including precious metals and fissionable materials like radium and uranium. Lunar mining was busily producing the raw materials and metals needed for space manufacturing, and there was work for nearly any geologist who wanted it. Dud and Dale were part of the U.N. Assay Office, which filed mining claims and kept the prospectors honest. There were 60 people in their office, and they were still overwhelmed with claims and permit applications. Mining had become a very big business on the moon.

Dud was trying to forget Nikki. There were enough people in the lunar colony that he could have had his pick of partners. Plenty of young, single females had migrated into space for the opportunities, and often to escape oppressive fathers, husbands, brothers, and governments at home. The public corridors and concourses of Luna City were crowded with women in saris, burkas, and veils, sandals, jeans, shorts, tee shirts and tank tops. Despite the feminine ocean lapping about him, Dud couldn't forget Nikki making love to him the first time on the rocks at Peterborg, taking him skydiving, flying him up to observe the singularity in a supersonic jet, or greeting him in his Tortola hot tub wearing only a brilliant smile. She had gotten to him, and he couldn't let her go.

Time and kindness heal all wounds. After nearly a year of living in bachelor quarters on the moon, Dud met an Indo-European geophysicist named Yasmin Mishra. She was about 40 and single, petite and slender with jet black hair and dark eyes. Her father was Indian and her mother Belgian, and the combination was simply stunning. Yasmin walked into Dudley's office at the U.N. Assay one day, and asked for help filling out a seismic permit. He found her fascinating.

Yasmin was part of a U.N. crew running seismic profiles across the moon to detect deep structures. They were trying to find the origin of the lunar "mascons," concentrations of denser material under the moon's crust that affected satellite orbits. Dud never had much interest in geophysics, which he generally thought of as little more than squiggly lines on a piece of paper. He did have quite a bit of interest in Dr. Mishra, however, and when

225

she invited him to visit their field site in Oceanus Procellarum on her third trip to the permit office, he jumped at the chance.

The Mascon Project was using Yasmin's seismic reflection data to delineate the size, borders and depth of the Procellarum mascon. The geophysics couldn't tell them what it was, however, although the velocity contrast with the surrounding basalts did suggest something dense and metallic, perhaps iron or nickel. To find out for sure, they were drilling down to it a few kilometers below the lunar surface. When Dud arrived for a visit, he learned that they were collecting drill core, but no one on the project was available to analyze it. The core was boxed up and stored for later examination.

This was perfect. The project needed an on-site geologist, and Dud Gardner was their man. They were drilling through volcanic rocks, and needed someone to tell them what kind of rock it was, and how it might change across the mascon boundary. Dud thought they were probably going to find a great, big nickel-iron asteroid that had slammed into the moon eons ago, and been buried in solidified lava flows. They would definitely know when they hit it with the drill bit. Still, it was a great chance to be posted at a field station with Yasmin, and maybe work on developing some kind of a relationship with her. He contacted his boss, who happened to be Dale, and asked for a transfer. Dale had been picking up on the whole Dud-Yasmin thing, and was worried about his friend ever recovering from Nikki's death. He thought a transfer to the Procellarum drilling project was a capital idea, and contacted the Mascon Project manager, telling her there was a geologist available to help guide the drilling. Since they were all U.N. people and it was all U.N. funded, and the project really needed a geologist, she told Dale they would be happy to have Dud on board.

226

When Dud told Yasmin about it, she asked him why he had transferred from Luna City to a field station. He told her it was so he could be closer to her, and held his breath. Dud figured she would either be delighted or totally creeped out, and he waited to see which. After a moment of surprise, Yasmin wrapped her arms around him, and gave him a passionate kiss. Things pretty much progressed from there.

Slowly, Dud's broken heart began to heal, as the memories of Nikki faded to a background glow.

****

It was nearly a year before the authorities got around to dealing with Finch. Two vehicles containing six grim-faced men armed with assault rifles and warrants arrived at the Geneva town jail one evening. They rousted Finch out of bed in the middle of the night and bundled him into one of the waiting black sport utility vehicles. None of the men spoke.

Finch protested loudly as he was shoved into the SUV. He demanded to know what was going on here, where they were taking him and on whose authority. The man in the front passenger seat, who seemed to be the leader of the group, made a brief hand motion to the armed man sitting beside Finch in the back seat. The second man acknowledged the order with a curt nod of his head, and Finch found himself quickly and professionally bound and gagged. Unable to struggle, and unable to make a sound above a whimper, he began to be frightened for the first time.

After ten minutes of driving on back roads and side streets out of Geneva and into the French countryside, the man in the front seat finally turned around and looked at Finch. The name patch on his uniform said Mohan. When he spoke, it was with a clipped and perfect Oxford accent.

227

"Dr. Finch, we are a special security unit of the United Nations Peacekeeping Force, operating under the auspices of Interpol. I am Inspector Mohan. You will do us all a favor by not struggling, or the next order I give to Gruppenführer Hoffmann sitting there next to you will be to knock you unconscious with a blow to the head. He has trained for years to do this efficiently and quietly, and I'm sure he would very much enjoy having an opportunity to show off his skills." Finch looked in panic at the huge man next to him. Hoffmann merely grinned, showing a gap-toothed smile.

"We will be in this vehicle for a number of hours," Mohan continued. "How many, I can't say exactly. We will be following a circuitous path across France into Belgium and then Holland. For security reasons, only Dmitri knows the exact route." He pointed to the big, blonde, Russian-looking driver. "The other vehicle will go a different way as a decoy. Believe it or not, many people want to kill you, and it is my job to ensure that they don't get the opportunity. That is the reason for the black-bag operation. If you will behave yourself, we can take the gag out after an hour or so.

"As for where we are going, if we can get you there alive, eventually you will be delivered to the International Court of Justice in The Hague. There, you will be put on trial for your unlawful and criminal acts that nearly destroyed the entire world, and were directly responsible for the death of U.S. Navy Lieutenant Commander Nicole Marie Shelton as she attempted to remediate the situation. The fact that Lieutenant Commander Shelton was successful in her attempt has no bearing whatsoever on the charges."

Mohan had a patch on his shoulder that identified him as a member of the legendary Ghurka Rifles. He had been highly trained by the British Army in a host of commando techniques, including covert operations, deception and concealment, and quick, quiet killing using guns, knives, letter openers, piano wire, poison or even his bare hands. The others were equally well-trained; Dmitry by Spetsnaz in the Russian Army and Hoffmann by NATO. A simple snatch and grab operation like this was almost beneath them. The Secretary General didn't want any screw-ups however, so she sent in her very best team.

"You might be interested to learn that the U.N. has reinstated the death penalty for this special case if the judge decides that the circumstances warrant it," Mohan continued. "You are in an enormous amount of trouble, Dr. Finch, and I hope you have a very good lawyer. You are going to need one."

The blonde driver turned around and grinned at Finch. "They're going to hang you high at Black Hole Creek, pilgrim," he said with a weird Russian-John Wayne accent.

****

The Afghan desert was quiet on this late spring night. It had taken former Chief Warrant Officer Ibrahim Mohammed many months to track down the jihadists who had interfered with the command and control of the Reaper drone carrying the second black hole. Mohammed had retired from the U.S. Navy and started this search with the imam in his local mosque, to whom he had given the sailing date and destination.

That imam was now dead; a casualty of war as far as Mohammed was concerned. The holy man had refused to cooperate, and would not give the chief any information about his contacts or where he had passed the

229

information. Mohammed was forced to use rather direct and somewhat severe methods of interrogation. He eventually got the name of the contact, but unfortunately, the imam did not survive the enhanced Q and A session. The chief carefully cleaned up all the forensic evidence, and drove the imam's car up to LAX airport with the body in the trunk. He parked it in the long term lot, and caught a flight to Morocco. Someone would eventually notice the smell and call the cops. They would probably figure out he was a suspect, but if they wanted to arrest him, he was going to be hard to find.

Morocco led to Tunisia, and then Algeria. Chief Mohammed moved from camp to camp in the northern Sahara Desert, seeking the jihadists who had hacked the drone. He was also gradually infiltrating his way into the jihad movement, pretending to be a true believer disillusioned with America, and supposedly carrying enough of the United States Navy's secrets to arm battalions of suicide boats. In truth, Mohammed only knew secrets about the Roosevelt's engine room with its ancient and cantankerous nuclear power plant. Still, it was enough to get him into the inner circles of the jihadist tribes, and moving ever closer to the men he sought.

Many months later, after passing through two Palestinian refugee camps and then into Syria, the trail finally led to Kabul and beyond, into the wild Hindukush Mountains wilderness of eastern Afghanistan. The jihadist group he sought was holed up in caves in the mountains. Careful negotiations with a small, heavily armed group of humorless men guarding the entrance eventually gained him admission to the main cave.

The cave was equipped with banks of lithium batteries recharged by solar panels mounted just outside the entrance. The batteries, which were designed to power electric automobiles, had been laboriously

230

transported into the mountains by donkey caravans. They now powered lights, satellite comlinks, and a number of notebook computers. This was the place Chief Mohammed had been seeking. It was the only group high-tech enough to have hacked into the drone's command and control software.

He wanted to find those who had been directly responsible for Lieutenant Commander Shelton's death. He was determined to visit death upon them as revenge for her killing. He couldn't be too obvious about it, or he would only bring death upon himself. Mohammed was not adverse to the idea, but he prayed to Allah to hold off until he had completed his mission. He carefully revealed the plans for the layout of a Lincoln-class aircraft carrier to the jihad group. The leader, a man named Nazir, was suspicious of Mohammed's motives for joining them. However, as the plans for the carrier became more detailed and complete, he began to trust Mohammed. Mohammed didn't bother to tell him that all the Lincoln class ships were obsolete and most had been retired from active duty in the fleet. The Roosevelt was the last one left, and it had been due to retire in less than a year before all this singularity business got started. Nevertheless, Nazir thought he was getting critical intelligence, and after a few weeks, he revealed that they had a nuke.

The single nuclear device was a relatively small, Chinese-made tactical battlefield weapon with a yield of only about 10 kilotons. Still, Mohammed reminded himself, that was half the size of the Hiroshima bomb, and it could still do a lot of damage. How the jihadists had gotten their hands on it was unclear, but seemed to involve a corrupt provincial official, a greedy Red Army colonel, lax security at a backwater military base, and lots of opium money. Since everyone at the time thought that the singularity was going to destroy the world in a few short months anyway,

231

no one was especially worried about the consequences of their actions. But that was then and this is now, Mohammed thought. Nikki Shelton had saved the world, and because she did, these bastards ended up with a working nuke.

They only had the one, and there was a great deal of debate among the jihad leadership about how and where to use it. The two frontrunners for targets were Tel Aviv in Israel and Orlando in the United States, with London as a back-up. Mohammed asked about Orlando, and Nazir told him that it was a much softer target than New York or Washington, and it had amusement parks and vacation attractions that the jihadists found repulsive. People should be spending their free time honoring Allah, not engaging in frivolity. Killing several hundred thousand international and American vacationers with a weapon of mass destruction would shock the world, and show it just how pious the jihadists really were. Chief Mohammed privately thought they were nuts. Blow up Disneyland? What the hell was wrong with these people?

Other suggestions for the nuke included Saudi Arabia for its ties to the west, Egypt for making peace with Israel, and Lebanon apparently just for the hell of it. One genius even suggested using the weapon on Iran to provoke the Iranians into counterattacking Israel and the west with everything in their modest but deadly nuclear arsenal. Because of the internal disagreement among the jihad leadership, the device had been stored in the cave for more than a year.

The other reason it hadn't been used was that nobody in the jihad could figure out how to set it off. It didn't come with instructions, and all the notations on the device itself were in Chinese, which no one could read. A French convert to the jihad named Phillipe, who was the most computer-savvy of the militants, had tried translating it on the Internet, with little luck. Mohammed immediately focused on Phillipe as the man who must have hacked the drone control system, and was the most directly responsible for the death of Nikki Shelton. He would avenge Nikki by killing Phillipe.

Mohammed could read and speak Chinese, thanks to an intense hypnosis course the Navy had put him through a few years earlier in preparation for some joint fleet exercises. His part in the exercise had been to babysit the half dozen Chinese sailors who were "observing" in his engine room, and keep their observations away from the sensitive and classified equipment. He had learned how to say "Please move away from there" in Mandarin pretty well.

Mohammed mentioned his language skills to Nazir, and a few minutes later, found himself staring at the outer casing of a Chinese Red Army model 8605, class II, "Teaflower" battlefield nuclear gravity bomb. Although he was not a weapons expert, Mohammed had served on a nuclear-armed carrier, and had acquired a basic understanding of the types of nuclear weapons and how they worked. His limited knowledge far exceeded anything the jihadists knew about the subject.

Here was his revenge, Mohammed thought. A gift from Allah. If he could get this thing to go off, down here in the middle of all of them, it would instantly take out Phillipe, along with Nazir, all the rest of the leadership and most of the foot soldiers in the jihad. The entire, callous killing machine would be reduced to isolated groups of leaderless criminals that local authorities could easily round up.

The nuke itself was an ugly gray-green cylinder, about a foot in diameter by four feet long. Mohammed thought the design looked like a simple uranium gun device, with a detonation charge designed to blast a

233

slug of uranium 238 into a uranium 238 target, creating a shower of neutrons within a critical mass and starting a chain reaction. This was the simplest of atomic bomb designs, and had in fact been the design of the first operational weapon dropped on Hiroshima.

A maintenance panel on the side was secured with four screws. Phillipe brought him some tools. Mohammed gingerly opened it up, and peered inside. Two switches, labeled in Chinese, were located under the access door. The red one said "arm" and the blue one "trigger." A short explanation on the back of the panel described these as the test switches in case the bomb was disconnected from the firing command and control system in an aircraft. Mohammed correctly surmised that the "arm" switch activated the electronics in the bomb, and the "trigger" switch would activate a pressure-sensitive altimeter when the bomb was dropped from an aircraft. At a predetermined height above the ground, the altimeter would detonate the device. He manually flipped the switches independently back and forth a couple of times, and could see the tiny lights on the status board inside the maintenance panel change. It was working. In actual combat, slung beneath the wing of a Chinese MIG, the device would be armed and the detonation altitude set remotely from the cockpit before the bomb was dropped.

Mohammed told Nazir that the bomb was operational, and could be detonated. He showed him the red switch and the blue switch, along with the dial to adjust the altimeter. He set the altimeter for sea level, surmising that they were high enough in the mountains that the bomb wouldn't go off, and flipped the switches on and off, instructing Nazir on how to detonate the bomb inside a crowded city. Once the altimeter trigger was set for a target city, all Nazir and his men would have to do was flip the red switch to arm the bomb, and then detonate it by leaving a martyr behind to flip the blue switch.

Nazir and Phillipe gathered up the men to come and view this wonder. In those brief few seconds when he was unwatched, Chief Mohammed quickly unclipped a wire from the blue switch and reattached it to the same pole as the other wire, shorting out the trigger. There was no way he was letting these crazies take this thing into a city. If Nazir and his buddies didn't notice the subtle change of two wires to the same side of the blue switch, which was unlikely given their lack of experience with the hardware, the next time they flipped the red switch to arm the device the shorted-out trigger would blow it up in their faces. Hopefully, before they ever moved it from this cave. "Allahu akbar!" Mohammed said quietly. "God is great!"

Mohammed peered into the access port and began adjusting a dial, following the Chinese instructions on the back of the access panel. They were at an altitude of about 10,000 feet in these mountain caves. He set the altimeter for 20,000 feet, which was higher than any of the local mountains. If the jihadists armed the bomb, it would go off, and there was nowhere high enough they could take it to avoid that.

Nazir came back over and asked what he was doing. He explained that he was adjusting the altitude settings so that they could take the device into any city in the world, and trigger it to explode.

Nazir nodded, and then rewarded him by shooting him.

Although Chief Mohammed was half expecting it, he was still surprised when the bullet ripped through his viscera. The intense pain sent him collapsing to the ground. As he lay there gasping, several of Nazir's

235

men dragged him roughly out of the cave complex and dumped him unceremoniously into the dusty Afghan desert.

Then Nazir stood above him, looking at him with pity. "I am sorry to have to shoot you, my friend, but a man with your knowledge is dangerous. I thank you for making the weapon operational, but after achieving this, you have become much more of a liability to us than an asset. We shall use this marvelous device to destroy many infidels, but you must enter Paradise ahead of us, because you are still an American, and cannot be fully trusted. I shall allow you to lie here and make your peace with Allah. If you have not died within the hour, I promise to come back and dispatch you quickly."

Nazir turned and walked back into the caves with his men. Chief Mohammed lay there in the desert with his lifeblood slowly draining out into the sand, wondering how long it would take Nazir to gather up his loyal followers and run through a demonstration of their new toy. As it turned out, it was not long.

Everything suddenly ended in silent light and white heat.

****

Gerd Hoffmann of the United Nations Peacekeeping Force took the call. It was Dr. Sophie Wu of the International Monitoring System for nuclear weapons tests. She asked to speak to Mohan. *Gruppenführer* Hoffmann fetched the inspector quickly. Calls from the IMS were not usually trivial.

"Yes, Dr. Wu. Inspector Mohan here. What can I do for you?"

"We have a standing order to inform the U.N. Peacekeeping Force of any unusual nuclear events. There was a large explosion less than an hour ago in eastern Afghanistan. It appears to have been nuclear, and located in the heart of the Hindukush Mountains. We show no nuclear assets or test facilities of any type there."

"Those mountains are full of jihadist terrorists. Could they be testing nuclear weapons? And what makes you so sure it was nuclear?" Mohan asked her, being thorough as usual.

"We have many sensors deployed in the area because of the proximity to India and Pakistan," Dr. Wu said. "We picked up the blast on seismic, hydroacoustic and infrasound detectors, and we are just starting to get satellite data on noble gases, particularly xenon-133, released into the atmosphere from the detonation. Xenon-133 is a very positive indicator of a uranium fission chain reaction. It was nuclear, all right."

"Do you have any idea which brand?" asked Mohan, worrying about the political fallout more than the radioactive fallout if the device happened to be from the wrong source for that part of the world.

"We only have preliminary data," Dr. Wu replied. "Until we can sample the fallout and get a fingerprint on the fissionable materials used, we can only speculate."

"And your speculation, Dr. Wu?" Mohan asked, pressing to get something more definitive out of her.

"Probably Chinese. The seismic signal and air blast were virtually identical to those from a Chinese tactical battlefield weapon, like a Teaflower. One of those is said to be missing."

"What exactly is a Teaflower?" Mohan asked. He could have looked it up, but this was quicker.

"A ten kiloton yield, uranium gun gravity bomb," she replied.

"A gravity bomb? How appropriate. We just got rid of the mother of all gravity bombs that would have crushed the Earth and everything on it. Now these jokers want to play with nukes." Mohan thanked the doctor and broke the connection.

"Gruppenführer Hoffmann," he called. "Gather up the men. We have to go search a site."

It took them better than a week to piece it together. At the detonation site there was nothing. Satellite images revealed that the location had previously been honeycombed with caves and tunnels, but all that remained now was a deep crater, approximately 750 meters across. Radioactivity levels were too high for them to remain there for more than a few minutes, and all they found was a bowl-shaped depression floored with dark green, cracked radioactive glass. They had better luck in the surrounding villages.

An old man who ran a shop in one village told them the jihadists had come in regularly for supplies. The last few times they had brought a black man with them, whom they introduced as a brother from Somalia. The elderly shopkeeper thought he looked and acted a lot more American than Somalian. He didn't know much else about the guy, except that he had come to Afghanistan to join the jihad.

It was slim, but Mohan and his men pursued it, along with dozens of other leads. They learned that the black American had come from Syria. More digging indicated that he had been in Palestine, Algeria and Morocco before that. Mohan even got a name from Syrian customs, who thought the man might be trying to smuggle something. He was clean, but it was unusual for a black man to enter Syria from Palestine. They remembered him. He had been traveling alone, and he knew things. The name was Ibrahim Mohammed.

International police records turned up more on Mohammed. A scrap of credit card receipt in a vehicle found in the long-term parking lot at LAX with a dead imam in the trunk placed Ibrahim Mohammed at the scene. The partial account number they were able to get matched credit cards belonging to Mohammed, a baker in Chicago, and a long-haul trucker out of Knoxville, Tennessee. The trucker's road logs proved he had been in Canada when the imam died, and the baker had never left Chicago. Mohammed was the most likely suspect. The last charge made on his account was a one-way airline ticket to Morocco. Mohan's men were also able to discover that Mohammed had been a member of the dead imam's mosque. The imam had a reputation for associating with known jihad terrorists. The clincher was that Mohammed had recently retired from the Navy, where he'd served as engine room chief aboard the Roosevelt.

Mohan smiled as he figured it out. Chief Mohammed feels guilty about the Roosevelt helping Nikki Shelton tame the singularity. He asks his imam for advice. The imam gets Mohammed to tell him where the interception will take place, and passes it on to his jihadi pals. They jam the drone, hoping the attempt will fail. Nikki Shelton exhibits great bravery and intervenes, sacrificing her aircraft and eventually herself to tame the singularity successfully. Mohammed finds out that he is indirectly responsible for the death of a fine officer, and vows revenge.

He retires from the Navy, and interrogates the imam. Although the body was in pretty bad shape, Mohan was certain that the imam died under some kind of interrogation. Mohammed then spends a couple of years worming his way into the jihad movement, and finally reaches the leaders.

239

Somehow, they've acquired a small nuke, but don't know how to use it. Mohammed does, and sets it to blow up in their faces. And that's the end.

So Nikki Shelton has been avenged, Mohan thought. Extraordinary woman. It was too bad she died while taming the singularity. He would have liked to meet her.

Epilogue

Nicole Marie Shelton was falling through space. Free falling like she was in an endless skydive, but never hitting anything. She was in this state for a long time, until a logical thought slowly came to her.

I'm inside the black hole event horizon. I'm not falling. I must be orbiting the singularity. Yes, there it was, off to her left. An incredibly tiny, bright, blue-white point.

Later, another thought.

I must be dead. I don't feel a body, and no living person could have survived the tidal forces and fierce radiation in that transition. All that's left is my consciousness...my soul, if you will. Circling. Falling. She knew that nothing escapes from a black hole, including electromagnetic radiation. And what was a soul, anyway, but an organized field of electromagnetic radiation?

Great. Trapped here forever or damn near. A singularity this size would take billions of years to evaporate. There wouldn't be much left of the universe when she got out.

Items popped into existence as they crossed the event horizon. She saw space junk. Mangled old rocket boosters, defunct satellites, pieces of exploded missiles. Everything seemed to pause for a brief moment, and then gradually pick up speed as it fell toward the bright white singularity. She thought for awhile (how slow one's thoughts are as a mere electromagnetic construct, without conductive nerves to carry the signals) and it occurred to her to wonder how she could see things. She was dead, she had no eyes, the eyes she had in life had been blinded, and how could there even be light inside the event horizon, anyway? Still, it was lit somehow by the tiny, bright singularity, and she could focus images, and there was the space junk, clear as day. One booster had CCCP stenciled in red letters on the side. Nikki realized that they must be using the black hole to suck up the debris in Earth orbit.

Oh, thank God, she thought. The Earth was still out there. The momentum she had added with her guns and afterburners must have worked. Her life was a small price to pay for saving the planet.

Still, she hadn't counted on this. She quietly watched the space junk disintegrate under tidal forces as it accelerated inward. She wondered again how she could see it, but this time for a different reason. By definition, each object had reached lightspeed, the velocity "c," when it crossed the event horizon. So how could she see something moving at the speed of light? The light from it would never be fast enough to reach her.

Einstein's general relativity theory was adamant that the speed of light could not be exceeded in the known universe. So, when an object falling into a black hole reaches a velocity of c, it leaves the known universe and disappears over the event horizon. That much was well-established, but nothing was known about the remainder of the journey from the edge of the event horizon to the final impact with the singularity, because no information could get back to an observer outside the event horizon. These objects Nikki was watching HAD to be moving faster than lightspeed as far as the outside universe was concerned. Yet here they were visible, and in fact, they were barely moving when they popped into existence. She suspected that some hitherto unknown aspect of relativity was responsible, keeping everything working within its own frame of reference. Maybe lightspeed was a lot faster here inside the event horizon than outside, and these objects were not breaking any cosmic speed limits. It looked like the rules got reset once something entered. How bizarre. This could be a whole separate little bubble universe, with its own laws of physics.

Suddenly, she felt another presence. Someone else had entered the black hole. She saw a body in a spacesuit torn apart by the tides fall into the singularity. But that person's soul, like Nikki's, orbited the black hole.

"Hello? Hello?" the voice echoed ghostly in her thoughts. "Is someone here? Who are you?"

"Yes," she projected back. "Someone is here. But since I was here first and you are intruding, perhaps you should tell me who you are."

"Yes, yes, indeed. I am, or perhaps I should say I *was* Dr. Geoffrey Finch, one of the greatest and most revered human scientists of all time. I constructed his singularity. And who is the entity I have the honor of addressing?"

"Oh my God. Finch, even dead you are still such a pompous ass that it makes me sick. If I could be sick, that is. I can't, because I don't have a body. This is just great. Of all the people to be stuck with for eternity inside the event horizon of a black hole, I could not possibly have done any worse. The greatest dipstick of all time."

"Of course," the new entity answered. "Only one other person has entered the black hole so far. Lieutenant Nicole Shelton, it must be you. Charming as always, my dear."

"Arrogant bastard. I was promoted to Lieutenant Commander before my last mission, so show some respect. I left you in a Geneva jail cell. How did you end up here, Finch?"

243

"After imprisoning me without charges for quite some time, the Philistines decided that I needed to be put through some sort of a show trial, a kangaroo court, if you will, at The Hague for the perceived crime of constructing a miniature black hole."

"Perceived crime? It was selfish, reckless, careless, and nearly destroyed the entire planet," she retorted. "You're lucky you weren't dragged through the streets and strung up like Mussolini!"

"Be that as it may, the singularity is now safely in high Earth orbit, and it is providing unlimited power to the planet below as it collects unwanted space debris," he said. "They never even thanked me for solving their energy needs for the next ten millennia. Anyway, as a sentence, they decided to drop me in here."

"Oh, that is just too perfect." Nikki wished she still had hands so she could clap them in glee. "Hoist by your own petard, so to speak. Execution by taking one long, last dive to infinity."

"Yes, yes." He was peeved, and she could hear it in his thoughts. "It was all done with great ceremony, of course, and legal formalities."

"But in the end, they just pushed you into the singularity." Nikki certainly didn't want to be around this guy, but she was glad they had executed him. He was far too dangerous to the human race to be left alive.

"Shot was more like it," he corrected her. "Out of the missile tube of a spaceship. So here I am and where does that leave us?"

"Stuck, professor. Stuck for most of eternity. Until the black hole radiates away from Hawking radiation, we can't get out. It could be a very long wait."

"Not as long as you might think. Time passes much more quickly outside, Nikki. It's been nearly two years since you disappeared."

"Two years? It feels like twenty minutes."

"Come, Dr. Shelton. You are inside the event horizon of a black hole, created by me, I might add. That alone makes me the greatest physicist of all time. But even a physicist of much lesser talent such as yourself should know that gravity slows down time."

Her reply was unprintable.

Later, he told her how they could escape.

****

The electromagnetic entity that was Finch moved away from her. He propelled himself downward into the singularity, and disappeared. She held back, not following.

Finch had told her that when the two singularities had collided, not only had forward momentum been transferred, but angular momentum as well. In other words, the formerly slowly rotating singularity now rotated at near relativistic speeds. Theory had it that a rapidly-rotating black hole would wrap the space-time continuum around itself, creating folds, creases and even wormholes through the fabric of space-time. These could lead to other places in the universe, or even to other universes altogether, if string theory and membrane theory were correct, making the known universe just one of many. Nikki thought that the singularity had recently proven a number of fairly bizarre and far-out theories in cosmology to be correct, so she listened to Finch.

If they fell into the singularity at a shallow angle and picked up its rotation, it might fling them out of the black hole and back across the event horizon. They could end up near Earth, in a different part of the universe far away, or in a different, parallel universe altogether. All they had to do was dive in.

She thanked Finch, but told him she didn't want to travel with him. She thought they ought to go their own ways. He gave her the electromagnetic equivalent of a shrug, and told her to suit herself. If she dove into the singularity separately from him, the odds were high that she would end up someplace else. The space-time folds were changing constantly, and there were an infinite number of parallel universes out there. If they left a few minutes apart, they should never have to see each other again.

Nikki gave it more than a few minutes. She agonized over how, when or even if she should do this. Finch was gone, and she could stay here in peace. But where was "here?" A volume of warped space smaller than a pea, dominated by a point source of light the size of an atom? She couldn't get back to the universe she'd known. There was nothing here except for the occasional piece of space junk falling into the singularity, adding to the mass.

In the end, Nikki decided that she would have a better chance for a meaningful existence in the afterlife if her soul was outside of the event horizon rather than in it, and the only way to get out was to dive into the singularity. Thus convinced, hours after Finch had left, she marshaled her thoughts and willed herself into a long, flat trajectory aimed at the singularity.

****

The soul of Nicole Marie Shelton passed close to the singularity, and it obligingly flung her out into a different universe. It was parallel to

246

the universe she had known, and similar in many ways, but it was run by different rules. Instead of being designed, constructed and run by a single God, this new universe had a Greek-like, polytheistic committee of a dozen Gods, who constantly fought, argued, squabbled and rarely got anything done. While they sat in endless meetings secretly planning ways to backstab each other, debating the fine print on contracts and agreeing to disagree, quite a bit of chaos went on around them. Galaxies collided, stars snuffed out or blew up, and life-bearing planets suddenly froze over or boiled away. It was a mess.

Several of the Gods had spotted Nikki when she entered their universe through the event horizon of a black hole in the center of a galaxy, and they brought her before the full committee. The group united for once and demanded to know who she was, where she had come from and what she was doing here. Nikki quickly realized that she was an unknown quantity to these Beings, and they were afraid that she might pose a threat to their committee. She decided to be truthful, but to also tread carefully.

Nikki told the Committee of Gods that she came from another universe run by a single, all-powerful God, who set up rules and got things done. She got the feeling they knew Who she was talking about, even though no one would admit it. They also seemed a bit embarrassed about the state of their universe, especially compared to the one she had just left. In a flash of inspiration, Nikki told them that this place was a disaster, but she could help them do better. A couple of the Gods sneered at her impertinence, but they were shushed by the others, who wanted to know what she had in mind. She said that her single God had designed His universe to follow orderly rules in predictable ways. People who studied those rules and learned how the universe worked were called scientists.

247

Nikki told them she had been one of these scientists, and offered to teach them the fundamentals of physics, along with some teamwork concepts and management theory. She gave them Newton's laws of motion and the Boyle's law gas equation for free, which they implemented with delight back at the creation of their universe, and then told them she needed some support before helping them further.

The Committee of Gods produced a contract and got down to business. The committee gave her the title Goddess of Science. Nikki tried not to chuckle, because the Committee wouldn't understand and might feel insulted. However, it seemed that her call sign Athena was going to follow her into another universe. At least she wasn't the Goddess of Love, one of the titles bestowed upon her by Dudley.

Nikki negotiated a fantastic salary, a substantial budget, decent hours, fabulous apartments in both Georgetown and Beverly Hills, a business jet, and a new body. They balked a little at that, because the twelve of them got along just fine as spirit entities, but eventually agreed after she told them that an organic brain would give her much more memory storage and allow her to think more quickly. The body was constructed following her design. It looked a lot like her former self at a youthful 29, the age at which she had died in the other universe. Nikki figured it was fair to pick up where she had left off, except this version was immortal. She also made herself a little bit taller, somewhat more athletic, and gave herself blonde hair with green eyes. What the hell – blondes have more fun, right?

Nikki discovered that the version of Earth in this universe was similar to her own, although her parents had never married here, so a parallel version of Nicole Shelton didn't exist. That was a relief – she wasn't sure how she'd react if she came into contact with herself. As an added

248

benefit, her annoying brother Stuart didn't exist here either. But there was another, more pressing concern. She needed to do something immediately about this universe's version of Sir Dr. Geoffrey Holmes Finch.

Because this universe also had the rule of Free Will, she couldn't just strike him down to stop him. However, it was easy for a goddess who could move about freely in time and space to plant small clues and indicators with the local Barney Freeman and Leon Hammermesh that raised suspicions about the motives of Finch. He had been less successful in this universe at obtaining grants for the ultradense matter experiments, and published quite a few physics journal articles explaining how such experiments could be run in the hopes of attracting the attention of funding agencies.

Certain publications found and read in a certain order made both Barney and Leon quite uneasy about what Finch might be up to, and they were able to get his privileges at CERN revoked before Finch could begin experiments with ultradense matter. He was incredibly angry at Freeman and Hammermesh for years afterward, publicly berating them at every opportunity. Barney and Leon both ignored him. Finch eventually succumbed to a stroke after a particularly fiery tirade against the shortcomings of the world physics establishment. So at least the singularity disaster was averted here.

Nikki learned that Dudley Gardner was essentially the same as in her universe, except that on the reference timeline here he was currently in the "living on Tortola in the middle of a messy divorce" phase of his life, which she needed to let him work through. She figured on giving him a year or so, and then making her move. She was a goddess after all, and she already knew what made him tick. It would be a piece of cake.

249

In the meantime, there was a variable star in the Whirlpool Galaxy that was causing extreme climate changes on its planets, making life miserable for the inhabitants. A densely populated planet in Andromeda was about to get smacked with an asteroid the size of Manhattan, and all the life forms in a solar system on the far side of the Milky Way were in imminent danger of perishing in a supernova.

Nikki got herself set up in a nice office in Alexandria just inside the D.C. Beltway, hired some staff, and set about saving the universe.

****

"I am sorry to say there is too much point to the wisecrack that life is extinct on other planets because their scientists were more advanced than ours." - John F. Kennedy